THE RUNAWAY MATE

SHIFTERS OF THE THREE RIVERS BOOK 1

KIRA NIGHTINGALE

ÉDITIONS SPOTTISWOODE

Book Cover by 100 Covers

Edited by Brigitte Billings

Published by Éditions Spottiswoode

Paperback ISBN: 978-1-7382838-0-4

Ebook ISBN: 978-1-7382838-1-1

First edition 2024

Dedication

Wow, I can't believe I have gotten this far! This book and these characters have been my baby for the last year, but I could not have done any of it without my family, and their superhuman ability to lend an ear when the plot got stuck, when I just wanted to give up, when I had to rant or when I needed someone to share in my squeals of delight when things clicked into place. To my husband, two kids, and my super clumsy cat Scout—you guys rock! This book is for you.

Trigger Warnings

This book contains some adult themes, lots of spice, as well as references to, and scenes involving, domestic violence.

CONTENTS

CHAPTER ONE

MAI

I wrinkled my nose as the scent of azalea and sage drifted toward me. I'd cracked open the car window half an hour ago, hoping to sniff out any danger here, but so far, all I'd caught was the scent of dusk flowers and the neighbors' yappy little dog. I couldn't stay in the car much longer. I had to get into my old apartment and try to dress some of my wounds.

It just brought back too many memories for me to deal with. I'd left here four years ago when I was eighteen and never thought I'd be back. From the outside, the apartment looked the same. Someone had put a new lick of paint on it, but my old bedroom window still had my Pokémon stickers stubbornly stuck to it. My parents had left the place to my brother Jem and me. I'm sure they never thought we'd inherit it so early, but then I doubt that they thought they'd get themselves killed, either. I'd been twelve, and Jem had been fifteen. We'd lost our parents and gained a tiny flat on Huston Road.

Jem wouldn't be here, but I knew my brother; he would never sell this place or tolerate anyone else living here. I'd kept an ear to the ground. I knew he'd killed Oliver after I left and, with his mate Hayley, they were the pair of the Three Rivers Pack.

The Three Rivers Pack. No matter how long I'd been away, it still called to me. It still felt like home.

I closed my eyes and saw again the scenery I'd driven through on my way here, the familiar landscape tugging at my heartstrings. The territory was a living tapestry where the Westfall, Coldbrook, and the Whispering Willow rivers converged in an intricate dance of nature. It felt like an organic fortress, the rivers like protective arms cradling the Pack's land, a natural haven that had once been the only place I knew. The small town of Three Rivers had been built at the apex, with a blend of tradition and modernity. Cobblestone paths led to boutique shops, quaint cafés, and historic buildings that told stories of generations past. The town square had been a magnet for community gatherings, a hub of life where the humans and Shifters who lived here could mingle, talk, and gossip.

I remembered evenings I'd spent there with Sofia Miller, my best friend. Both of us watching the four Shaw brothers, hoping they would notice us. Jem was often there, as well. At least in those days. Now he was Alpha, I doubted he skateboarded around the fountain, flicking water at everyone.

Jem wouldn't be here. But even as I thought about him, I could sense the larger forces that had shaped both of us. The Three Rivers Pack was not just a place; it was a living, breathing land that had given us much and taken away even more. It was a place of rich resources, from the fish-laden Westfall River to the Coldbrook's raging currents and the surrounding forests, full of wildlife and timber, each providing in its unique way for the Pack's needs. Yet it was also a land that demanded vigilance, its strategic importance, where roads from the north converged before making their way to the bigger markets and cities down south, making it a jewel that many coveted. I had a history here, but so did the Three Rivers Pack—a history steeped in alliances, betrayals, and the ceaseless struggle for dominance.

Stifling a whimper, I reached over to grab my bag. I knew my arm was broken, probably a few ribs, too, and my left knee wasn't looking too pretty right now. I could do this, though. I had to. I'd escaped Seth, my scumbag ex-boyfriend, and driven twenty hours to the only place I knew I'd be safe from him. There was no need for me to see anyone from my old Pack; I could camp out in my old apartment, lie low while Seth cooled off, then plan where I could go to start afresh. Again. I'd done it once when I fled this Pack after Ryan... I couldn't think about that now. I had to get inside and try to reset my arm.

I ground my teeth together as I hauled my bag and my body out of the car. I closed the door behind me and took a deep breath. The scents of the forest, the rivers, and the Pack filled my lungs. It was a heady mix, a blend of serene beauty and underlying tension, a mirror of the challenges and triumphs that had shaped me. I was home, and yet I was on edge. But then, that's how it always was in the world of the Three Rivers Pack.

I limped up the steps. I didn't have a key, but I knew if I jiggled the lock a few times, it would slide back. I'd done it enough times when I came back from school, and Hayley, Jem's mate from hell, had locked me out.

The trick still worked, and I stepped through the door and inhaled. It smelled like home. Hell, it looked like home. It hadn't changed at all. Our couch was here, with the same rip on the left armrest. The carpet was the same, old stains and all. It was open plan with a small kitchen

3

to the right and a hallway straight ahead that led to the bathroom and the three bedrooms. Jem and Hayley were hardly here for the year before I disappeared. They were too busy plotting their challenge on Oliver, the previous Alpha. Of course, Jem hadn't really been around before that, either. He'd made his way up the ranks to the Beta spot and left everything at home for Hayley to handle. I don't know if he didn't realize what a flaming bitch she was to me or if he didn't care. Either way, I was used to being alone here. Hayley never wanted to be far from Jem's side, so she left me to it as much as possible. It was my one sanctuary when Hayley wasn't around, and I felt, for the first time in the last forty-eight hours, that maybe everything was going to be okay.

I dumped my bag on the couch and eased myself down. I needed food, medical supplies, and sleep, but there was no way I could head out again. I'd been up for thirty-four hours. The shock of being attacked was wearing off, and the pain of my injuries was seeping into my bones.

I slipped my phone out of my pocket and hit the Takymora Delivery site, hoping they were still in business. If you wanted anything from the shops in town, you ordered it with Takymora, and they'd collect what you needed and deliver it to your home.

I clicked on enough food to last me a couple of days and added some supplies from the family pharmacy in town, then dozed on the couch until I heard a car pull up outside.

I hobbled into the kitchen and grabbed the biggest knife I could find, then opened the door just enough so I could smell who was coming up the stairs.

I relaxed when I realized it wasn't Seth. Or Hayley or Jem. The scent was vaguely familiar, though, but not one I could place.

I opened the door fully to see better.

A kid, maybe about seventeen, stopped at the top of the steps. With blond hair, deep blue eyes, and freckles across his nose, he'd be a looker in a couple of years when he grew into his height and didn't look so gangly.

"Mai? Is that you?"

Crap. I hadn't bargained on anyone recognizing me so soon.

"Jase?" I asked, beginning to put this guy together with Sofia's little brother. In high school, Jase had been an annoying wisp of a kid who thought it was funny to steal our bras and sell them to his friends.

"Fuck, Mai! You look like shit."

"Thanks." I managed a weak smile. I needed to get Jase gone. "Is that my stuff?" I pointed to the three bags he was holding.

Jase frowned at me, then walked forward. I could allow him to get in my space or I could step back, letting him into the apartment. I wasn't ready for anyone to be near me right now, so I backed up. Jase took a quick glance around, then headed to the kitchen, where he dumped the bags on the counter and started to unpack.

"I don't smell anyone else. You here alone?" he asked as he opened the fridge and put away the meat and milk.

"I don't remember Takymoras doing such a full service. Aren't you supposed to drop the bags and run?"

"Yeah, well, a lot has changed since you left." He looked me up and down, scowling at what he saw. "Fuck, Mai."

"You said that already."

"I guess I did. You gonna tell me where you've been and who the hell did this to you? Your brother's gonna flip. Ryan's gonna—"

"I don't want them to know I'm here!" I held up the knife I'd been holding and waved it at him with my good arm. "You promise me, Jase Miller, right now, that you're not going to tell, or I'll cut your balls off before they get the chance to sow those famous Miller oats in every girl from here to Yellowknife."

Jase grinned and held up his hands. "Fuck, Mai. You're still the same badass you were when you left. Alright, you got me. I won't tell."

I hesitated for a moment, then lowered the knife. "And stop saying 'fuck.' Your sister would slap you upside the head if she knew you swore so much."

"You should hear the words that come out of her mouth these days. You know she's working at the Bottley Bar? Picks up all sorts of interesting new phrases there."

I didn't know she was working there. I hadn't been in touch since I left; too scared Jem would use her to track me down. Sofia would be great at the Bottley Bar. It was a mixed place for Shifters and humans, and she would keep them all in line.

"You're gonna need help setting that arm."

I looked down. My arm was still useless from where Seth had held me down and twisted it. There was dried blood all over my clothes, rips in my shirt and jean shorts, and I was pretty sure my face was a lovely blue-green color.

"Sit." Jase gestured to the couch as he started unpacking the medical supplies I'd ordered.

"I can do it." I just wanted to be alone.

"Not a chance," Jase replied. "Sofia would kick my ass if she knew I left you in this state."

"Really, I'm fin—" The room started spinning, and I crashed

6

heavily to the floor, jarring my bad knee. "Fuck! Fuckity, fuck, fuck!" I yelled.

Jase picked me up and gently placed me down on the couch.

"Who's swearing too much now?" he teased.

"Fuck you!" I said through gritted teeth. I'd had enough of the pain, of bossy fucking werewolves, of being helpless and beat up, and of feeling so damned sad. I wanted to take the painkillers and pass out.

Jase took hold of my wrist in one hand and my shoulder in the other and then twisted.

The pain was blinding for a second, stopping my breath and causing the nerves in my entire body to fire in protest. It was only for a moment, though, as then I lost consciousness.

CHAPTER TWO

MAI

W hen I came to, Jase was standing over me, his phone in his hand.

"No! You promised," I growled at him. I would have leaped up and snatched his phone away, but my body was not cooperating right now.

He looked at me, his face full of indecision.

"Please, Jase." I softened my tone. "I can't deal with all their bullshit. I just want to recover and move on."

Jase sighed. "I'm going to tell Sof, but I won't let the big guys know."

"Deal."

Jase disappeared out of my eyeline and came back with painkillers, water, and a blanket that smelled of Jem. I took the pills and lay down with the blanket.

"You're a good kid, you know that?"

Jase snorted. "Mai, I'm really not a kid anymore."

"You'll always be a kid to me and Sofia," I mumbled, as sleep called to me.

"Feel better, Mai. I'll be back tomorrow to check on you."

I drifted off to sleep, the painkillers making my thoughts muzzy. I thought of this flat and how happy I'd been here while my parents were alive. I'd believed nothing could ever touch me here. I thought of Jem and how much he changed when he left school and was working his way up the ranks. How he'd devoted all his time to making it to Alpha and had left me in Hayley's care.

Hayley, who had lost her parents, too. They died just after she was born, as part of the last war with the Bridgetown Pack. She was raised by an aunt, who was overjoyed to get a new kid that she could make the servant of the family. Jem realized Hayley was his fated mate in Grade Ten, right after our parents died, and he took her out of her aunt's place as soon as they got together.

At first, she'd been nice to me, the kid sister who was suddenly an orphan. But she soon tired of that. She saw me as a rival for Jem's love and quickly found ways to put a wedge between us. Hayley was unyieldingly determined and ambitious, driven by her absolute need to be both an Alpha, so that no one would ever tell her what to do again, and the center of Jem's attention. She wanted to be in charge, with all the benefits that would bring. No more bowing down to anyone or having others expect her to cook, or clean, or iron, or do the washing.

Soon, Hayley barely tolerated my presence. She was obsessed with Jem, and if he was in the room, Hayley had to have his whole attention. If it wandered, she would do things to bring it back. She would start an argument or start kissing his neck. That one worked a lot in the early days, but after a couple of years, the arguments got better traction.

Ryan had always made me feel better when Hayley and Jem were off in their own room, fucking their brains out or off fighting again. Ryan was Jem's best friend. They were tight, had been since kindergarten when Ryan broke Andrew Webb's nose for stealing Jem's lunch. Ryan Shaw, whose mom was dead, killed by Oliver at the same time he got our parents killed, and whose dad never gave a fuck about him or his three younger brothers. Ryan became their *de facto* parent when he was fifteen. He stole food for them, worked odd jobs, mostly illegal ones, after school and on weekends, just to keep the heating on in their flat. Jem had tried to help as much as he could, and the Shaw brothers pretty much lived in our tiny flat with us.

My mind slipped in and out of sleep. The past and present blurring. For a few moments, I thought Oliver was still my Alpha and my parents would walk through the door at any second.

Oliver. He'd been a nightmare of an Alpha and had been responsible for our parents' deaths. He sold faulty guns to a werewolf Pack down south, thinking it didn't matter, that they were too far away to retaliate. He thought wrong. The southern Pack attacked us one afternoon. They sneaked into our territory and hit us where we were weakest; the farthest point in town from the Alpha compound where all the enforcers were. They killed anyone they came across. My parents. Ryan's mom. Oliver's mate, Romy, had been dropping off food at the local food bank. She heard the screams and came to protect her Pack. She took down ten of the attackers before they killed her, too. Oliver lost it, killed the attackers, hunting down any who escaped. It didn't mean shit to me. I'd lost both my parents because of some stupid, fucked up decision Oliver made to make himself more cash. I hated him with my entire soul.

Oliver had always been harsh, but after Romy died, he was a different Alpha. Not all Alphas keep governing after the death of their mate. Some do, though, and continue to protect and strengthen their Pack. Not Oliver. He became unstable. Unpredictable. He was brutal, mean, and liked to see people suffer. We all learned pretty quickly to stay out of his way, but he let his enforcers do what they liked. Jem and Ryan knew this wasn't how life was supposed to be. They spent their nights plotting to take over the Pack. But you could only challenge for a Pack if you were an Alpha couple.

Jem and Hayley were serious contenders to be the Alpha pair. Jem challenged and won the Beta position, and I think Oliver thought that would temper Jem's ambitions for a while, but it only made them stronger. The Pack was in a bad way. It was all I'd ever known, but even I knew that. Oliver had everyone cowering and afraid. If Oliver didn't like the way you looked at him or the way you spoke or the way you ate, or even the way you walked, he would give a nod, and his enforcers would beat the shit out of you. Oliver would watch, laughing as his crew crushed bones and sliced skin. The whole Pack was scared. Then Oliver started making deals with the drug lords in the neighboring county. He wanted in and used our Pack to transport the merchandise and sell it to the humans who lived in our town.

School got worse and worse. It was never good to begin with, but Sofia and I stuck together, and the bullying was low-level—tripping us in the corridors, sticking notes on our backs. After Jem became the Beta, though, school became unbearable. We all knew the fight was coming. Families couldn't come out openly in support of Jem—it was too dangerous—but all those who supported Oliver knew I was Jem's little sister and was an easy target. The Madden family, in particular, hated us. Jem had defeated Lionel Madden to become the Beta of the Pack. His son, Brock, was in my year at school.

A week after Jem won the Beta spot, Brock Madden and Tracy Hua held me down in the canteen and made everyone walk past and empty their unfinished lunches on top of me. Some plates were still steaming with whatever they had been eating; some were cold and slimy. Their food piled up on top of me like dirt. There were spilled chicken wings, beans and rice, fries, cartons of orange juice, and tuna sandwiches. The human teachers knew their place and bugged it out of there as soon as Brock grabbed me. Sofia was going ballistic, trying to get to me. I could see Brock's friends, Ben and Roscoe, holding Sofia back, and I'd just hoped she wasn't hurt. After everyone was done, they all stood and watched, some groups whispering and giggling, some silent with pitying eyes. Brock laughed, his voice bouncing off the walls in the canteen.

"Now everybody knows what I know, Mai. You're our trashcan. Your family is dirt. You have no fucking right to even think you can be Alphas. This..." He gestured to me. My clothes were soaked and stained yellow and brown. The smell of spaghetti, brown gravy and mayonnaise, wilted lettuce and orange peels, meat scraps and soda filled my nostrils and made me choke. "This is all you'll ever be, Mai."

I scraped what I could off myself and walked out, ignoring Brock's voice that followed me, shouting that I'd better know my fucking place from then on. I didn't tell Jem. He was working so hard trying to stay one step ahead of Oliver, and most nights, he didn't come home. When he did, he and Hayley wanted privacy to do the things that mates do. So, they'd take off, and the Shaws would turn up to keep an eye on me. We had to be careful with Oliver and his enforcers just looking for an excuse to take any one of us out. Anything to weaken Jem. So, we'd cook, order food, play games. Ryan would listen to me talk about my classes, or my favorite TV shows, or what I was reading. He called me his chatterbox. I didn't care. I'd talk about anything just to hear him reply.

Ryan, beautiful Ryan. Six foot two, dark hair, perfect jaw, muscles sculpted from hours of training with the enforcers, honing his body into a fighting machine, and smoldering eyes that stared right into my soul. His eyes were like the ocean, deep blue and full of life, and always moving. He constantly scanned the environment around him, searching for threats, but when he looked at me and smiled, it was a smile so stunning and bright that it almost hurt to look at it.

I'd known Ryan all my life, and I'd always known he was the one for me. For werewolves, sometimes you just know who your mate is. Sure, we can sleep around, even seriously date others, but we're always searching for the one who fits. I didn't need to search; I'd known at my parents' funeral when Ryan draped his coat around me to stop me shivering, gave me a daisy he'd picked, and stayed by my side the entire day. The coat smelled of Ryan, and his warmth and scent followed me everywhere. It kept me grounded and made me think that I could get through the day. I never did give that coat back. He never asked for it, and I'd kept it in my closet. When I was alone, I would put it on. Mostly when I had a crap day at school. I'd wrap myself in that coat, lie on my bed, and just breathe in the scent of him.

I hovered just on the edge of sleep now, thinking that I could almost smell his scent, like he'd sat on this couch a couple of months ago. It was tantalizing, just out of reach, and yet just smelling it, I felt safer than I had in weeks.

CHAPTER THREE

RYAN

S omething was wrong. I couldn't work out what the fuck it was, but there was something off in the Pack bonds.

"Ryan, are you listening to me?"

I glanced across the table at my brother Derek. What was he babbling on about? "What?"

"The Bridgetown Pack, they're recruiting again."

We were "out" to the humans, but we weren't supposed to draw attention to ourselves. The Bridgetown Pack had turned their town into a top tourist destination, with humans flocking there hoping to see and, more often than not, sleep with a Shifter. They were up to something, though. The humans never saw behind the screen that Michael, the Bridgetown Pack Alpha, wanted them to see, but it wasn't an adult Disneyland over there. They'd been recruiting humans and wolf Shifters for the last year. I couldn't help the feeling he was building an army.

"Any intel on what their end game is?" I asked Derek. At twenty-three, he and his twin Sam were the youngest of the four of us Shaw brothers, but he'd risen up the ranks quickly. His time in the army had taught him skills we'd needed in the last year.

"No, but I've got an asset inside. We should know more soon."

I grunted, that feeling of unease sweeping over me again.

"You alright? You've been acting funny since yesterday."

I leaned back in my chair and tapped the desk absentmindedly. "You don't feel anything? In the bonds?"

Derek went still for a moment, and I knew he was paying attention to his bond to the rest of the Pack.

"I don't pay much mind to it these days, not with Hayley causing trouble," he said softly, though I could tell his mind was still elsewhere. He was right; I knew most of the Pack tried to block the bond these days. The sooner we came up with a solution to Hayley, the better. It weakened us as a Pack.

Derek shook his head. "No, I don't feel anything. You think something's wrong? Well, more wrong than usual?"

I nodded. "I can't shake this feeling. It's a warning; something dangerous is coming. It's pulling me, getting more urgent."

Derek's expression turned serious as he leaned forward, resting his elbows on the table. "Alright, let's assume something is wrong. What's our move?"

I took a deep breath, steeling myself. "I don't know." I could hear the frustration in my voice. "I can't pinpoint where it's coming from. Is it Hayley? The Bridgetown Pack? Something new?" I resisted the urge to stand up and start pacing. I knew it would make Derek worried.

Derek looked at me for a moment, and I knew he was weighing up what I'd just said. He was always the thoughtful one of us four Shaw brothers. It was why he'd been so good in military intelligence.

16

"I'll double the patrols. As for the Bridgetown Pack... We need to gather more intel on what they're up to."

I nodded in agreement. "We can't let them build up an army without knowing their intentions."

Derek nodded, standing up from the table. "I'll call in the asset and see what they've got. In the meantime, listen to your Pack bonds; see if you can narrow it down. If you get anything, let me know."

I watched my brother leave the room, feeling a slight sense of relief knowing we were taking action. But the unease was still there, gnawing at me. I tried to focus on the Pack bonds, reaching out with my mind to feel for any broken currents.

That's when I felt it. A sudden jolt of pain, like a knife to the gut, followed by a need so urgent that it took my breath away. My wolf was howling inside of me, demanding release. He wanted out. He needed something that was vital to his very essence. He hadn't been this agitated since Mai left.

Wait, what if—

"Ryan!"

I turned to see Jem in the doorway. He looked tired, more so than usual, but there was a fierce light in his eyes.

"Have you found her?" Jem barked at me.

I frowned, confused. "Who?"

"Mai! She's back."

And just like that, the bottom dropped out of my world.

Chapter Four

Mai

I jerked awake to someone banging on my door. For a moment, I was back in Cocrane, Seth drawing his foot back to kick me in my ribs again. I took short, shallow breaths, the panic coursing through me.

Safe, I was safe here.

I looked around at my old apartment, the familiar scents settling me. Seth had never been here, so there was nothing to remind me of him. My eyes focused on a dent in the wall, made when Jem tried to do a 360 jump on his skateboard off the couch and instead rammed into the wall.

The door slammed open. I tried to get up, but my knee buckled, and I collapsed onto the floor.

Fuck!

Sofia marched into the room and stood over me. "I always thought you'd come groveling back and apologize for the way you just upped and skedaddled out of my life, but this is taking it a bit far, Mai."

I glared up at her. "You're hilarious. Now help me the fuck up, would you?"

As she bent down to pull me up, I noticed Jase coming into the apartment with a box full of food. He switched the box to one hand, then shut the door.

"How did you get in, anyway?" I asked Sofia.

"Dude, you think you're the only one who knows that lock jigging trick on the door? I'm pretty sure Jem has refused to get it fixed all these years, just in case you came back."

I groaned in pain as Sofia tried to place me as gently as possible down on the couch.

She crouched down in front of me and looked me straight in the eyes. "You gonna tell me who we're killing?"

And that was why I loved Sofia. It didn't matter that four years had passed since I'd last seen her or that I hadn't been in touch since then. She had my back, no matter what.

"He's not relevant. I escaped, and I have no intention of ever seeing that motherfucker again."

She stared at me for a beat, then nodded. "Okay, but you just say the word, Mai, and I'll bring the shovel."

God, I'd missed her. My eyes started to well up, and I looked away before I embarrassed both of us.

"So," Sofia said, as she stood up and glanced around my apartment, "this is still the same shitpit."

"Yeah, I guess Jem moved out and didn't look back."

Sofia shook her head. "No, Jem moved out, and he and Ryan threatened the Pack with instant death if anyone touched this place. They wanted it to be just like you left it in case you ever came back. Man, they are gonna blow when they find out you're here."

"That's not going to happen," I said, breathing through my mouth and wishing the pain would fuck off already.

"Mai, you're delusional. Ryan has been looking for you for years. He'll find out you're here sooner or later. You need to prepare yourself; you can't run from him. Not again."

I scoffed, "Wanna bet?"

"Jase told me your plan. Stay off the radar, right? Heal up, then ship out again. That's a dumb-ass plan, and you know it."

"Really? Seems like you and Jase just brought me enough food to last a month. I have everything I need right here; I don't need to leave the apartment. No one but you two know I'm here. As long as neither of you snitch, they'll be none the wiser, and I can clear out in a couple of weeks."

"Brilliant plan. Except you forgot one thing, Mai," a deep voice said from the doorway.

I turned, and all the breath left my body. Ryan was here.

CHAPTER FIVE

MAI

Ryan. My Ryan. My heart stopped. He was here. Was he real? His eyes bore into mine, pinning me in place. And suddenly, I was transported to that day four years ago when my entire world shattered.

───※───

Four years ago

It was just after my eighteenth birthday. I'd promised myself that I would wait until I was twenty before I told Ryan that he was my mate. Mates recognize each other; our wolves recognize each other. There is no escaping it. But for some, it took longer than others. I didn't think he knew, not yet. He'd never made any moves, never given any indication that I was anything other than Jem's little sister. I'd watched him date others and stamped down my jealousy with the knowledge that I was his only true mate, and one day, he'd be all mine. That and slitting Karen Eastley's car tires, stealing all of Macy Daring's left shoes, and filling Nancy Hampton's car with popcorn and whipped cream. It took her and Ryan two days to get it all out and it stank for months afterwards, long after she and Ryan split up.

There was something about Sarah Conley, though. She'd been sniffing around Ryan for weeks. Sarah worked as an assistant manager at the bank in town. She wore sophisticated skirts and tight blouses and had flawless make-up. I could barely afford my second-hand trainers. Jem let Hayley control all our money, and new clothes for me weren't a priority, not when they were trying to buy snitches in Oliver's enforcers. Sarah was everything I was not. I was skinny, short, scrappy, had bad hair that hadn't been cut in two years, and dressed in Hayley's old jeans and T-shirts. I had no life plan other than to get to graduation, so I wouldn't need to hear Brock Madden calling me the "skanky trashcan bitch" anymore. Sarah had a job, money, her family had power in the Pack, she was curvy in all the right places, was well-liked in the Pack, and would make Ryan the perfect mate.

Sarah started slow, brushing past him too close when she walked by him, then moved up to lingering touches on his hands, his arms, his chest as she talked to him. My wolf watched every move, and it was all I could do not to let her loose and rip Sarah's throat out. I didn't know what was wrong with me. I'd put up with his other women, knowing I was too young, that I wasn't ready for a relationship. What was so different this time?

It happened at the Alpha meet. Once a year, all the northeastern Packs got together to discuss issues and build alliances. Sometimes, this was on neutral territory, but some years, a Pack hosted. This year, Oliver had volunteered the Three Rivers Pack to host the meeting. Everyone was on their best behavior, trying to impress and not cause any trouble.

At the first evening welcome party, the whole Pack was instructed to be there and make nice with the other Packs. There could be no hint that things were anything but perfect. Sarah was there, of course, and she was dressed to kill in a tight, dark blue dress that left little to the imagination. She kept close to Ryan all evening, whispering in his ear and trailing her fingers down his arm. It was a clear message to everyone there. She wanted him, and she was going to stop at nothing to get him.

I felt my wolf clawing at my skin, begging to be released. I was shaking with rage, and I knew that if I didn't get away from them soon, I would lose control. I headed to the door, but Brock Madden and his crew were there, and Brock was watching me carefully. I knew he wouldn't let me just slip away. I turned, heading for the fire exit on the other side of the bar. I kept my head down, pushing through the crowds. Until a hand gripped my arm, stopping me in my tracks.

"Not leaving so soon, are you?" Brock's voice whispered in my ear. "I thought you and I could have some fun later."

My stomach turned. Sweat was starting to run down my back with the effort of keeping my wolf under control.

"Fuck off, Brock." I yanked my arm back.

"Aw, don't be like that, Mai."

I ignored him, turned, and slammed into Oliver's chest.

"Mai Parker." His voice was full of disdain, like I was a bug he'd found on the bottom of his shoe.

"Alpha." My eyes were rooted to my feet.

"Well?" he asked.

My mind went blank. Well, what? I sneaked a peek from under

my eyelashes. Oliver was standing with an Alpha pair who I didn't recognize. I could feel their power flowing off them in waves.

"Um..."

Oliver's eyes were cold and calculating. My heart was hammering against my ribs, and I knew he could hear it.

"Come see me in the Alpha compound tomorrow," Oliver commanded, then pushed me out of his way. I spun around, and that's when I saw them. Ryan and Sarah were just five feet away. Ryan was staring at me. He had heard what Oliver said. Jem was going to be so pissed. Rule number one for me was to stay away from Oliver. Don't draw attention, don't get on his radar. Sarah sidled up to Ryan, placed her hand over the six-pack I knew was hidden under his shirt, and pressed herself into his side. Her entire body was touching Ryan.

It was too much for me. Before I knew it, I'd darted forward and shoved Sarah away from him. She staggered back and looked at me with such surprise I almost laughed. Everyone discounted me. Everyone just saw me as Jem's quiet kid sister. I heard the gasps from those around us. Sarah's breathing was shallow. She kept her eyes locked on me. Her legs tensed, ready to spring at me. I growled, and then Ryan stepped between us. He grabbed hold of me and dragged me away from Sarah.

"What the fuck, Mai?"

I struggled against his hold, my wolf raging inside of me. "She was all over you, Ryan! Why are you letting her touch you like that?"

Ryan's expression hardened, his grip tightening on my arms. "That's none of your business, Mai. You need to calm down."

I glared at him, my heart pounding in my chest. I couldn't stand the thought of him with Sarah, of anyone taking him away from me. He was mine, even if he didn't know it yet. I struggled against his hold, trying to break free.

Suddenly, a voice cut through the chaos. "What's going on here?"

I turned to see Jem standing there, his eyes taking in the scene before him. His expression was cool and collected, but I could see the anger simmering beneath the surface. He walked over to us, his eyes flickering between Ryan, Sarah, and me.

"Mai?" he asked.

I was unable to control the words that spilled from my mouth. Without taking my eyes off Ryan, I blurted, "You're my mate."

A shocked silence spread out from us.

"Bullshit!" Sarah growled, walking toward us. "Tell her, Ryan. Tell her she's fucking delusional."

I glanced up at Ryan, afraid to look at him but needing to see his reaction. Was he pleased? Finally, he would have a fated mate. He had to be happy. Everything was going to be okay now that he knew.

Ryan's grip on my arm tightened. His face was blank, no emotion there at all. I frowned, confused.

"Ryan?"

"Mai, you're a fucking kid. We're not mates. We'll never be mates. You don't understand how this works. You will, one day when you grow up, but this is just a little girl's fantasy that's gotten out of hand."

His words hit me like a punch in the gut. I staggered, my heart shattering. How could he say that to me? He was supposed to be my mate, my other half. I looked at him, my eyes pleading for him to take it all back. But his expression was cold.

I yanked my arm free and stumbled back. "Why are you saying this? You know the truth, Ryan. You know I'm your mate."

How could he not feel it? How could he do this? My wolf was whimpering inside of me. Ryan's rejection of everything we had ever dreamed of confused her. It wasn't supposed to be like this.

"Mai." Ryan took a step toward me, but stopped when Sarah placed her hand on his waist.

I glared at her hand, willing Ryan to shrug it off. He didn't. I saw him glance around the room before he carefully put his hand over Sarah's.

Jem strode forward to stand facing me, blocking my view of Ryan and Sarah. "Mai, go home." His voice was harsh, disappointed. "Go cuddle your teddies. We'll talk about your behavior in the morning."

That was when I heard the laughter. Brock, Ben, and Roscoe had wandered over and had heard everything.

"Oh my God, this is fucking priceless. Even her own side doesn't want anything to do with the trashcan bitch. You know, Mai," Brock raised his voice so everyone in the room could hear, "if you beg, and I mean really beg, I might take you in as my plaything."

I couldn't take it anymore. My chest felt like it was going to explode; it was heavy, and there was such pain there. Pain I couldn't explain, couldn't get rid of. It felt like I was breaking apart, and the one person who should be there to hold me up was the one holding the hammer. I turned and sprinted out of the room, Brock's laughter trailing behind me. I ran home, went straight to my room, and locked the door. I collapsed on my bed, not able to stop the tears, to stop the whining of my wolf who wanted me to go back, to go and shake some sense into our mate.

I don't know how long it was before Hayley came home. I heard a soft knock on my bedroom door, followed by a voice that seemed too gentle for its owner. "Mai, it's Hayley. Can I come in?"

I hesitated, not really wanting company, but I knew she wouldn't go away until she said whatever she wanted to say. I clicked the lock.

The door swung open, and Hayley walked in, her eyes meeting mine briefly before she looked away. She sat on the edge of my bed, her posture straight, every inch the Alpha female she wanted so desperately to be.

"I heard about what happened," she began, her voice laced with sympathy. "I'm really sorry, Mai. No one should have to go through that."

I swiped angrily at the tears that were starting to fall again. I didn't want Hayley to see me crying.

"Ryan," she sighed. "Ryan is a complicated person. He's had to look after his brothers since his mom died and his dad checked out of the whole parenting thing. He's got a lot of responsibility. He doesn't need another kid on his plate, you know? But he really could have handled the situation with more care."

"I'm not a kid!" The tears wouldn't stop. Oh Goddess, why wouldn't they stop?

"Sure, you're not. But that's the way Ryan sees you. The way he'll always see you. I don't want to hurt you, but you need to know the truth, Mai. When Ryan is with Sarah, he lights up. He's happy, Mai. She's good for him."

I felt like Hayley had stabbed me in the heart with an icepick. It hurt so much to hear her say that Ryan was happy with someone else. That he was meant for someone who wasn't me.

Hayley reached out and stroked my hair. She had never done that before. Never shown me any physical affection. "I know you. I know

29

you love Ryan and will want to do what is right for him. Sometimes, life gives us signals, Mai. Signals that maybe we're not where we're supposed to be," she continued, her eyes searching my face for a reaction.

"What do you mean?" I whispered, not sure I could take much more.

Hayley sighed, her eyes flicking to the door and back to me. "What I mean is, maybe this is your chance to get out, to see the world, to grow up, to escape this... smallness," she waved her hand vaguely around the room, "and discover who you really are."

"Run away, you mean," I clarified, my voice tinged with disbelief.

She shrugged. "Call it what you want, but sometimes, running away is running toward something better, something that's actually worthy of you. Do you want to stay here? To always be the kid who thought she was Ryan's mate and got rejected in front of all the Packs? Your little scene will sustain the gossips for months, years even. This news will spread across the northeast in no time. Who'll take you now, Mai? If you stay, no one will want you. You'll always be the delusional kid pining for the mate she can't ever have."

Hayley was right. Nobody would touch me now. I would always have to live with the rejection, the humiliation. But could I really leave everything behind? My home, my Pack, my brother? Ryan?

Hayley seemed to sense my struggle. "You could always come back. But you'll come back stronger, wiser, and who knows, maybe even out there, you'll be able to find someone who truly values you for who you are."

Her words were wrapped in a layer of sweetness, but something in her tone set off alarms in the back of my mind. Was she really concerned about my well-being, or was she just trying to get rid of me?

Still, her words hit a nerve. She was offering me an out, a way to escape the humiliation and heartbreak. And part of me, the part that wanted to stop feeling this unbearable pain, wanted to take it.

She stood up to leave, her eyes locking onto mine one last time. "Just think about it, okay? You deserve so much more than this, Mai."

She left the room, closing the door gently behind her. I don't know how long I stayed there, my feet rooted to the floor. But by the time I wiped away my tears, I knew what I was going to do. I packed a small bag and left that night. Everyone was at the party, and the border patrols were on skeleton crews—all the enforcers were in the center of town to protect the Meet. I was able to slip out of our territory without seeing anyone. I ran... and ran far. Only stopping two years later, when I reached Cocrane and tried desperately to forget all about Ryan.

CHAPTER SIX

MAI

And now here he was, standing in my fucking doorway.

Ryan. My Ryan.

No! Not mine. Never mine.

My wolf was clamoring inside me. She wanted to go to him, to be kissed and touched in a way that she never wanted with Seth. I reined her in, but it hurt more than my broken arm or twisted knee. He'd rejected me, and now he was just standing there. I could feel his eyes on me, his gaze piercing through me.

"Ryan," I whispered. Shit, I so wasn't ready to see him again. I didn't think I'd ever be ready to see him again.

Ryan looked me up and down, his arms crossed over his chest, his blue eyes laser-sharp in their gaze. He wore blue jeans and a black T-shirt that stretched tight across his broad chest. Muscles bulged in his arms; not the sculpted muscle built by weightlifting. No, this was powerful muscle corded into shape by hours of fighting and ripping through his opponents. His jaw was clenched so tight I thought he might break his teeth.

Goddess, he looked good. His dark hair was shorter than I remembered, only about an inch long on top. It made him seem more severe, less the boy I knew, more manly somehow. His face was hard, and a muscle twitched in his cheek when his eyes passed over my injuries. His whole body was rigid and tight, like he was desperately trying to hold himself back from moving. Yet his presence seemed to invade the whole space. You always knew when Ryan was in the room; you could feel his energy spreading out and taking all the available oxygen.

"How did you know I was here?"

"Your brilliant plan didn't take into account that Jem's the Alpha now. He feels it when any of us come into his territory."

Right. For a milli-second, I regretted not cutting my bond to the Three Rivers Pack. After I left, I couldn't bring myself to do it. I figured if I just shoved it down inside and pretended it wasn't there, then I wouldn't need to think about it. I knew that if an Alpha concentrated on a Pack member, they would know exactly where we were within our territory. It was something about the magic of the Pack bonds and the link to our land, our territory. But this nifty little trick didn't cross the boundaries of our land. I knew when I left that if I just made it to our border, then Oliver couldn't track me. So, I'd never seen the need to sever the bond. It wouldn't have kept me safer.

Of course, Seth had despised it. He hated that his Alphas had given me long-term resident status in the Cocrane Pack and let me live and work there without needing to bond to their Pack. It was common enough in Cocrane. The city was a haven for people like me, those passing through, trying out life in a Pack to see if we liked it. Most joined the Pack eventually, and their policy of no pressure meant drifters like me had the time to put down roots, learn to like the place, and then feel comfortable joining.

It drove Seth up the wall that I hadn't joined his Pack. I didn't tell him I came from the Three Rivers, but he'd ordered me to cut my previous bond and join the Cocrane Pack. I'd refused, but he kept at it. In the end, we'd been having daily arguments about it. I hadn't wanted to give up my freedom, hadn't wanted to be tied down to another Pack. I liked the fact that I didn't belong to any and could leave if I wanted to. But there was no way I was going to be reclaimed by the Three Rivers Pack, either. I'd worked too hard forgetting about this place.

I shook my head at Ryan. "Us? I'm not one of you. I'm not part of this Pack."

Ryan lifted one eyebrow. "You're Jem's sister. You'll always be part of this Pack."

Right. Jem's little sister. That's all I'd ever be. Anger surged up. Just because Jem and I shared the same blood, that didn't mean I was part of his Pack. Of all people, Ryan should have known this. He rejected me, had driven me away. Or had he forgotten?

"Besides, if you really didn't want to be part of this Pack, you'd have severed your bond. That Jem felt it when you came back means it's still there, Mai. You still want us."

That cut a little too close to home and veered into an area I'd spent the last four years purposefully not thinking about. I had to change the course of this conversation. I stood up, using the edge of the couch to help me. I didn't want to be sitting lower than Ryan right now.

Narrowing my eyes at him, I said in a bored tone, "What do you want, Ryan? What are you even doing here?"

I swear to the Goddess, for a moment, it looked like his head was going to explode. His nostrils flared, taking in my scent. His gaze hovered on my cuts and bruises, and a green sheen flashed in his eyes. His fists were clenched so tightly that I was pretty sure his nails were going to leave some serious marks on his palms.

"First, I'm taking you to the Pack doctor," he growled. "Then, Jem wants to see you."

I did not think so. "No. No fucking way. I'm not seeing the doctor. I'm not seeing Jem. Hell, I'm not even seeing you." I waved a hand in front of my face. "Look, this is just a bad dream. I'm going to count to three, and poof, you'll be gone." I closed my eyes, hoping he'd take the hint and leave. "One, two, three."

I opened them, and Ryan was standing right in front of me, so close that if I moved more than an inch, my lips would touch his. His scent washed over me, and I couldn't help but breathe it in. I felt dizzy, almost hypnotized by the smell of him. His eyes were blazing with an odd intensity, and his voice was low and rough when he spoke. "You're coming with me, Mai."

Er, no.

I tried to back away from him, but the pain in my knee made me stumble. His hands reached out to steady me. His touch was electric, sending shivers down my spine. For a second, I had the urge to lean into him, to soak up the heat of his body and forget everything else. Damn it. I thought I was over Ryan. He wasn't mine and never would be. I had to remember that. I glared at him and opened my mouth to tell him where to shove it when Sofia, the little traitor, jumped in.

"Ryan's right, Mai. You need to see a doctor."

I shifted my glare to her.

Sofia held up her hands in a don't-blame-me gesture. "You need to get checked out. I'll come with you if you want. Keep the big bad boys off your case?"

I loved her for offering. I took a breath and shook my head. I'd just wanted to hide here for a few days, give myself time to heal and recover. I didn't want anything to do with this Pack. I didn't want to see my brother and his bitch of a mate. I didn't want to deal with Pack politics. I definitely didn't want to see Ryan. But it looked like my plan had blown up, and was raining debris all around me. Fine. They wanted to see me, I'd see them. But I'd show them I wasn't a kid anymore; I wasn't the girl who ran out of here.

"No, it's okay, Sofia. I can handle it."

I lifted my chin, limped past Ryan and out of the door.

Chapter Seven

RYAN

I stood there, almost bursting out of my skin, wanting to go to her. To hold her, kiss every fucking inch of her. But first, I had to make sure Mai was okay and that she wouldn't bolt again. My heart—and wolf—wouldn't survive it if she did.

When she agreed to see the doctor, my wolf calmed. He knew she would be looked after. It took all my self-control not to pick her up and carry her to the car. Instead, I had to watch her hobble down the stairs and across the yard. My wolf was going crazy, but I had to hold it together. I had to find out who hurt her and tear that fucker apart.

When she stumbled at the curb, I'd had enough. I scooped her up, ignoring her startled yelp, and placed her gently in the passenger seat.

"I can get myself in a car, you know!" she growled at me.

I ignored that, too, and got in the driver's side.

As I pulled out onto the road, I couldn't believe she was actually here. Her scent—of honeysuckle, mint, and aspen leaves—was real, not just the hints I'd dreamed about for years. Her face had refined, grown out of her teenage looks, with features that were sharper, more angled than I remembered. Her beautiful brown eyes somehow seemed bigger in her face now, giving her a more vulnerable look, though that might just be my wolf reacting to her broken arm and bruised body. Ebony hair, always cut short back in the day, now flowed round her face and down to her shoulders. She was pale, her face a mix of pain and anger and something else. It took me a moment to place it. I knew that look; it was the one she always got when she was determined to do something on her own without anyone's help. But this time, she couldn't. She needed me, and I wasn't going to let her down.

I pulled up at Thomas's house. He'd been our Pack doctor for the last eighteen months. Jem had found Thomas and his mate Wally when they were on the run. They'd gone rogue and left a Pack down south without permission. The other Pack hadn't been too happy that Thomas's mate was a man. Jem assured Thomas and Wally that they'd be safe here, safe and accepted, and promised Thomas that he would have full control to treat whomever he wanted. At his last Pack, only those the Alpha pair approved of could get medical attention. I scooped Mai out of the car and carried her to the front door.

"Put me down right now, Ryan Shaw!"

Holding her this close was torture. Her scent was intoxicating, even with the faint aroma of blood and pain mixed in. It was the scent of home, of safety, and of desire.

Thomas swung open the door before I had the chance to knock. He took one look at Mai, and his face twisted in concern. "What happened?" he asked.

"This is Mai, Jem's little sister."

Thomas's eyes flashed to mine. He knew about Mai, had heard the rumors of Jem's lost sister, the one Jem and I were searching for.

He knew I was saying he had to take good care of her. Not that he would treat her any differently from anyone else. He took great care of everybody who walked in his door.

"Come in, come in." Thomas ushered us inside his office.

Mai winced in pain as I helped her onto the examination table.

"Out you go, Ryan," Thomas said. "We need privacy."

"I'm not going anywhere." I crossed my arms and glared at him. I'd just found Mai again; no way was I letting her out of my sight.

"Ryan, I can't go anywhere. Please just back off, okay?" Her scent was full of pain now.

"I'll be outside. Thomas, I'm putting her safety in your hands." I knew there was a dangerous edge to my voice, but I couldn't help it.

Thomas nodded, but I saw the flash of anger in his eyes. I'd just insulted him, and normally he would give me a tongue-lashing over it—I might be the Beta outside, but in here, he was the boss and a damn fine doctor—but he knew what Mai meant to me. To all of us.

My wolf growled inside me, restless and angry. I went outside and paced back and forth, my mind racing with thoughts of who could have hurt her and why.

My phone rang.

"Well?" Jem's voice was harsh and impatient.

"She's with Thomas."

"Thomas? What the fuck, Ryan?"

"She's hurt. I'm not sure how bad, but not badly enough to stop her bitching at me."

I heard Jem's sigh of relief. "What happened?"

"I don't know. She's been beaten pretty bad. A broken arm, certainly. Something is wrong with her knee. I'll know more once

41

Thomas has finished."

"Okay. Bring her here as soon as he's done." He hung up. Jem never was one for goodbyes.

It felt like an eternity before Thomas finally emerged from the room and straightened up. Thomas was a big werewolf. At six foot five, he towered over most of the Pack. I often saw him at the gym, and even now, I could see the muscles bulging through his shirt. He'd been trying to bulk up ever since he got here, and at this rate, he was going to need a bigger shirt soon. His size intimidated some of the other wolves, though, especially the more skittish members and especially when they first saw him. We'd had trouble persuading some of them to see Thomas, but I'd heard that after their first appointment, most of the Pack was keen to come back. He had a sharp tongue for us enforcers, but he was gentle and kind to the rest of the Pack, and he took a lot of care during his first meeting with a new patient to be as unthreatening as possible. I'd seen him roll his shoulders and scrunch down to appear smaller and less threatening. As he stretched his back, I knew he had done that with Mai. Thomas walked over to me, a serious expression on his face. Given I was the Pack Beta, Thomas should be averting his eyes. Eye contact was seen as a challenge to those higher up the hierarchy of the Pack than you, but as the Pack doctor, Thomas got a lot of leeway.

"She's going to be okay," he said. "She has a broken arm, two broken ribs, and her knee is sprained. But the rest of her injuries are superficial. I've reset her arm, wrapped her ribs and given her painkillers. She'll need to stay off the knee for a day or so. She's lucky werewolves heal quickly."

I nodded, relieved she was going to be okay, but the anger was still simmering inside me. "Who did this to her?"

Thomas looked down, probably sensing my rage and not wanting to provoke me further. "She didn't say."

I ran my fingers through my hair in frustration.

"You need to go softly with her, Ryan."

I glanced wryly at him. "Is that your professional opinion, Doc?"

Thomas stood up straighter. "Yes, actually, it is. This is typical of domestic abuse victims. You need to tread carefully; don't spook her. We all know how much she means to you and Jem, but if you want her to stay, you need to go slow."

My blood went cold at his words. "You think someone she knew did this to her?"

"From her evasive answers, the fact that she ran here—to the very Pack she fled from four years ago in order to hide from this person—and that she has no offensive wounds, which means she didn't fight back..." Thomas shook his head. "I have no doubt that she knew her attacker and was probably close to them."

I stared at the house, my anger mounting. I heard the echo of my heavy breathing and the growling of my wolf. My hands clenched as I tried to keep him in.

"Keep it under control, Ryan," Thomas said sharply. "You can't help her if you lose it."

Soon, I told my wolf, *we'll hunt them soon.*

He knew I'd keep that promise.

"I need to take her to the compound. Jem wants to see her."

Thomas nodded. "I'll get some crutches that she can use."

Chapter Eight

Mai

As Ryan drove me to the compound where Jem and Hayley lived, I couldn't help but feel nervous. What would I say to Jem after all these years? Would Hayley still hate me? I had to make sure that they knew I wasn't here to stay.

I'd never been inside the Alpha compound before. I'd just turned eighteen when I left and had never been there. As we approached the entrance, I could see a network of cameras and sensors covering the perimeter. There was a guard stationed at the gates. Ryan wound down his window and nodded to him. The guard looked at Ryan, then at me, then back at Ryan. His face showed no expression. Right.

The guard talked into his radio, "Open the gate." Then tapped on the roof of the car two times.

We drove through, and I was surprised to see that the compound was more like a small town. There were several large houses scattered around a central square. All of them had well-maintained, spacious gardens in front.

In the center of the square was a fountain surrounded by benches and a ring of Japanese maples. The fountain was beautifully crafted, with intricate carvings of rabbits, fawns, and squirrels.

Each house was different. Some were modern, with grand windows and sleek lines, while others were more traditional, smaller, with thatched roofs and beautiful rustic stonework.

The largest one, which I was guessing was where the Alphas would stay, was a sprawling, three-story house with a wide veranda and a garden full of colorful flowers. There were bean bags and two hammocks on the veranda, and I could just picture Jem chilling out in one in the evenings.

Ryan parked the car in the driveway.

"We're here," he said.

No shit.

"Mai, I—"

"Don't start. I just want to get in there, listen to whatever Jem has to say, and get the hell out."

Ryan stared at me for a long moment, his jaw tight. I knew he wanted to say more, but thankfully, he got out without saying anything. I blinked, and he was at my door before I'd even opened it. These crutches sucked.

"Here, let me—"

"I've got it, Ryan. I don't need your help, so back off."

I hobbled past him toward the door. It was awkward, but I made it to the front door. Ryan walked straight in. I guess Jem had an open-door policy. I followed him and was immediately struck by how cozy and welcoming the house felt. There were soft pastel rugs on the floors and bookshelves full of books lining the walls. I didn't remember Jem as a big reader. That was always my thing.

Ryan steered me into the living room. It was spacious, with high ceilings and large windows that let in plenty of natural light. It was decorated in warm, earthy tones, with plush couches and chairs arranged around an imposing fireplace. Then, my eyes met the gaze of the man standing in the middle of the room. My brother. Jem.

I hadn't seen him in so long, and I could hardly recognize the boy I once knew. I could see the weight of the past four years etched on his face. There were lines around his eyes and mouth that hadn't been there before. He was taller, broader, and just oozed confidence that I guessed came with being an Alpha. His eyes, the same deep brown as mine, were filled with emotions that I couldn't quite decipher.

For a moment, we just stared at each other, unsure of what to say or do.

Then, without warning, Jem strode forward and pulled me into a tight embrace. I felt his strong arms wrap around me, and I breathed in the familiar scent of him. It was a mix of coconut and earth, with a hint of something that was uniquely Jem.

I forgot about everything else. I forgot about the pain in my leg, about Seth and the fact that he was still out there, about why I left in the first place. All I could feel was the warmth of Jem's embrace, and an overwhelming sense of relief washed over me.

"Mai," he said softly. "I'm so glad you're back."

Tears were prickling at the corners of my eyes. I had missed him so much. All those lonely days when I didn't know when my next meal would be or if I'd find somewhere to sleep that night, I'd think of Jem—there was no way I'd let my thoughts go to Ryan, there was too much hurt there—and wonder if he was okay. When I heard the rumors that the Three Rivers Pack had a new Alpha pair, I knew it was Jem, and he'd finally done it. Jem was always the strong one. He'd plotted and prepared, he'd kept us safe, and when the time was right, he and Hayley had challenged Oliver. Me? As soon as things got hard, I'd run.

I took a deep breath. I didn't want to break down in front of him.

Jem must have sensed my hesitation. "It's okay," he whispered. "You're safe now. I won't let anything happen to you."

"I can't stay," I mumbled the words into his shirt.

"We can talk about that later." Jem pulled back. "What did Doc say?" he asked, looking at Ryan.

"Broken arm, two ribs. Twisted knee. She'll be fine in a couple of days."

Jem looked at me again. "Who?"

I stared back at him. "This isn't why I came. It isn't your business. I'm handling it." I had to set the boundaries now, before I fell into being his kid sister again, one who needed protecting.

Jem's eyes bore into mine, and I knew he was not happy with my answer.

"Does that trick work on all your minions?"

Jem's jaw clenched, and then he sighed. "Normally, yes. I glare. They spill. That's how the whole Alpha gig works. Apparently, it doesn't work on sisters, though. I'll have to come up with something different just for you."

I grinned at him. Man, I'd missed him.

Jem grinned back at me. "You must be exhausted. Why don't we get you settled in your room?"

"What room?"

"You can't stay in our old apartment, Mai. I haven't seen you in four years. Please, stay here with me so we can catch up properly before you leave again."

He had me. He knew he had me. I couldn't go back to the apartment now.

"Is Hayley—?"

Jem cut me off. "Don't worry about her. She's hardly here these days."

That didn't sound good, but I wasn't going to dwell on it. Spending some time with Jem actually sounded good. Maybe we could catch up; maybe I could get some closure before I moved on. Maybe we could even get to the position that when I did get settled somewhere else, I could call him once in a while and hear his voice.

"My stuff—"

"Sofia packed it up and brought it all here while you were at Doc's," said Ryan.

Oh, did she? She and I were going to have words.

"I have to move a couple of meetings, Mai. Ryan can show you around, and then you can rest. I'll see you for dinner, okay?" Jem leaned down and kissed my forehead, gave Ryan a look that I couldn't decipher, and then strode out of the room.

Chapter Nine

MAI

R yan led me out of the living room and into the rest of the house, walking slowly so I could keep up with my crutches. I hobbled through a gorgeous kitchen with a large island in the center. The countertops were made of dark granite, and the cabinets were in a light wood. There was a huge oven designed for people to do proper cooking.

"The fridge is always stocked up." Ryan pulled open the double doors on the biggest fridge I'd ever seen. "Everyone helps themselves. You hungry?"

I shook my head. I knew I should eat, but the adrenaline from seeing Ryan again, from coming here and meeting Jem after four years away, was seeping out of me, leaving me feeling tired and sore. My whole body ached, and the stabbing pains in my knee were back.

"You sure? I can make you something. Omelet, toast? I can whip up a curry; you used to love my green Thai curry when you were a kid."

I had loved it. Ryan used to make it for me and his brothers when Jem was off with Hayley or doing missions for Oliver. I hadn't had a green Thai curry in four years. One time, when we were dating, Seth had taken me to an Asian restaurant. I'd feigned feeling sick and had gone straight home alone. I couldn't face the memories that the taste of a curry would have brought back to me.

"You know, I'm feeling really tired, Ryan. Can you just point me in the direction of my room? Then you can get back to whatever it was you were doing before Jem ordered you to pick me up."

"Jem didn't order—"

"Really, Ryan, you don't need to do this. I just want to lie down. Please."

There it was again, that flash of green blazing in his eyes before he got a hold on it. I was pissing him off, but I wasn't sure how. He must have better things to do than show Jem's kid sister around. I was just telling him he was off the hook; surely he would be pleased? But I guess this was excruciating for him, too. Me claiming he was my mate in front of all the Packs, in front of Sarah, must have embarrassed the hell out of him.

Goddess, why did I think about Sarah? I didn't want to think about Sarah. About how she was probably at Ryan's home right now, waiting for him, maybe with three mini-Ryan's bouncing around. Or at her job, about to call and check in with Ryan, see how his day was going. Fuck, I could just imagine that conversation when he told her who was back in town.

Ryan's gaze stayed on me for a moment, then he nodded. "I'll show you the way."

I hopped upstairs, growling at Ryan every time he took a step toward me. I knew he was getting impatient, keen to get out of here, and he just wanted to pick me up and carry me to the top, but I couldn't let him touch me again. It sent electric shivers through my body, and I just wanted to lick him all over. I needed space away from Ryan. Time to get my fucking hormones and wolf under control. Thomas had given me spare pills so I could sleep, and that was exactly what I was going to do. What I really needed was to Shift, but I didn't feel safe enough here yet.

"There are six bedrooms up here. Jem and Hayley have the master at the end of the corridor. Yours is one of the spare rooms in the middle. My brothers and I live next door, so you'll be able to just holler if you need anything."

"You live here, in the compound?" I asked, surprised that Sarah would want to live with the three other Shaw brothers. Before I'd left, I'd seen how messy their apartment was and how much mess they made every time they came over to ours.

"I'm the Beta now. Jem finds it handy to have the Pack hierarchy all living here."

"Doesn't that keep you separate from the rest of the Pack? All of you tucked away behind these walls, living in luxury?"

Ryan grimaced, and I knew I'd hit a sore spot.

"Hayley insisted. As half of the Alpha pair, he can only overrule her so many times. There have been bigger issues that were more important for Jem to win."

There it was again, a hint that all was not good in the Three Rivers Pack and their Alpha pair.

"How does Sarah find it, living with you and your brothers?"

And why did I ask that?

Ryan frowned. "Sarah? Sarah who?"

"Sarah Conley." There. I said her name without breathing fire.

"Why on earth would Sarah...? Oh! No. Fuck no, Mai. I think we need to get some things straight."

My heart froze. No? He wasn't with Sarah? For the past four years, I'd assumed he and she had mated up. Not true mates, because even if I was a delusional little kid back then, I'd always known Ryan was my true mate. But I figured he'd shacked up with her, maybe had some puppies by now. Of course, whenever I thought of that, I'd get blindingly drunk just to get the images out of my head and to quieten my wolf howling inside of me. But if he wasn't with her, that didn't mean he hadn't shacked up with someone else. And I definitely wasn't up for hearing about that right now.

"I think I'm pretty straight. Besides, I'm really tired, Ryan. Is this my room?" I pointed to the door in front of us.

Ryan sighed and opened the door. It was a kick-ass room. Bigger than most of my apartments for the last four years, with a large bed in the middle and full-length windows offering a view of the gardens. The walls were painted a calming shade of blue, and the bed was covered in soft, fluffy blankets. There was a small desk in the corner, with a bookshelf to the left of it. My eyes hovered on the books. They were all my favorites from when I was a teenager. Who would have done that? Certainly not Hayley. Jem? But he never took much notice of me; had been too busy keeping us all safe and plotting to take on .

My bag of things was sitting in the middle of the bed, and the room smelled faintly of Sofia. Maybe Sofia had brought the books?

"Wow, that bed is bigger than my apartment."

Strangely, Ryan's fists clenched at my comment. I was too tired to try to work out what I'd said to piss him off now.

"Thank you for showing me around. I'd like to take a nap now."

There, job done. Ryan was off the hook and could leave. Me, I'd take Thomas's pills and pass out.

Ryan looked at me for a moment, his blue eyes searching mine. His jaw was tight, and I thought he was going to say something, but then he looked at my arm and then my leg. "I'm going to give you this, Mai. But we are going to talk. Whatever fucked up version of events has been in your head for the last four years needs to be straightened out. I've waited all this time to tell you the truth, and you aren't going to push me away, Mai. This is going to happen."

What the hell was he talking about? I frowned, then stifled a yawn. My eyesight was going fuzzy. I needed sleep. Then, I could put a new avoid-Ryan-at-all-costs plan into action. I yawned big this time and slumped down onto the bed.

"Christ. Get some sleep, Mai." Ryan turned and walked to the door. "I won't be far. Call, and I'll be here."

I watched blearily as he closed the door, then I laid down on the bed.

Just hide and heal, then run away. My plan was so simple. And so utterly fucked. How had I ended up seeing Ryan and being installed in the Alpha's compound? It hadn't escaped my notice that all the security on the way in meant the chances of me slipping away unseen again were zilch.

If I was going to make a run for it, I'd have to come up with something more sophisticated than packing a bag and driving off this time. Fuck! My car wasn't even here; it was still at the apartment. I couldn't have messed this up any worse. I giggled. It was either that, or cry and I'd done all the crying I was going to do driving myself here. I sighed, too tired and weary to think anymore, and fell asleep.

Chapter Ten

Mai

When I woke up, it was already dark outside. I had to admit, the bed was incredibly comfortable. I sat up and stretched. Then winced as my broken ribs asked what the fuck I was doing.

"Mai? Are you awake?" The voice came from the other side of the door.

Hayley.

I hesitated for a moment, but I couldn't hide in this room forever.

"Yeah, I'm awake," I replied, my voice a bit hoarse.

The door opened, and Hayley walked in. She was wearing a casual outfit of dark, fitted jeans and a plain white shirt, and her long blond hair was pulled back in a messy bun. She looked older, more aged than the four years since I'd seen her should have shown. She had always been tall and slender, like a toned marathon runner, but now she was bordering on the side of skinny. It wasn't a healthy look for a werewolf.

Hayley looked around the room and then finally at me. "So, you're back."

"It looks like it," I replied, wondering briefly if I should avert my eyes. She was a Pack Alpha but I bristled at showing her that respect.

"Don't worry, I'm not staying long."

We stared at each other for a moment and I felt her Alpha power sidle round me. Her eyes bore into mine, willing me to look down. When I didn't, her eyes flashed before they flickered over my injuries. "You should stay, Mai. As long as you need to," she said, her voice soft.

I tilted my head, wondering if Jem was within hearing range. Hayley used to pull this trick before, playing nice whenever Jem was around and making certain I knew I wasn't wanted whenever he was out.

"I mean it," she insisted, almost like she could read my thoughts. "Things are different now that I'm the Alpha. Jem has struggled with you being gone. It'll be good for him and the Pack if you stick around for a while."

A knot formed in my stomach at her words. The last thing I wanted was to get involved with the Pack again. But I knew I couldn't just run away this time. Not with security all around the compound and Ryan hovering over me like a mother hen. Maybe I was going to have to face my past.

"I'll think about it," I said, trying to keep my voice steady.

Hayley nodded and then sat on the edge of the bed. "You know, Mai, I always admired you. When you left, I knew you were strong enough to make it on your own. It takes a lot of courage to walk away from everything you've ever known."

Did it? I'd done it twice now, once when I fled from Ryan and again when I escaped Seth. Was it courage or cowardice that made me run from them? I didn't know anymore.

I did know that I wanted to steer this conversation away from me. "You seem to have gotten everything you wanted, Hayley. You're

Alpha now. You live in the big house. No one to tell you what to do." That had been so important to her after growing up with her aunt's family. I really was happy for her that she had that security now, that she had what she always wanted. A shadow crossed her face at my words. If I'd blinked, I would have missed it. What was going on with her and Jem?

She paused for a moment too long, then laughed airily. "It certainly has its perks."

I wasn't falling for it. Hayley was not a happy wolf. Did I care enough to try to find out why? No. I had to look out for myself. Heal up, find a way to make a run for it again. Nothing had changed. I couldn't stay here with Ryan around every corner, his delicious scent drifting on the air, always just out of reach. I still knew that he was my fated mate. It would drive me mad to stay here and see him every day, knowing I couldn't touch him, not in the way my wolf yearned to do.

"Come on." Hayley got up off my bed. "Jem's waiting, it's time for dinner."

Hayley stayed in the corridor while I got dressed and freshened up. She didn't offer to help me down the stairs, something I was grateful for. I didn't like to feel like an invalid who couldn't look after herself. Going to school with Brock Madden and living on the streets for months after I'd left here had taught me the dangers of looking weak.

I followed Hayley into the dining room. She walked straight to a chair next to Jem. Jem was sitting at the head of the table, with Ryan next to him. I felt a stab in my chest at the sight of him. Okay, so the sleep didn't make it go away. Fine. I'd deal with it. No fucking clue how, but I would work something out so I could at least cope while I was here.

Jem stood up as I entered the room, a smile on his face. "Mai, how are you feeling?"

"Better, thank you," I replied, trying to keep my voice steady.

"Good. Mai, you remember the Shaw brothers, right?"

Ryan and his three brothers, each of them tall and muscular men, stood up. With their Alpha standing at the table, Pack hierarchy dictated they were not allowed to be seated.

"They're all Pack enforcers now," Jem continued, "although Mason and Sam also run a private investigations firm on the side."

"Sure." I felt Ryan's gaze on me, but I avoided it and looked around at the rest of the Shaw brothers.

Sam and Derek were twin brothers and had been in the year above me in school. They'd left by the time Brock had held me down and got everyone to pour food on me. Otherwise, they would have broken both of his legs.

Although they were twins, it was clear that time had accentuated their differences. Derek had always been the more serious of the two and had just left for the army by the time I'd done my vanishing act. His time there seemed to have left its mark on him. He sat tall and confident; his dark brown hair was cropped short, and his steely gray eyes seemed to take in everything around him. Next to him, Sam appeared more approachable and easygoing, his warm smile and bright green eyes giving off a welcoming vibe. His light brown hair was longer than Derek's, falling into his eyes in a charmingly disheveled manner. I remembered how Sam had always been the more outgoing twin, and I thought it was a smart move, joining forces with Mason in a PI firm where Sam could use his knack for connecting with people to help solve cases.

Mason was sitting nearest to the door. He was the oldest, after Ryan. It had been four years since I last saw him, but I couldn't help but marvel at how much he had changed. He must be twenty-four now, and he'd certainly filled out. I guessed he was at least 6'3" when he stood up, his muscular and athletic build probably down to rigorous training I knew enforcers went through. His short, jet-black hair appeared slightly tousled, giving him a rugged and effortlessly attractive look that I hadn't noticed before.

Mason was always one to put family and Jem first. He'd backed Jem and Ryan one hundred percent with their plan to take over the Pack. I remembered his dry sense of humor and how he'd share a joke or crack a sly smile, but only with those close to him. Although he often came across as intimidating, I knew that beneath that tough exterior, Mason would always help those in need.

I turned to Sam and before I could blink, he had encased me in a bear hug. His scent of wood smoke, dark chocolate, and a tinge of citron enveloping me. "Mai. Girl. We missed you!"

"I missed you, too."

"My turn," Derek said, tugging his brother off me and pulling me into his arms. I'd only ever seen Derek truly relax when he was around Sofia. His hug was the same. Where Sam was an all-in kind of hugger, Derek held me carefully for a moment and then backed off.

"Hey," Mason said, striding toward me and kissing me on my cheek. "Sam's right. We missed you, Mai."

The sound of glass breaking and the scent of fresh blood made me turn around. Ryan was glaring at his brothers, a broken wine glass in his hand.

"For fuck's sake, Ryan," Hayley hissed as she started mopping at the spilled red wine on the table.

"Shit, man, you okay?" Sam said, going over to Ryan.

My wolf nipped at me, wanting me to go to him, but I pushed her back.

"It's fine," Ryan replied, gruffly grabbing a napkin and wrapping the cut on his palm. "Just a little cut."

"What happened?" asked Mason as he picked up the pieces of glass that were strewn on the table.

"An accident, that's all." Ryan's tone made it clear that was the end of any discussion. He took the pieces of glass from his brother and strode into the kitchen.

I watched him go, wanting desperately to follow him to make sure he was okay.

"Why don't you sit, Mai?" Jem said as he gestured for me to take a seat. "We were just about to start dinner."

I hesitated for a moment, my eyes darting to the kitchen, then I nodded.

"Sure."

Jem had gestured to the only seat left, and the universe seemed to be conspiring against me. It was right next to Ryan's. With a deep breath, I slowly made my way there. I could do this. I just needed to avoid smelling Ryan. Avoid touching Ryan and avoid talking to him. Easy, right?

As I sat down, a trim middle-aged woman with short brown hair and three earrings in each ear started to put dishes on the table. The woman's warm brown eyes took in the scene, and then she cursed. "Well, not the best start to a meal. But no matter. The food will more than make up for it."

"Mai, this is Sylvie, our housekeeper and chef extraordinaire," Jem said.

As the delicious scents of lemon chicken, sage potatoes, salad, and freshly baked baguettes wafted around the room, it was clear that Sylvie's culinary skills were not to be underestimated.

Sylvie smiled at me. "I've heard all about you, Mai. It's lovely to finally meet you in person."

I smiled back at her just as Ryan came back and sat down next to me, his hand in a clean bandage. I ignored Ryan and the way his body was mere inches from mine. He was so close. His scent was suddenly all I could smell, overpowering everything and everyone else in the room. I swallowed, looking down. His leg was almost touching mine; I couldn't even see daylight between them. The image of me running my fingers up his leg and slowly undoing his belt jumped into my head.

No!

I shoved the image away. Food. People. That's what I had to think about. I had to concentrate on this meal and then get the hell away from Ryan.

Sylvie put the last dish on the table. "There you go. Enjoy!"

Before Sylvie had even left the room, the sound of clattering plates and cutlery filled the space. My stomach growled involuntarily, reminding me that I hadn't eaten in what felt like days. I reached out for the potatoes, but Ryan got there before me.

"Here," he said, loading them onto my plate.

Okay. "Thanks. Can you pass the chicken?"

Again, Ryan took the dish, and instead of passing it to me, he loaded enough chicken to feed everyone at that table directly onto my plate.

Okay, then.

I opened my mouth to ask for the salad, but Ryan beat me to it.

"Sam, don't hog all the salad. Mai wants some. Pass it here," Ryan said without even looking at his brother. Immediately, the huge salad bowl, full of lettuce, tomatoes, bacon, croutons, peppers, olives, and a dressing that smelled amazing, was in Ryan's hands, and he was spooning it onto my plate.

"Either you're trying to fatten me up to...?" Eat me? Hell, no, I wasn't going to go there. "Cook me in a pot, or you need glasses."

"You need to eat."

"I'm going to eat, but everyone else needs food, too."

"Don't you worry, Mai, there's lots more food in here!" Sylvie's shouted reply from the kitchen made Sam and Mason laugh.

"I promise, Mai. When you eat your first bite, you'll be thanking Ryan for giving you the best food this side of the Rockies," Sam said.

"Aw, Sam, you always were my favorite!" Sylvie shouted.

I frowned at the kitchen doorway, wondering why Sylvie wasn't in here eating with us.

Jem saw me looking and leaned toward me. "It's not a rule. She doesn't like to eat with others."

I nodded, glad Hayley hadn't created a "Downtown Abbey" atmosphere here, then took a bite. They were not wrong. I almost moaned in pleasure at the flavors that were being set off in my mouth.

Out of the corner of my eye, I saw Ryan smile, but valiantly ignored him. Instead, I focused on my plate, letting the conversation wash over me.

"How's Shaw Investigations getting on? Any new cases?" Derek asked, breaking off a piece of bread and slathering it with butter.

"It's pretty quiet at the moment," Mason replied.

"Yeah," Sam agreed, a mischievous twinkle in his eye. "So quiet we even had time for a chitchat with Tanya today when she made her deliveries."

"Who's Tanya?" asked Hayley.

"Oh, just a Bridgetown Pack wolf Mason has his eye on."

"I do not have my eye on her! She's Bridgetown. That says everything there is to say about it."

"Oh, really?" quipped Sam. "Coz I'm pretty sure I heard you flirting like a pro with her earlier."

"There was no flirting," Mason growled, making it clear to all of us that there was indeed flirting. "And maybe if you did less eavesdropping and more work, we'd actually make some money for a change!"

I laughed. I couldn't help it. Unless Mason had had a complete change of personality, he couldn't flirt even if he had a university degree in it. Everyone at the table, apart from Mason, knew Sam was teasing him.

Jem leaned over to me. "Don't listen to them, Mai. I know for a fact that Shaw Investigations does very well for itself."

Hayley remained silent, eating her food and glancing out of the window every now and again.

"We've been hearing rumors that Bridgetown are recruiting again, though," said Mason.

"I've been hearing that, too. Did Tanya confirm it?" Derek looked at Mason.

Mason managed to glare at his brother and look uncomfortable at the same time. "She's seen the new recruits. Delivered to where they are being based. She could give us an idea of how many there are, but we need to go slow with Tanya. She's loyal to her Pack. She likes gossip, which is where we get some intel from her, but it always needs to be confirmed with our other sources. Her use is more in giving us a feel for Bridgetown; the state of the Pack, how people are feeling about things that their Alphas are doing. She sometimes confirms things we have heard elsewhere, but I don't want to push hard with her unless it's an SOS situation."

"Michael and Camille might be allowing her to deliver to you, knowing she will plant false information."

Mason raised an eyebrow. "Sure, Derek, we definitely hadn't considered that."

"Alright." Derek grinned and held up his hands in surrender. "Just checking. The Bridgetown Alphas are clever."

I knew Bridgetown. Its territory bordered our own. When I left, it was already a pretty big Pack. Oliver had always forbidden us to interact with them, but if Tanya was making deliveries here, I guessed Jem had changed that. "Do you think Bridgetown is looking to expand their territory?" I asked.

Why did I ask that? I didn't want to know, didn't want to care, or be drawn back into the Pack and what was going on here.

Jem looked pleased at my question. "It's a possibility. We're keeping an eye on the situation. Derek, Mason, and Sam have been gathering intel to find out what their intentions are. We should know something for sure soon."

Mason chimed in, his deep voice steady, "It's important we know what their plans are. The Pack comes first. Always. But we also need to make sure our clients and those we care about are safe. We don't want any surprises or unnecessary confrontations. We need to be prepared for anything."

"Anything except you turning up again after four years," Sam said, a cheeky glint in his eyes. "So, Mai, you gonna tell us where the fuck you have been all these years?"

Chapter Eleven

Mai

Sam's voice was light-hearted, but everyone in the room tensed, including me.

"Er, let me think. No, Sam, I'm not."

There, that should shut him down.

"Come on, Mai. We missed you. You left. Ryan went crazy. Jem and Hayley killed Oliver. We've purged the old enforcers and built the new Pack, all so that it was safe and welcoming for when you eventually came back. You gotta give us something."

I froze as his words sunk in. Ryan went crazy? They built the new Pack for me?

"What?" I whispered.

Mason's voice was sharp. "Drop it, bro. Now's not the time."

"What does that mean? You built the new Pack for me?" I looked at Jem, knowing he'd answer me.

Jem threw a sharp look at Sam before answering. "We looked for you, Mai. For years. Ryan ran down every lead we ever got. It soon became clear that you didn't want to be found, but I knew that you'd come back sooner or later."

Jem paused, his gaze softening. "We wanted to create a Pack that you'd feel comfortable returning to. One where you'd be safe and welcome, no matter what had happened in the past."

"The school is closely monitored now," Ryan said, his tone gentle. "The children of our enforcers do not hold sway there simply because of who their parents are. The teachers are not too scared to speak up or punish those who bully others. Jem has restructured the whole Pack. All enforcers get vetted now. It's not a case of who your father or mother was or who owes who a favor. Each enforcer goes through rigorous tests and training, and we keep an eye on them. Anyone looking to take advantage of those weaker than them is thrown out. All Pack members get a basic income. Anyone who has the Three Rivers bond is entitled to it. We put a hydro dam in the Coldbrook River. It runs the whole town, cutting down our costs, and we sell a chunk of it back to the grid at a premium price. Shaw Investigations is funded by the Pack. Sam and Mason run a tight outfit with over fifty employees. They offer security services to human and Shifter businesses on the whole east coast, and they do a lot of work in the conclave cities."

The conclave cities were those that allowed both humans and Shifters. There were still human-only places, and some of the Shifter towns up north refused entry to any non-Shifter.

"The Pack is doing well," Ryan continued, "and we make sure we look after all our members. We knew it was what you would have wanted."

I swallowed hard, my heart racing. I didn't know what to say, the enormity of their actions washing over me like a tidal wave. "Why? Why would you do that?" I looked at Jem. "I wasn't... I mean, I was just your kid sister. I left. People do that all the time."

"That night, Mai, the one when you—"

"We are not going to talk about that night," I said, my voice harsh and my eyes darting to Ryan. I couldn't talk about the single most humiliating, heart-breaking moment of my life in front of everyone.

"That's it," Ryan growled, rising abruptly. "I'm done." Without warning, he scooped me up and strode out with me slung over his shoulder.

"What the fuck, Ryan? Put me down! Now!" I yelled. I could hear Jem and Ryan's brothers laughing in the dining room. I wasn't going to get any help from them.

"No," he said as he marched up the stairs toward my room. "I've had enough. We need to talk."

Ryan held me securely as he carried me up the stairs. I could feel the heat of his body pressed against mine, and despite my protests, there was a part of me that loved being so close to him.

"We're not talking. We don't need to talk. I don't want to talk, and you can't make me."

Did I just say that? How old was I? Five?

As we reached my room, Ryan gently set me down on my feet. His fingers dug into my hips, holding me in place. His blue eyes locked onto mine, their depths swirling with a mixture of protectiveness and passion.

What the fuck? Was I imagining the desire in them? Did I want him so badly that I was making it up now?

"We're going to talk, Mai," he repeated, his voice firm. "If you want to keep your mouth shut and just listen, that's fine. Probably better that way. There won't be as much yelling."

I glared at him, but he ignored my laser-intensity beams.

"You have to know the truth about that night."

I braced myself, trying to suppress the embarrassment and shame I felt every time I thought about him telling me I wasn't his mate and it was all some kid's fantasy. "I already know the truth, Ryan," I said through gritted teeth. "I was there. It's not something I can forget, even though I've tried. I've tried really fucking hard."

"You don't know shit. I had to reject you. It was the only way to keep you safe."

Safe?

Wait, what? "What are you talking about?"

"We were at war with Oliver and his enforcers. Jem and Hayley were nearly ready to challenge the Alpha, and Oliver knew it. He and his crew were looking for any way to weaken us. You know how hot on security Jem was. None of us went anywhere alone. Oliver was just looking for an opportunity to take any one of us out and pretend it was an accident. You were already on their radar as Jem's sister. If I had admitted that you were my mate as well, you would've become target number one for Oliver and his enforcers. And if he killed you, both Jem and I would have lost it."

My heart froze. Did he just say what I thought he just said? "Admitted? As in—"

"I know you are my fated mate, Mai. I've known for years."

My heart started beating again in a rush of blood and a thumping sound that echoed in my ears. What? Was he really admitting that I wasn't just a crazy kid with a crush?

"I told Jem. He and I decided that I had to ignore it. I couldn't tell you. We couldn't risk putting that kind of a target on your back. Then you announced it in front of everyone. You caught me off guard. I thought I had to reject you to keep you safe."

The pain of that night was still raw and fresh in my memory. "You flirted with others," I whispered, my voice trembling.

"I had to," Ryan admitted, a pained expression crossing his face. "I had to keep the focus off you until Jem had taken over the Pack. Then, we could finally be together. I never wanted to hurt you, Mai. I just wanted to protect you."

I jerked free of him and stepped back. I felt so confused. Everything I had believed to be true for the last four years was bullshit.

Ryan took a step toward me, but I held up a hand, and he stopped. It didn't stop him talking, though. "After the meet, I told Sam to go after you. He made sure no one followed you home, made sure you were safe, then he came back to help us deal with the fallout."

I shook my head. "What fall out?" I had so many emotions crashing around inside of me that I was struggling to keep up with what Ryan was saying.

"We had to smooth things over with Oliver. The night was supposed to be perfect, showcase the Pack as stable, no infighting, no dramas. The other Packs had started to ask questions about Oliver's gun business. He needed the meet to show he was an Alpha with power so that they would back off. He was not happy about the scene we caused. Jem and my brothers made sure he didn't suspect you were telling the truth, made sure the other Packs were appeased and saw Oliver as an Alpha in total control.

"We waited until the Packs left, then I told Jem he could stick it. I was done with the lies, with pretending to be someone I wasn't. I came over to see you. But you weren't there. Jem and I thought that Oliver had taken you as punishment. We raided the compound that night, and Jem and Hayley challenged for the Alpha spot. It was only after they won that Hayley mentioned you said you wanted to leave. I don't think that Jem has ever forgiven Hayley for not saying something sooner. He's always thought that if we had looked for you straight away, we might have found you."

Tears threatened to spill from my eyes as the enormity of his revelation washed over me. For years, I had felt abandoned and betrayed. Had felt that I didn't deserve to be loved. "I thought you didn't want me."

Ryan closed the distance between us, one of his hands encircling my waist while his hand cupped the back of my head and pulled me to him. I could feel the heat coming off him and his corded muscles hard against me.

"You're my mate, Mai." His voice was rough, demanding. "There is no one else for me. Not then, not now, not ever."

As his warm breath ghosted across my skin, my heart pounded in my chest. All this time, I had thought he'd rejected me. That he'd taken one look and decided that he didn't want anything to do with me.

"You absolute asshole, Ryan Shaw!" I shoved him away from me. "You and Jem decided, did you? Where was my choice in all this? You humiliated me in front of the whole Pack. In front of all the other Packs. And you knew! For months, you knew that I was your mate! You could have told me. We could have worked it out, kept us both safe. But, no, you and Jem had to know better, didn't you? Have you any idea what I went through? You tore my heart out!"

"Mai, I—"

"Get out!" I pushed against him with everything I had. He didn't shift, not even an inch.

"Out!" I yelled again.

He stared at me, seeming to drink in my appearance with such longing in his eyes it made my knees weak. Then he turned and left.

Chapter Twelve

RYAN

"Well, you certainly made a right mess of that," Hayley said. She was waiting for me at the bottom of the stairs.

I was in no mood for her bullshit. "Mai had to know the truth."

"Your brothers are making bets on how long it will take for her to forgive you, you know."

"I've got two years!" shouted Sam from the dining room.

The thought that she might never forgive me hit me, and I stumbled just as Jem walked toward me.

"Hayley, leave Ryan alone."

She whirled to him. "Of course, that's your reason for living these days, isn't it? To ruin all my fun."

"Hayley—" Jem took a step toward her, his hand outstretched.

"Don't bother, I'm not interested," she said and strode out of the front door.

Jem watched her go, his face full of regret. They really needed to get their shit together. This ongoing feud between them was hurting the whole Pack.

Jem turned to me. "Mai will come around."

I nodded, but I wasn't sure he was right.

"You tightened security around the compound?" I asked.

"Of course. She isn't going anywhere tonight."

"Not when you dramatically carted her out of here and forgot her crutches." Derek appeared, carrying them.

"Fuck!" I yanked a hand through my hair. What if she needed to come downstairs? I had effectively trapped her in her room.

"Don't worry, I'll leave them outside her door," Jem said, watching me carefully. "She needs time, and so do you."

My wolf was restless, stirring within me. He was eager to escape; the emotional turmoil of today causing him to push against the boundaries of my control.

"I need to run," I muttered, the urge to Shift growing stronger by the second. Jem nodded, understanding my need for release.

"Go ahead. We'll keep an eye on things here," he reassured me, his hand briefly clasping my shoulder.

With a grateful nod, I headed out the door and out of the compound. The cool night air was soothing on my heated skin. But I didn't want soothing. Mai was right. I should have told her years ago. I should never have hidden it. All of this, all those years that she'd been out there, alone, and it was my fault.

I slipped into the forest behind the compound, feeling the call of the wild grow stronger within me. The need to let my wolf take over was overwhelming, and I could no longer resist the urge. I tore off my clothes, not caring where they fell, and took a deep breath. I felt the power of my wolf coursing through my veins, and I willingly relinquished control. My bones cracked and shifted, rearranging themselves to accommodate the change. The pain was intense, but

I welcomed it. My skin prickled as thick fur sprouted from my skin, quickly covering my body in a dense, warm coat.

My face elongated, transforming into the muzzle of a wolf, my human teeth giving way to the sharp fangs of a predator. My ears shifted to the top of my head, becoming pointed and alert, twitching with every sound that filled the forest. My fingers and toes formed the powerful paws of a wolf, equipped with claws that could tear through flesh with ease.

I could feel my senses heightening, my wolf's instincts taking over. The scents of the forest became more distinct, the sounds of the night more vivid. My connection to the earth beneath my paws was electric, and the energy of the moon above filled me with a primal strength.

I retreated into my mind and let my wolf take over. My powerful limbs propelled me through the dark forest, the scent of damp earth and pine filling my nostrils. My heart raced as I leaped over fallen logs and dodged low-hanging branches, the exhilaration of the run providing a break from the heavy emotions filling me.

As I moved through the woods, Mai's beautiful face was etched into my mind. The thought of her forgiveness was both tantalizing and terrifying, and my wolf growled in frustration. He was clear that I should have told her as soon as I knew she was my mate. The memory of that moment when I'd realized that she was the one was burned into my soul.

It was an evening in late September. Mai had just turned seventeen. The sun was setting, and the sky was a deep orange. I'd been out for a run, on two legs this time, and stopped to catch my breath. In the distance, I saw Mai talking to Hayley, a frown on her face. They never did get along. I needed to talk to Jem about it again. I knew something wasn't right there, but Jem refused to listen. He loved Hayley and couldn't see the way Mai reacted whenever she was around.

I wiped the sweat from my brow. Mai shifted to the side, and the sun's rays caught her face. My wolf stirred in excitement. I stepped closer, watching as the light danced off her delicate features. As if sensing my presence, Mai looked up at me with a questioning expression on her face. Our eyes locked for one brief moment before she turned away, but it was enough for me. It was like a thunderbolt had struck, and I stumbled backward, unable to breathe. Time stopped. I don't know how long I stood there, caught in that moment, but when I looked up, Mai and Hayley had gone, and I was left with the absolute certainty that I had just found my true mate.

The wind howled through the trees as I ran, remembering that moment. I pushed myself harder, my muscles rippling beneath my fur as I raced through the moonlit night, seeking solace in the freedom of the run. My wolf had wanted to go straight to her that day, and we almost did, but then Jem had found me. I told him where I was going, and he grabbed hold of me. I punched him in his jaw when he told me I couldn't say anything to her. My wolf was going crazy, but Jem always did have a way with words. He convinced me that Oliver would kill her if he knew. That keeping it hidden was the right thing to do. That it was the only way to keep her safe. He was wrong, though. We both were.

⚜

Eventually, exhaustion began to set in, and I slowed my pace, panting heavily. I couldn't go far; my wolf needed the run, but he wouldn't allow me to be long without checking on Mai. I turned back and headed for my clothes.

CHAPTER THIRTEEN

MAI

I woke up and stared at the ceiling for a long time. Fucking Ryan. How could I be so mad at him and, at the same time, just want to feel his hands sliding along my body, touching my skin, and making me pant with need? I desperately wanted to know what his lips felt like on mine. What they'd feel like kissing every part of me. I wanted to run my hands through his hair, over his chest, and down toward the bulge in his jeans that I'd spent years fantasizing about.

My vibrator had not been one of the essential things that I'd grabbed on my escape from Seth, although I was regretting that now. Maybe if I took care of myself, I could just be mad at Ryan and not think about what it would feel like to have him thrusting inside of me, filling me completely with his cock, and making me scream with pleasure.

I moved my hand down my stomach and then drifted lower, skimming under the waistband of my panties to the skin beneath. A spark of heat ignited at the contact, warmth spreading through my belly, and I bit my lip against a quiet moan.

This was what I craved. What I needed. A reprieve from the anger and heartache, a chance to simply feel.

My nipples were tight peaks beneath my tank top, sensitive and wanting. I rolled one between my fingers and moaned.

My other hand slipped beneath my panties, questing fingers finding my clit. I rubbed slow, teasing circles, pretending they were Ryan's fingers instead of my own. The coil inside me wound tighter, pleasure building with each touch.

I dipped two fingers inside, imagining the stretch and fullness of Ryan filling me. My breaths came fast and shallow; my heartbeat raced as I drove myself higher. Ryan would grip my hips, thrusting deep and hard, growling my name against my throat—

My orgasm hit like a thunderclap, wringing a strangled cry from my lips. I shuddered against the mattress, aftershocks rippling through my body in waves. This was bliss. No thinking. No worries. Just this feeling of calm and peace.

And then the door swung open.

Ryan stood in the doorway, shoulders braced against the frame. His eyes were fathomless pools that gave nothing away. But there was a tightness to his jaw, and the way he held himself hinted at barely leashed control. Oh, Goddess, how long had he been outside my room, hearing me pleasure myself while thinking of him? Humiliation and anger warred inside me.

"Enjoy yourself?" The harshness of Ryan's tone made my hands clench into fists.

"Get out," I spat. My face flamed, and I was acutely aware that I wore only a tank top and panties. I crossed my arms over my chest as if I could hide what he'd already seen. What he'd heard.

Ryan prowled into the room, closing the door behind him with a loud click. "I don't think so. We have things to discuss, you and I." Ryan stopped in front of me, looming over my smaller frame. His eyes glowed like embers in the dim light from the window. "Did you think of me when you touched yourself?"

"Don't flatter yourself, Ryan." I swung my legs out of the bed and grabbed a pair of jeans from the floor.

"You want me as badly as I want you, Mai. Deny it all you like, but your body betrays you." He reached out, tracing a finger down my jaw in a feather-light caress.

I jerked away from his touch, heart pounding. "I didn't think of you. I didn't think of anyone. I just had fun. You should try it sometime. It might make you less of a jerk."

A smile tugged at the corner of Ryan's mouth. "I'm looking forward to you showing me fun, Mai. But I'm not wrong." His gaze raked over me, hot as a physical touch. "You're mine. And soon, you'll admit that to yourself."

I swallowed hard, refusing to give him the satisfaction of a response.

Ryan leaned in closer, his breath warm against my ear. "I could smell your arousal, Mai. I heard every gasp, every moan."

Heat flooded my cheeks. I shoved at his broad chest, but he didn't budge. "Fuck off, Ryan," I said through gritted teeth.

"Not until you admit this is bigger than both of us." Ryan caught my chin in his hand, forcing me to meet his gaze. "We're mates, Mai. We're meant to be together. No matter how much you fight it, I won't let you go. Not again."

I wrenched my chin from his grasp. "There is no us. There never will be an us."

Something dangerous flickered in Ryan's eyes. In one smooth movement, he pinned me against the wall, hands on either side of my head. I sucked in a sharp breath, heart rabbiting against my ribs.

Ryan leaned in until his lips brushed my neck. "Keep telling yourself that. But we both know the truth; you want this as much as I do." Ryan nuzzled my neck, and I shuddered despite myself. "Say it, Mai."

I squeezed my eyes shut. I couldn't give in. I wouldn't.

Ryan nipped at the sensitive skin of my neck, and a helpless moan slipped from my lips.

"Say it," he repeated, voice rough with desire.

Every inch of me was on fire for him. I couldn't remember why I was fighting this. Fighting us.

No, wait, I did remember.

I stubbornly lifted my chin. "You're delusional. This is just a fantasy you've concocted in your mind."

"Really?" Ryan slid a hand down my side in a slow, deliberate caress that made my breath hitch. "Your heart is pounding. Your cheeks are flushed. And I can smell how wet you are for me." His hand ran across the gap of bare skin between my tank top and panties. "Tell me you don't want this. Tell me you don't want me."

I shoved against his chest again, panic and longing warring inside me. Ryan still didn't budge.

"Let me go," I whispered.

He leaned in closer to me. "The next time you come, it'll be because I'm fucking you, Mai."

More heat rushed to my cheeks. I opened my mouth to protest, but no words came out.

A smug grin spread across Ryan's face. "You can pretend all you want, but your body knows the truth. It craves me, just like I crave you."

Okay, I had to shut this down. Now. Nothing had changed. Yes, Ryan acknowledged that I was his mate. But he'd rejected me four years ago. Had lied to me for months and made me believe I was unlovable. Ryan admitting the truth didn't change anything. I didn't trust him, could never trust him. My plan was still in place. I was going to heal and then get the fuck out of here.

"Ryan—"

A knock at the door stopped me.

"Mai, you up yet?"

Jem. He had freaking brilliant timing.

"I'm up!" I yelled back, my frustration mounting.

"I'm heading out. I've got some meetings in town. Do you want a lift to the Bottley Bar? I've had six texts and three phone calls from Sofia this morning, asking when I'm going to let you out from your 'luxurious prison,' as she seems to have nicknamed my home."

"Yes!" I shouted, scrambling out from Ryan's hold and ignoring his chuckle. "Hell, yes!"

"I'll be downstairs in ten, then. Be quick!" Jem said.

I turned, limped into the bathroom, and slammed the door. I heard Ryan leaving the room as I stepped into a deliberately cold shower.

CHAPTER FOURTEEN

MAI

I hopped on my crutches into the Bottley Bar and Coffeeshop, instantly feeling the warmth and welcoming atmosphere of the place. The scent of freshly brewed coffee and homemade pastries filled the air, as soft jazz music played in the background. The walls were decorated with eclectic artwork, and the mismatched furniture gave the place a cozy, lived-in feel.

Sofia was behind the counter, her vibrant red hair falling in loose curls around her shoulders. Her eyes sparkled with excitement as she caught sight of me, her full lips curling into a wide grin. She had always been the life of the party, her infectious energy and caring nature making her the best friend a girl could ask for. She jumped the counter and bounded up to me, arms open. I sucked in a breath as she wrapped her arms around me and squeezed.

"It is so good to see you, Mai. You're looking much better than yesterday!"

"Need... need to breathe..."

"Oh, shit!" she exclaimed, letting me go. "Sorry!"

"No problem. I missed your hugs!" I did, too. My ribs? Not so much.

I slid onto a stool at the counter, my heart swelling as Sofia poured me a cup of coffee.

"So, tell me everything. What did Ryan say to you? Did you see Jem? What do you think about the Alpha's compound?"

I grinned. "You haven't changed, you know. Always wanting the gossip."

"Duh!" Sofia grinned back. "Why do you think I work here? The day lot gossip like old men, and at night, one sip of alcohol and they blab everything! This is gossip central! I get to know everything that happens in the human and wolf world. So don't let me down, Mai. Spill."

So, I did. I told her about the compound, about Hayley and Jem. About the Shaw brothers. About what Ryan had said to me, and what happened this morning.

"Holy fuck!" she whispered.

"I know! Can you believe that guy?"

Sofia looked at me for a moment, then leaned in closer. "You should know that Ryan hasn't touched anyone since you left. He hasn't even looked at another person—werewolf or human—in that way. That night, when he, you know... and then you left, he went mental. When he found out you'd gone, his wolf took over, and he lost it. It took all of his brothers and Jem to subdue him. When he Shifted back, he didn't say a word. Just walked right into the Alpha compound and attacked Oliver. Luckily, his brothers, Jem and Hayley followed him. But they'd spent months plotting how to take down Oliver, and Ryan blew it all in one night. Thank the Goddess, they came out on top."

He did what?!

"I... I don't know what to do with that information," I confessed. It was too overwhelming right now. What I'd thought to be right all these years, that Ryan was an asshole who rejected his true mate, that I wasn't worthy of being loved, that maybe there was something wrong with me, something that made Ryan not want anything to do with me, was bullshit. I had to rethink everything about that night, about what I thought about Ryan and what I thought about myself for the last four years.

"I know, chickee. It's a lot. But your leaving changed everything for us. Jem and Ryan wanted to change the Pack so you could come home and feel safe. They both felt that they'd failed you. I know they hoped you would hear that they were in charge and would come home," she continued. "Day by day, though, the rest of the Pack watched as they lost hope, and it was heart-wrenching. It drove Hayley nuts."

I snorted. "That I can imagine."

"I know, right? She was happy at first; she was finally the Alpha, and we all knew how much she wanted that. But they never gave up looking for you, Mai. They started to change the Pack so it was the kind of Pack that you should have grown up in. That wasn't what Hayley wanted. She wanted more of the same, just with her in charge, living it large in the big house, and finally being the one telling everyone else what to do."

"Yeah, that sounds like Hayley."

Sofia nodded. "She doesn't care about us, Mai. Not like Jem does. And she hated that Jem was doing things for you. In her mind, it should have been just her and Jem ruling everything. Not Jem trying to make things better for the rest of the Pack. Not Ryan constantly out there searching for you. She's a bitter woman, Mai. You need to watch your back."

"She's bitter, but she's harmless, Sofia. I'm not a kid anymore, and she's not my guardian. She doesn't have that kind of power over me."

"Just be careful, okay? You're going to have to watch your back with Hayley and watch that your panties stay on when Ryan is around."

I knew she was trying to cheer me up, but I was just so overwhelmed by it all. "I don't know what to do with any of this," I whispered.

Sofia reached out and touched my arm, knowing exactly what I was talking about. "You don't need to do anything with it. Take time. Think about it. I won't tell you to give Ryan a chance; what he did was unforgivable, but know that he has tried to make amends, even if you weren't here."

I looked down at my hands and tried to steady my breathing. Everything was so complicated. I didn't know what to do or who to trust.

As I lifted my head, I saw Ryan outside the bar, leaning against his car and staring right at me. His eyes were filled with a dark intensity that sent a shiver straight to my core.

Sofia followed my gaze. "I can tell him to fuck off, if you want?"

"No," I shook my head. My wolf was pining for him, and I knew she felt safer knowing he was near. "It's alright. I'm sure he's got better things to do than hang around outside a bar all day. He'll get lost soon enough."

Chapter Fifteen

Mai

Ryan did not get lost and was still there an hour later. In between serving her regulars—both humans and Shifters—Sofia was finding it hilarious. I was getting more and more pissed off. It wasn't just Sofia who had noticed. Most of the Shifters came into the Bar on edge. Their Pack Beta was lurking outside, a scowl on his face, radiating a talk-to-me-and-I'll-break-your-legs vibe. As soon as they saw me, though, they'd relax and grin, a knowing look on their faces. A few had even winked at me! It was all I could do not to go out there and throttle Ryan. If he was going to follow me around wherever I went, my being back was going to spread through the Pack in no time. Did he not have a job to go to?

"How you holding up?" Sofia put down a coffee in front of me.

I breathed in the scent of smoky dark roast. "Thank you, you're a lifesaver!"

"Just doing my job."

I took a sip and sighed in pleasure. "Well, you're amazing at your job. Is the owner around so I can sing your praises?"

Sofia slid into the booth. "Nah, she pops in now and then, but she leaves it to me most days."

I watched as Sofia took in the elderly Shifter couple sharing a slice of carrot cake, the human dad with his five-year-old kid who was drinking a baby cappuccino, the ones that were just frothy milk, and had a splodge of white froth on the end of her nose, and the other barista, a sixteen-year-old human goth who'd been introduced to me as Brian, who was humming a Taylor Swift song as he wiped the tables. Sofia smiled.

"You like it here."

She looked back at me. "Yeah, I do. I get to talk to different people here. Doesn't matter if they're human or Shifter, if they are office workers, pizza deliverers, CEOs, or cleaners. I get to watch their faces light up when they take their first sip of coffee or bite into the homemade muffins. Life is stressful, Mai. In here, they get to take a break for a while. Relax. Just enjoy the small things, you know?"

"Plus, everyone talks to you, and you get to know everyone's business, sometimes even before they do," I guessed.

Sofia laughed. "Yeah, there is that."

"What about your parents? Do they come here, too?"

Sofia's parents had never liked me. They weren't exactly supporters of Oliver, but they were quiet people. They didn't want to rock the boat, stick their necks out, or bring any attention to themselves. Especially the type of attention Oliver gave. Me? I was trouble. As Jem's sister, they could see that being my friend would only put Sofia in the firing line. They forbade her to see me. Something she completely ignored.

"Ah, yes, my parents." Sofia tucked a stray bit of hair behind her ear. "They moved two years ago. Went out west to join my mom's sister."

"I didn't know she had a sister."

"They didn't like to talk about her much. I've only met her a couple of times. She married a witch, so they went off the radar for a long time."

Witches and werewolves mixing was frowned upon. Witches were even banned from practicing in the northeast ever since a witch called Simon Webster tried to create a spell that would put all werewolves under his control. He nearly succeeded, which freaked out the Wolf Council and led to a purge of all witches in a thousand-mile radius of where Webster lived.

"They had a couple of kids. The daughter got into trouble a couple of years back, and Mom and Dad moved to help my aunt deal with her."

I blinked. "Your parents? Moved toward controversy and attention?"

Sofia laughed. "I know, right? They were all 'fuck no' when I wanted to stand up for what I believed in, but as soon as Jase and I moved out, they packed up and moved to help their niece, who was making waves with Wolf Council and threatening to burn the whole thing down. And they're helping her do it! Can you believe it?"

"I'm sorry."

"No, it's okay. Mom and Dad saw the difference that Jem and Hayley made here. They knew how unhappy I was when Oliver was the Alpha. I think they realized that keeping their heads down and ignoring things didn't make anything better. If you want to change things, you have to step up. This is them stepping up."

"For your niece and aunt, though. Not for you or Jase."

Sofia shrugged. "In their own way, they think it is. They want to change how the whole Wolf Council is run. They think that will make things better for everyone, me and Jase included."

"Well, I'm impressed as hell. I never thought of Mr. and Mrs. Miller as agents for political change or guerilla fighters wanting to change the system! You weren't tempted to go with them?"

"We weren't exactly on speaking terms when they left. Besides, Jase was here, and he needed a place to stay."

"He lives with you?"

Sofia nodded. "We have an apartment upstairs. It works for us. Though I could do without his numerous girlfriends leaving their bras lying on the couch."

My eyes widened. "I can't picture little Jase Miller dating!"

"Trust me, you don't want to picture it. Or see it in person. It will scar you for life."

"What about you? Any boyfriends hanging around?"

"Me? Goddess, no! Men are way too much trouble. I'll stick with my pink rabbit; it sorts me out better than a guy ever could."

I raised my eyebrows and was just about to ask about Derek when the door swung open and a group of six office workers walked in, their chatter filling the whole room.

"Got to head back. I'll come catch up when the lunch rush is over."

I was sipping my coffee, still reeling from the revelations Sofia had shared with me, when my phone buzzed on the counter, an unknown number flashing on the screen.

"Hello?"

"Where the fuck are you?"

Fear gripped me, and I froze. Out of the corner of my eye, I saw Ryan sprinting toward me.

"Well? Answer me, Mai!"

I flashed back to the last time I'd seen Seth, me on the floor, bleeding and about to pass out. Seth standing over me, his face grim, saying, "You gotta learn, Mai. You gotta learn."

I twisted to the side so that Sofia and Ryan couldn't see my face. "I'm out of your reach, Seth," I whispered. "Don't look for me."

"You can't escape me, Mai. I will find you."

My phone was snatched from my hand. I turned as Ryan held the phone up to his ear, rage boiling off of him, but I could hear the dial tone. Ryan's fingers squeezed my phone.

"Please don't break it, Ryan. It has all my clients' contacts on it."

He looked at me, his jaw tight. I don't think I'd ever seen him this angry. "Who was that?"

I shook my head, not ready to explain. I didn't want Ryan to know what an idiot I'd been for staying with Seth, even after I saw the warning signs.

"I'm handling it, Ryan. This doesn't involve you."

"You're my mate, Mai. Of course it involves me," Ryan growled.

A jolt of electricity zipped through me at his words. I'd dreamed of him saying those words, that I was his mate. It was a shame that now he was admitting it, I just wanted to throw something at him.

"Back off, Ryan, I've got this."

"Clearly, you don't. You're going to have to let me in, Mai."

"Not a chance in hell, Ryan Shaw."

We glared at each other, neither one of us backing down.

"You know," Sofia moved in front of Ryan, breaking our eye contact, "as delightful as this stand-off is, there's a new phone shop that opened last month on Boddington. Why don't you get a new number, switch the contacts across, then ditch this one."

I glanced at her. It wasn't a bad idea. Maybe I should go all out and get a new phone. Seth knew people who could track phones. I needed to get rid of it.

"He isn't going to touch you. I won't let him hurt you, Mai," Ryan said fiercely. "You're safe here, I promise."

I wished that were true. But Seth had shown me that I couldn't trust anyone. "No one can make me safe, Ryan. I have to do this on my own," I whispered back.

CHAPTER SIXTEEN

RYAN

S he'd looked so fragile, telling me she had to do this alone. Whoever this guy was, he'd done a number on her, making her think that. Werewolves were drawn to Packs for a reason. We were a team, one that looked after everyone in it. I should have been there to protect her. Hell, she never would have been there in the first place if I'd handled our whole mate thing properly four years ago. This was my fault, and I was going to do everything to protect her now.

"Come on," I said. "I'll drive you to the phone shop."

She nodded, said goodbye to Sofia, and let me lead her to my truck. I opened the door, picked her up, and settled her into the passenger seat, ignoring her glare.

She was silent as I drove, her face turned to the side, staring out the window, lost in thought. She looked really pissed off, though.

She had that same look earlier when I told her the next orgasm was going to happen because of me. My cock twitched at the thought of her making herself come this morning. Her scent, her moans drove me wild. It was all I could do to wait outside her room until she was done. I'd wanted to walk in there and lick her pussy until she was moaning my name, begging me for more.

I'd gotten to her this morning, though. She might deny it, but she wanted me. Now her walls were back up, thinking about whatever fucker had beaten her up.

I had to track this bastard down, make sure he could never hurt Mai again.

When we got to the phone shop, I could feel the tension radiating off Mai as she swiveled out of the car, her movements stiff with pain again. We needed to stop by Thomas's on the way back, see if he could do anything for her.

I followed Mai into the shop, my senses on alert for any hint of danger.

Mai limped to the desk and spoke with the clerk. I scanned the street, keeping one eye on Mai. There were dark circles under her eyes, and her skin was paler than usual, but her eyes were clear and focused. I could see the determination in them, the same determination that had made her run four years ago.

The clerk showed her some phones. I walked over and picked one up.

"This one."

"What?" Mai frowned at me.

"This one," I repeated. "We use it in the Pack. It's the best one for security."

I saw her eyes widen as she glanced at the price tag.

"She'll take this one," I said to the clerk. "Charge it to the Pack."

"No!" Mai turned to me. "That's not—"

"You're part of this Pack, Mai, whether you like it or not. Your safety is pretty fucking high up on our priority list right now. You're going to take the phone because it's the best one there is, you're going to let Derek give you a briefing on how to keep it clean so no one can use it to track you, and you're going to let me take you out for dinner."

Mai's mouth opened, then closed. Then opened again. It would almost be cute if I didn't know she was only speechless because she couldn't decide what to yell at me first.

"You—"

"Give the man the phone, Mai. You can yell at me later." I turned, pulled out my own phone, and walked outside. I had calls to make. I couldn't wait any longer. I was going to track down that motherfucker.

I'd just ended my last call when Mai came out of the shop. She glared at me, then hopped to the car. She was certainly getting faster on her crutches.

I bleeped the locks but didn't pick her up this time. I knew better than to get in range of those crutches right now. Knowing Mai, she'd swing one at me.

I got in and set off for Thomas's.

"You okay?"

"Do I look okay?" she snapped back.

"No," I said, patiently, "that's why I asked."

Her shoulders tensed. "I don't want to talk to you right now."

"I know. But I'll be here when you do."

She narrowed her eyes at me. "Stop treating me like the kid who left here four years ago. I'm a grown werewolf, for fuck's sake. I can handle my own shit, and I don't need you or anyone, for that matter, to be sticking their noses in my business. I'm not the same person who left here, Ryan. You don't know me. Not anymore."

"You're right. I don't. But I'd like to." I tilted my head and gave her my most charming smile. "So, is that a yes for tonight?"

"No, that is not a yes!"

"Ah, so it's a maybe? I'll take a maybe."

"Ryan—"

"Look, you need to eat. I need to eat. Let's eat in the vicinity of each other. You can yell at me. I'll apologize profusely for whatever you say I need to apologize for, and then I'll take you to the bedroom, and I'll—"

"Don't finish that sentence," she warned.

I grinned at her as I pulled up at Thomas's house. "Say yes, or I'll finish that sentence in explicit, and I mean explicit, detail."

Mai crossed her arms and glared at me. "Fine. But only because I need to eat."

"Great. I'll pick you up at seven." I jumped out and opened the door for her.

Thomas met us at the front door. "Mai, good to see you again. Let's give you a quick check-up, then you can try Shifting."

I watched her go, feeling a wave of frustration. I knew I was pushing her too hard, but I couldn't help it. I'd spent four years hoping she'd come back, and now that she was here, I couldn't bear the thought of losing her again. I knew I should be patient and let her come to me on her own terms. But I'd done enough waiting. She was mine, and I was going to make sure she knew it.

CHAPTER SEVENTEEN

MAI

Thomas declared I was okay to Shift. I welcomed it. I didn't want to think anymore. I wanted the peace that always came when my wolf took over. I could retreat to the back of my mind and just feel the movement of our body.

Thomas led me out the back of his house, down the garden to a small wooden cabin. He opened the door, and a wave of warmth and security washed over me. As I stepped inside, the familiar scent of earth and pine filled my senses. Floor-to-ceiling French windows filled one wall. Shelves full of clean clothes for after a Shift stood on one side of the room, while off to one side stood a narrow bench for my personal belongings.

"Go ahead and Shift, Mai," Thomas said, his voice soothing. "The French windows can be opened with a slight push and lead out to the forest. If you go west, it's well-protected for five miles. The enforcers do regular sweeps of the boundaries, but they know not to come in. It is for my patients and for them alone. I'll be here when you get back."

I nodded, feeling a sense of relief as I began to undress. The Shift was always a release, a way to escape the complexities of the human world and embrace the raw power of the wolf. I closed my eyes and let myself go, feeling a rush of energy coursing through my veins. My bones cracked and contorted; my skin tore as fur burst forth. It was always painful, like a plaster being ripped off, but this time, with my injuries, it was excruciating. I let out a howl of pain.

Suddenly, I heard a loud thud and then voices outside, harsh and angry. Ryan trying to get to me.

"You'll make it worse, Ryan. Stand down. She isn't in any danger. She needs to do this to heal properly, and you'll mess it up if you storm in there. She has to feel safe. If you charge in with your scent and emotions this riled up, you'll freak her out. She needs to remain calm, Ryan, and she can't do that with you like this. Come on, come back inside."

I tuned them out, the pain all-encompassing now. Bones broke, skin stretched, then pulled tight, like a band forcing me into a smaller and smaller position. Finally, the pain left me. I lay on the floor, panting from the effort. As I took a few deep breaths, I felt my wolf form settling into a calmness I hadn't felt in a long time. I shook off the lingering discomfort and inhaled. Scents flooded my senses—the earthy aroma of damp soil, the tangy scent of fallen leaves, the rich musk of nearby wildlife. And, underneath it all, a familiar fragrance—the Three Rivers. It was like coming home after a long journey, the bond with my territory flaring to life, filling me with a warmth I hadn't realized I'd missed. I could feel the other members of the Pack, distant but connected, their lives tiny threads woven into the tapestry of my own existence.

My paws touched the wooden floor as I padded over to the French doors. I nudged them open, stepping into a world amplified. The night air was crisp, electrifying, as if welcoming me back. I took off, my paws barely touching the ground, the wind singing through the trees, leaves dancing in nocturnal celebration.

The night was mine, and I was free to explore. The trees flew past me. Every step was a thrill. My ears picked up the distant call of an eagle, the soft hooting of mourning doves, the scuttle of a small mammal in the underbrush, the whispering of the trees sharing their secrets. And my paws, oh, how they relished the feel of the earth beneath them—the gritty texture of soil, the soft give of moss, the unyielding solidity of rocks.

It was like nothing else mattered, nothing else existed except for the moment that I was in.

As I ran, the tension in my body dissipated, replaced by a sense of peace. For the first time in a long time, I felt truly free. The human world, with all its feelings and dangers, the Pack's dramas, my confusion about Ryan, and Seth's threats, felt a million miles away.

Here, and in this form, I didn't feel weak. My injuries were gone. There was no one here to cower from. No one here to beat me or make me feel like I was less than I was. I'd run in these woods as a child, in both forms. I knew this place, and it knew me. The forest filled me up, and I knew that I belonged.

I didn't want to go back. I could have run and run. But my wolf had other ideas. She had none of my conflict over Ryan. He was our mate. That was it.

She padded back into Thomas's cabin and started to Shift back. It wasn't painful this time; my injuries were healed, and after taking a moment to recover, I slipped back into my clothes. I hesitated at the door. I had to face Ryan, but I still didn't know how I felt. I was so angry with him, yet my wolf was singing with joy every time she saw him.

Luckily, Thomas was the only one there when I came out of the building.

"I've sent Ryan to wait in the car. He was finding this, um, challenging, shall we say?"

I smiled at the doctor, surprised that Ryan would obey an order from a doctor. "Really? And he listened to you?"

"Yes. He knows what's good for the Pack. It's possible I've threatened, on a number of occasions, to leave if he pissed me off enough. I'm not under Pack obligations. You see, that was my condition for coming here. I can leave any time I want or any time the Pack enforcers annoy me too much. Not that I would. I like it here too much, and despite some people here, this Pack is better than most. But don't tell Ryan that. I like to threaten them with leaving every now and again to keep them on their toes."

I laughed. I liked Thomas and the fact that he'd found a way to keep the enforcers and Jem off his back.

"Come into the house. I want to do a final exam if that's okay with you? But it's looking like everything has healed up nicely."

I swung my arms back and forth, then hopped up and down on my bad leg.

I grinned at him. "As good as new."

Chapter Eighteen

MAI

I followed Thomas into the house and let him do a quick exam, testing my muscles and bones.

Just as he was finishing, I heard the front door open and a man yell, "Thomas? You here?"

"He knows full well I'm here," Thomas whispered to me. "He does that every time he smells I'm with someone new. He doesn't want to spook them, you see. You're not spooked, are you?"

"No," I whispered back.

Thomas sighed. "Maybe he's right, then, and it does help."

"Of course, it helps," said a voice from the doorway.

I turned to see a man there, almost the opposite of Thomas. Whereas Thomas loomed no matter how hard he tried not to, this man was skinny and small, though maybe he just seemed that way next to Thomas. He obviously took a lot of care in his appearance, with a crisp light-blue shirt, perfectly ironed black trousers, and polished leather shoes. His skin was light brown, his dark hair was combed back, and his bright eyes stared at me with a sparkle of mischief.

"Well, hello there. I'm Wally, Thomas's mate." He strode forward and offered me his hand.

"Hi, I'm Mai."

"Mai?" He darted a questioning look at Thomas. "*The* Mai? The one who has been missing for years and is now back and making Ryan all hot and bothered? That Mai?"

"Um—"

"Leave her be, Wally. Now is not the time for your gossiping."

"Shush! Don't be silly. I hold the title of town gossip, so it is my duty, my darling. Therefore, it is always time for my gossiping." Wally turned to me, his eyes sparkling with curiosity. "So, Mai, tell me everything! What brings you back?"

"Everything? To the self-declared town gossip?" I joked.

Wally put one hand on his hip. "Did you see the sign on your way in?"

I couldn't remember any sign outside. "Um, no?" I said, not sure where he was going with this.

"Well, trust me, there is one. It says 'Thomas Merdais, Doctor,' then some letters afterward, but they're not important." He waved his hand as if to demonstrate how unimportant they were.

Thomas snorted.

"But that sign means that anything you say in here is covered by doctor-patient confidentiality."

I opened my mouth to point out that Wally was not a doctor, but he continued, "And I take that oath seriously on behalf of my gorgeous hunk of a husband. So that means that anything you say here does not leave these fine lips of mine."

I glanced at Thomas, and he nodded. "Wally won't repeat a thing."

I hesitated, unsure how much to reveal. But I had to talk to someone, and Thomas and Wally didn't know me. They weren't here when Ryan rejected me; they didn't know the person I was before. They wouldn't know just how idiotic I'd been to believe in Seth or how stupid I'd been in staying with him so long. Oh, Sofia and Jem would be sympathetic if I told them, but I'd see it in their eyes, that judgment of what a fool I'd been.

"After Ryan rejected me, I thought maybe I couldn't be loved by anyone. I ran. I spent time bouncing from town to town, just wanting to put distance between me and the Pack. I used different names, took on temp jobs—waitressing, barkeeping, cleaning rooms. I slept in the streets, in back alleys, cheap motels, and bedsits."

"That sounds tough." Wally put his hand on my arm and gave it a gentle squeeze.

"I coped. I just wanted to escape from the heartbreak. I didn't care what I did or where I stayed as long as I could keep busy and not think about Ryan or the Three Rivers. Then, in one town, I saw an advert for an online coding class. I fell in love with it. It was challenging but straightforward. I felt like maybe, just maybe, I could do something with my life. I worked to pay for more classes, and when I thought I was ready, I started my own web design business. It started small at first but then took off. I had my regular clients, whose sites I'd build then maintain, and new clients were calling me every week. It got so I started turning people away. The money was good, and I was able to rent a cute flat in the center of Cocrane.

"I've been there!" Wally said. "It's a nice town, good Pack Alphas if I recall?"

"Kara and Ajak. Yes. They're good people. Their Beta is a wolf named Korrin, and Korrin has a son, Seth."

Wally leaned forward. "Uh-huh, I just know we're getting to the good bit now."

I nodded slowly, remembering the first time I'd seen him. "I was in a coffee shop, working on a website. He sauntered over and said, 'Impressive,' in a deep, growly voice. I thanked him, and he said he was talking about me, not my work. I was flattered, you know?"

Wally nodded. "You hadn't had much male attention before, had you? And then Ryan's mishap made you feel that maybe there was something wrong with you?"

I glanced at him, wondering how he knew that from what I'd told him. He must have read the question on my face.

"It's what I would have thought."

I blinked. Was it that obvious?

"Go on, what happened with Seth?" Wally urged me to continue.

"Seth made me feel special and appreciated, something I hadn't ever felt before. We started seeing each other. No red flags. He was attentive, kind, and seemed genuinely interested in my life. But things changed over time. He became controlling—commenting on my clothes, discouraging me from making friends. I put it down to him being tired or stressed with work—he was being trained as an enforcer. His dad wanted him to take the Beta spot one day, but Korrin is a hard man to please. He was always telling Seth he wasn't good enough, that he had to be better. Seth tried to hide it, but it really got to him. He wanted nothing more than to get his dad's approval. I thought that was why Seth was so on edge all the time, and I knew exactly what things would annoy him, so I started to avoid doing them, or saying them, or wearing certain clothes.

"It wasn't until Seth started trying to control my work schedule that

I realized how toxic our relationship had become. With my business, I can set my own hours. For me, the best time of day is the early morning; I love watching the dawn come up with my laptop and a mug of coffee. But Seth, he began to get angry about it, insisting that I should stay in bed with him until he decided to get up. I finally realized how much of myself I'd changed to fit around Seth, and now he wanted me to change how and when I worked, too. It felt suffocating; I needed to end it."

"I'm guessing that did not go well."

I shook my head. "He wasn't angry at first. He just laughed at me. I told him I was serious, and he stared at me with this look of betrayal on his face. Then he punched me. I was so surprised, I didn't do anything. Just curled up as he started kicking me. He... he..."

Wally squeezed my arm again. "It's okay."

I took a deep breath; the room was filled with the scent of my fear and adrenaline.

"After... after he said, 'You're never leaving.' Then he slammed my head against the floor, and I passed out." I stopped there, unable to go on.

"Here," Wally said gently as he handed me a tissue.

I frowned, then touched my cheek. It was wet.

When did I start crying?

"You're safe, Mai. He can't hurt you here."

I wiped the tears with the tissue before continuing, "When I came to, Seth wasn't there. It took me a while to crawl to the couch and get myself up. But I knew what I had to do. I grabbed a few things, then got to my car. I was so scared that he would come back before I could get away."

"But you did. You escaped him," Wally said gently.

I nodded. "I drove out of Cocrane and came straight here."

Chapter Nineteen

Mai

"I'm so sorry you had to go through that. But you're here now, and we're not going to let anyone hurt you ever again, are we, Thomas?"

Thomas nodded. "You're safe now, Mai. You're strong. I have no doubt you'll find your way. And remember, you've got a whole Pack here to support you. The Shaw boys might be a handful, but they're good at their jobs. They'll track down Seth and make sure he leaves you alone."

"No! I don't want them to know. I'll handle Seth if he shows up."

Wally looked at me, a horrified expression on his face. "Girl, what are you talking about? Of course you need to tell them."

I shook my head. "I can't. I feel... I feel so stupid. I should have seen the signs. Why didn't I leave? Why did I stay with him for so long? And when he started hitting me, what the fuck did I do? Nothing. I'm a fucking werewolf. Ryan trained me to fight before I left, and I kept training wherever I went. I even trained with Seth's best friend, Isaac. Every Thursday, we'd hit the gym, and I'd learn how to beat the shit out of him. Yet when Seth started hitting me, all I did was curl up in a ball."

"Someone you loved and trusted just hit you; of course you did nothing!" Wally looked like he wanted to shake some sense into me. "That's not something to be ashamed of."

"No? Well, I feel ashamed. Ashamed and embarrassed. I don't want people to know what an idiot I am. I don't know how I feel about Ryan, but I don't want to see pity in his eyes when he looks at me," I pleaded with him. "They can't know. If I have any chance of looking at myself in the mirror, then I have to deal with this by myself."

Wally studied me for a minute. "How?"

"How, what?"

"How are you going to deal with it?"

"I... Well, I just will." Okay, even I knew that was a lame-assed answer.

"Girl—"

"Not now, Wally," Thomas interrupted. "Give her some time."

Wally glared at him. "We don't know this motherfucker, Seth. We don't know if she *has* time."

"Wally," Thomas said again, more firmly this time.

"Fine, fine." Wally threw his hands up in defeat. "But this conversation is not over, girly. I think you need to tell them, and I intend to keep telling you that."

"Thank you," I replied, relieved that he was going to drop it for now.

"But in exchange, I do have a question I want an honest answer to."

I narrowed my eyes at him. "What's the question?"

"What are you going to do about that big heap of drooling wolf that's sitting outside our house?"

I frowned. "What?"

"Ryan, girlie, what are you going to do about Ryan? It's all over town that you're back, and everyone knows that you're his mate. So, what about it? You gonna jump that thang?"

My heart thumped in my chest. "Everybody knows?"

"Sure, everyone's talking about Jem's lost little sister who Ryan rejected and then spent the last four years pining after."

Wally's words hit me like a ton of bricks. Everyone in the northeast knew about my rejection, but now they also knew I was back and that Ryan had been pining for me? It made me feel exposed and vulnerable.

"So? What's the plan?"

"I don't know," I whispered, feeling my cheeks heat up.

"But you want this, right? You guys are fated mates."

"Yes, we're fated mates, but honestly, I don't know what I want anymore."

"Well, you better figure it out soon. That man is head over heels for you. And let me tell you, I don't know Ryan particularly well, but I know enough that Ryan is not the type to let the woman he loves slip through his fingers twice."

I swallowed hard, feeling a mix of emotions stir in my chest. Anger, hurt, confusion, and desire all battled for supremacy within me.

Wally's eyes softened. "Did Thomas tell you about how we got together?"

I shook my head.

"I knew he was my mate the first time I set eyes on him. I was visiting his Pack for a business meeting, and something happened when I looked at him. I felt hot and cold, I couldn't breathe, it was like, in that moment, a part of me knew that my world had turned upside down and nothing would ever be the same again."

His words stirred something within me—a familiar blend of excitement and dread that I'd felt before but tried to forget.

"But I was scared," Wally continued. "I didn't know what it meant, and I didn't know if I was ready for that kind of commitment." He paused, looking at me with earnest eyes. "Thomas never gave up on me. He was patient, kind, and he always knew when to push and when to back off."

As he spoke, my mind snapped to Seth. Patience wasn't his strong suit. He'd tried to dictate every facet of my life until I became a shell of who I once was. The thought of giving someone that kind of influence over me again was terrifying, even if it was Ryan.

"Eventually, I realized that I couldn't run from this. We were fated mates; it was meant to be, and I couldn't imagine my life without him."

Meant to be? Like I didn't have a choice anymore?

Wally must have seen the panic on my face. "Look, where have you left it with Ryan?"

I shrugged. "He explained everything about why he rejected me, but it's not that easy. He can't just say, 'Oops, my bad, let's start again.' Too much has happened. I've changed too much. I'm not the person who ran out of here. I'm sure he isn't the same person he was four years ago, either. And now he wants to have dinner tonight. Dinner. Like a date!"

Wally grinned at me. "That boy moves fast! A date is exactly what you need right now. Why don't you go? Forget about everything else for one night?"

Forget? How could I? My past was a tapestry of experiences that had shaped me, and Seth's dark thread was woven through it all. I didn't know how to move past it, to even consider writing a new story with Ryan and not let Seth's shadow darken everything.

"Ignore the past, Mai. Just go and get to know him. Let him meet the person you are now. No baggage, no anger, for one night, just you and him and leave all this stuff at the door. Get to know Ryan for who he is now, and let him see the strong woman you've become."

I thought about it, about forgetting the past for one night and just being with Ryan. I was tired of being angry, of being scared, of feeling confused about everything. Maybe if I just switched off for a night, showed Ryan who I was now, found out who he was, then maybe I could decide what to do next.

"I guess I could try."

"Good." Wally smiled at me, a satisfied look on his face.

I looked out of the window. Ryan was in a familiar position, leaning against the car, arms crossed, glaring at the house.

"He might not think so," I replied, nodding toward Ryan. "He has no idea what he's let himself in for."

CHAPTER TWENTY

MAI

I sat on the plush couch in the Shaw brothers' cozy living room as Derek tapped away on his computer. My new phone was plugged into it, and he'd just finished giving me the 101 of how to be a spy. At least, that was what it felt like.

I'd told Ryan about Wally's idea on the way back.

"Sounds good," he'd said, holding my gaze for a moment and making my stomach do a flip. "I'll take anything I can get."

"Alright, then," I'd replied. "Pick me up at seven, and don't be late."

When we made it back to the compound, Derek had been waiting for me, and Ryan slipped off "to make some calls."

My eyes followed Derek as he shut his laptop with a definitive click. "Okay, your digital life is now Fort Knox," he announced, looking pleased with himself.

"Fort Knox, huh? I feel safer already." I smiled. "Seriously, thanks for setting this up. It means a lot."

Derek leaned back in his chair, eyeing me with a smirk. "You do realize that 'password123' isn't the epitome of cybersecurity, right?" His eyes twinkled with mischief.

I rolled my eyes. "I know that now. It's a process. I'm evolving."

"Evolving, you say? Can someone who always clicked on the 'You've won a million dollars' emails evolve?"

I grimaced, remembering my younger, more hopeful self. "Okay, fine. I get your point. This isn't the flip-phone era anymore."

"Exactly," he said, getting serious for a moment. "With the kind of attention you're attracting, you can't afford any digital vulnerabilities."

I leaned back to mirror his posture. "Alright, Mr. Cybersecurity, any other wisdom you'd like to share?"

"Just remember to update your apps, especially the security ones. You don't want to be that person who ignored the update notifications and got hacked."

"Updates? Like, I have to nurture this thing?"

His smile was genuine, warm. "Think of it as a pet that doesn't poop but can bite you if you neglect it."

I laughed. "Fine, I promise to be a responsible phone owner."

"I'll believe it when I see it." Derek chuckled. Then his face turned serious, and he looked me dead in the eyes. "You know, Mai, I'm really glad you're back. We all are. Ryan hasn't been the same since you left."

I raised an eyebrow. "Oh? How so?"

"He got harder—more ruthless. He's always been protective, but these last few years, it's like he's got something to prove. He'll do anything to make sure the Pack is safe. He'll do anything, and I mean anything—even if it pisses you off—to make sure you are safe."

I really didn't want to have this conversation right now. "Derek, I get that you're rooting for him, but he rejected me four years ago, remember?"

"I know, I know. Just, listen, okay? I've seen him smile more since you've been back than in the last four years put together. He messed up, Mai. I'm not defending him. But you guys are meant to be. I want you to be happy, both of you. And I reckon that'll only happen if you are together. So I'm going to do anything I can to help you guys."

"Why?" The word escaped before I could stop it.

"Because you bring out the best in him, even if he's too stubborn to see it. And because you deserve someone who'll fight his way to the ends of the earth to make sure you are happy."

I sighed, letting Derek's words sink in. "I don't know if I can forgive him, Derek. It's complicated."

The sound of footsteps echoed down the hallway, growing louder until the door swung open, and Ryan stepped in. The moment he entered, the room's atmosphere changed. Tension thickened the air like a gathering storm. His eyes met mine briefly, then flicked toward Derek, who was still sitting next to me. Derek quickly looked at the floor but I could see the muscle in Ryan's cheek twitch.

"Derek, you finished showing Mai the security features?" His voice was deceptively calm, but I felt his annoyance from here.

"Yeah, she's all set up," Derek replied as he stood up and moved a few steps away from me.

What was going on?

"I'll leave you two to catch up. Got some things to take care of." He cast a knowing smile at me and then glanced at his brother, who was still standing rigid, like a sentinel.

"That alright?" Derek asked Ryan. Derek was blocking my view of Ryan, so I couldn't see either of their faces. They stood facing each other for a moment before Ryan moved to the side and let Derek leave the room. He turned just before he closed the door and winked at me.

The room felt smaller with Derek gone, the tension between Ryan and me now an entity of its own. Ryan seemed to take all the oxygen in the room. His presence was overwhelming my senses, making my heart beat faster. Ryan's stance remained taut, his eyes still fixed on me, scrutinizing my every expression. I felt like I was under a microscope, my emotions and thoughts laid bare, whether I liked it or not. Silence enveloped us, and I suddenly felt unsure.

Ryan must have seen something in my face, as he made a visible effort to relax his posture. He broke eye contact and walked, oh so casually, over to the couch I was sitting on. "So, Derek got you sorted with your new phone?"

I looked up from where I was sitting, my eyes meeting his. "Yeah, he did. Apparently, my phone is now a fortress no one can breach." I kept my tone playful, but I couldn't forget why the security was needed.

Ryan smiled, his eyes meeting mine with a momentary softness. "Derek knows his stuff. He'll make sure you aren't vulnerable."

The word hung in the air, charged with unspoken emotions and memories. There it was, confirmation that the Shaws all saw me as a weak link.

As if he had read my mind, Ryan said, "Mai, being cautious doesn't make you weak. It makes you smart."

I cocked an eyebrow, leaning back on the couch. "Smart, huh? So why does it feel like you're gearing up to bubble-wrap me?"

Frustration etched the lines on his face. "I'm trying to keep you safe, Mai. Can't you see that?"

"Oh, I see it. I just don't need a knight in shining armor, Ryan. I've been managing just fine on my own."

"Just fine? Was it not you who I had to drag to the doctor with some broken bones and a twisted knee?"

I exhaled sharply, my hands clenching. "I didn't ask you to! I had it under control. It was you who stuck your nose in my business and got insufferably bossy."

"Fuck, Mai! Why do you have to make everything so damn difficult?"

Me? What planet was he on? He was the one making everything, even a damned conversation, so challenging.

Ryan ran his hand through his hair and sighed. Almost unconsciously, he picked up a water bottle from a side table, unscrewed the cap, and set it down beside me. I stared at the bottle and then back at him as he turned away. He was oblivious to what he had just done. It was such a simple act but no one had offered me anything, not even a water bottle, for years. I had always been low down in the Pack hierarchy, here with Oliver as Alpha and in Cocrane. It would have been seen as weak for anyone higher up to offer something to me.

"Look, Mai, I don't want to fight anymore," Ryan began, but before he could continue, his phone vibrated on the coffee table. He glanced at the screen. His eyes narrowed, and the tension in the room seemed to ratchet up a notch.

"What's wrong?" I asked, nodding at his phone.

He pocketed the phone and looked back at me, his face softening. "Nothing. Are we still on for dinner tonight, or have I messed that up?" His voice was casual, but the tension was humming beneath his words like a tautly pulled string.

I glanced at the water bottle in front of me. "Annoying as you are, dinner still sounds okay," I said, forcing a smile. And it did. I wanted to get to know him again. To leave all my baggage behind for one night and just be me. Besides, he promised I could yell at him, and my wolf would kill me if I backed out now.

Chapter Twenty-One

Mai

It was six thirty, and I'd heard Ryan arrive ten minutes ago. He was downstairs talking to Jem. I couldn't hear enough to work out what they were saying, though, which I found annoying.

I'd spent the last two hours finishing the project I'd been working on, then emailing all my clients with my new phone number and a message saying I was taking time off for the next couple of weeks. I had some money saved up, enough to get me through a month without work if I was careful about it. It wasn't what I had in mind for that money, but I needed a break, needed to sort my head out, and make a new plan. When I knew where I was going, I'd email them back and say I was open for business again.

I was dressed in a simple, turquoise dress that hugged my curves in all the right places. After Derek's lesson, I'd called Sofia and dragged her away from the bar to help me shop. She'd insisted this was the dress for me. She was right; I loved it. It made me feel confident and ready to face whatever the night threw at me.

I opened my door to find Hayley waiting in the corridor. Her hair was up in an elaborate braid, but there were loose strands escaping, giving her a slightly disheveled look. The Hayley I remembered always had perfect hair and make-up. She had on a lot of make-up, and I mean a lot, but it couldn't hide how tired she looked, like she hadn't slept in days.

"Well, well, don't you scrub up nice." Her tone was even, but it had an edge to it.

She'd been nice to me last night, telling me I should stay, but this was the Hayley I knew.

"Thanks." I kept my voice even as I walked past her, hoping that it was the end of our conversation.

"I bet you think you have it made now, don't you? Finally, back where you belong, with everyone running around after you, making sure you're happy."

I paused at the top of the stairs, then pivoted and strode back to her.

"You told me to stay, Hayley. Just like you told me to run four years ago. What? You changed your mind again?"

"I... I didn't tell you—"

"Don't, Hayley. I'm not a kid you can manipulate anymore. You took advantage when I was at my lowest. You told me I should run." A thought occurred to me. "Is that what the problem is? Ryan said that you told them I wanted to leave. And now you're scared I'm going to tell Jem the truth, that you urged me to run?"

Her face paled, and I knew I was right.

"That's why you were so nice to me when I got back. You were trying to figure out what I was going to say. What? Not enough patience to follow it through, Hayley? Now you're going straight back to being a bitch again. What's the plan this time? Make my life miserable, so I'll leave and won't have time to rat you out to Jem?"

"Go ahead," she said, her voice wavering. "He won't believe you over me."

Maybe, but Jem would always wonder. I couldn't do that to him or to the Pack.

I shook my head. "You can relax, Hayley. I'm not going to tell him. I've only been back a few days, but even I can see how messed up your bond is and how it's hurting the whole Pack. Me telling Jem would only make it worse for everyone."

I caught the relief that flooded her gaze before she could hide it.

"I don't know what you're talking about."

"Mai!" Jem's voice floated up from the bottom of the stairs. "Ryan's here."

Before I could respond, Hayley turned on her heel and walked away.

My stomach did a triple pirouette as I took a deep breath and made my way downstairs. Ryan was there, looking every bit as pant-wettingly gorgeous as I remembered, in smart black pants and a pale pink shirt unbuttoned at the top. His brown hair was styled to perfection, his blue eyes sparkling as he looked up and saw me.

For a moment, neither of us spoke; we just stared at each other in silence. All I could think was how much I wanted to run my fingers down his broad chest, kiss every line on his stomach, and finally touch what was hiding in his pants. Ryan broke my train of thought when he took a step toward me, his hand reaching out to touch my arm. A jolt of electricity raced across my entire body.

"You look stunning," he said softly, his eyes never leaving mine.

I felt a blush creep up my cheeks as I smiled at him. "Thank you.

Right back at you."

Oh, my Goddess, were we really going to be able to go a whole night without arguing?

Ryan smiled, his hand still on my arm. "Are you ready?" he asked. I nodded, and he gestured toward the door. "After you," he said.

"Not so fast," Jem's voice was abrupt, reminding me that I wasn't alone with Ryan, not yet.

"You look beautiful, Mai. Have a good evening, and if Ryan doesn't treat you right, just let me know, and I'll make him do five thousand push-ups a day for the next year." He kissed me on my cheek, slapped Ryan on the back, and watched as we walked out the door.

As we made our way outside, I thought about Wally's words from earlier. Could I really forget about everything that had happened between us for one night? Could I pretend this was just a first date without any of the history or baggage we brought with us?

Ryan opened the car door for me, and I slid into the passenger seat. His eyes met mine as he shut the door, and I could see the intensity in them. It was like he was looking right inside me, seeing all my fears and doubts and desires. I swallowed hard, trying to keep my nerves at bay as he climbed into the driver's seat and started the car.

We were both silent as he drove. Now that we were finally here, I didn't know what to say. Ryan's knuckles were white as he gripped the steering wheel, and I could feel the heat rolling off him in waves. I kept stealing glances at him out of the corner of my eye, taking in the way his jaw was set and his muscles were tensed beneath his shirt. It was like he was holding himself back, fighting against some powerful urge. Every time our eyes met, I felt a spark ignite between us, a connection that I was finding increasingly impossible to ignore.

If my wolf had been a cat, she would have been purring. We were exactly where she wanted us to be. But it wasn't that easy for me, and every time I opened my mouth to say something, I quickly shut it again. What to say that wasn't off-limits? I couldn't ask about his brothers, or work, or Jem. Did he have a hobby? I couldn't ask that; it sounded so lame. I had to ask something, though, before this got even more awkward.

"So where exactly are you taking me for our past-free dinner?"

Ryan looked over at me, then nodded his head at the Bottley Bar. "Here. I thought you'd be comfortable at some place you knew."

I glanced out the window at the packed bar and froze.

Chapter Twenty-Two

RYAN

I pulled up outside the bar, and I could see how busy the place was. Mai froze, and it hit me that she would have to face all these people. There would be people she'd known her whole life in there, watching us, trying to work out where she'd been, why she was back now, how our date was going.

Great fucking plan, Ryan.

We couldn't eat here without our history being shoved in our faces all night.

I pulled a U-turn and set off in the direction of the compound.

"It was a bad idea. Sorry. But I have a Plan B," I said, glancing over at Mai.

She nodded, her scent full of relief, but I caught her frown when I turned into the compound. "You're taking me back?"

Dinner with Jem and Hayley around? No fucking way.

"I'm taking you to my home. Mason and Sam are working on a case out of town, and Derek told me he'd be at the office all night. We'll have the place to ourselves."

"Oh." She swallowed nervously. "Okay."

"Relax, I'm not that bad of a cook."

"You still cook?" She looked so surprised that it made me laugh.

"Of course. What? You think there is a Sylvie at all the compound houses?"

She shook her head. "Well, yes. Either that or you order in."

"I like cooking. I liked cooking for you and my brothers, and I still like cooking now. It relaxes me. It always has."

From the way she fell silent, I knew I'd messed up by bringing up the past. She'd been clear that she wanted tonight to be just us getting to know each other now, with no mention or reminders of our history.

"I've been living with my brothers for over three years now," I said softly. "We're all busy, but I realized pretty soon that we couldn't live off takeaways. We all cook. We take it in turns now, but I make a mean steak with hollandaise potatoes."

She turned, her beautiful eyes staring right at me, and fuck me if I didn't want to pull over and claim her right here.

"Alright, I'll risk it," she said, her tone light and joking, and for a moment, I thought she had read my thoughts. "I haven't had steak in years."

My wolf growled. Mai should have all the steak she wanted whenever she wanted. What had that fuckhead been doing? The sooner we tracked him down, the better. All my brothers were on it. Derek had hacked Mai's phone and laptop, and we'd been able to trace her life back to a town out west called Cocrane. Mason and Sam were headed there now.

We pulled up at the house. I'd never really thought about how it looked; it was just home. But I saw Mai studying it. The outside was clad in dark, weathered wood siding, which blended in with the surrounding trees. A large porch wrapped around the front and one side of the house, offering a spot for us to relax in the evenings and keep an eye on the compound.

I led Mai up the steps and opened the door. "You want a quick tour?"

"Inside the Shaw brothers' secret den? I bet most of the people in town gossip about what's inside here, so, yeah, I do!"

As I showed her around, I realized my wolf was nervous about her reaction. I didn't know why, but it was important that she liked it. The house was a modest two-story building with a spacious living room and an open kitchen. The living room had a large stone fireplace that was always lit during the winter and a huge leather couch that could fit all four of us comfortably. The kitchen was my favorite place. Modern and sleek, with stainless steel appliances and a long, marble-topped island where my brothers and I could catch up with each other while we were cooking. Finally, I showed her our office. We did a lot of our work here or at Jem's house. Mason and Sam had their own offices at their firm, but they had desks here, too.

I could see Mai taking it all in, her eyes darting around the room as she smiled.

"It's nice," she said, her voice soft and warm. "I'm guessing this is your desk?"

I narrowed my eyes and looked at the four desks.

"I'm right, aren't I?" she teased.

I nodded. "How?"

"It was easy. This one is Derek's. It's empty. There is nothing personal on it at all. He was in the military, and habits are hard to shake. I'm guessing he locks everything away whenever he's finished working. Mason and Sam work as enforcers, but they also run a PI firm. I doubt they meet clients here, so they must do that in their other office in town. Here they can have some personal things. Sam always loved Star Wars," she pointed to the R2D2 on his desk, "and Mason always needs to have something in his hands to fiddle with when he is thinking." She swung her finger around to point at the tennis ball, the exercise hand grip, and the kid's fidget toy on his desk. "That leaves this desk; it has a computer and a laptop, but there is nothing neat about it." She looked pointedly at the scatter of pens and paper that covered one end of my desk.

"I have a system," I said, my voice flat.

She looked at my face and laughed. "Sure, you do."

I watched as she walked toward it and ran her fingers along the edge of the sleek, polished wood. Her eyes traced the curves of the chair, and for a moment, I wondered if she was imagining me sitting there, typing away on my computer. The thought sent a shiver down my spine, and I had to remind myself to stay focused. This was just dinner, nothing more.

As we walked back through the house, Mai's eyes drifted to the huge TV that took up most of one wall in the living room.

"Sam's a big gamer," I explained. "He bought that last year so he could hook it up to his console."

"Do you play?"

"Me? I don't have much time for it, but yeah, we sometimes have family tournaments. Sam kicks everyone's ass, but I can hold my own."

"Maybe after dinner, you could show me?" She smiled, a glint in her eyes. I remembered how good she used to be, especially with the fighting games, and I had the feeling she was setting me up. I didn't care. Anything to have her smile at me like that.

"I'd like that. You hungry?"

"Starving," she replied. "Thomas said I need to eat twice what I usually do for the next couple of weeks to replace the weight I lost when... Well, you know."

I nodded. Keeping our history out of tonight wasn't going to be as easy as I thought it would.

Chapter Twenty-Three

MAI

I followed Ryan to the kitchen and watched as he pulled out some steaks from the fridge and a couple of frying pans from a cabinet. "You need help?"

"Nah." He shook his head. "You could get us some wine, though."

I could feel his eyes on me as I followed his instructions, finding some glasses and opening a bottle of red wine. My hand shook as I poured the wine. Why was I so nervous? It was just dinner, nothing more.

The sizzle of the meat filled the air. As Ryan cooked, I watched him, entranced. He moved around the kitchen with effortless grace, his muscles flexing beneath his shirt as he flipped the steaks and cut the potatoes. The smell of cooking meat and herbs filled the air, making my stomach grumble. I couldn't remember the last time I'd had a meal like this. It was decadent and indulgent, and I fully intended to enjoy him.

It.

Enjoy it, not him.

What was I thinking, coming here, being so close to him and his oh-so-kissable lips?

Ryan looked up and caught me staring. "What?" he asked.

I blushed and looked away. "Nothing," I muttered, taking a sip of wine.

"You're cute when you blush," he said, and my heart leaped in my chest.

"I'll get you a refill," I said, stepping away. I needed to clear my thoughts. Yes, this was one night with no baggage, where the past didn't matter, but that didn't mean I should jump him to see if the sex would be as good as I always imagined it to be.

Oh my God, did I just think that? The wine was going to my head; that had to be it. I couldn't afford to be thinking about sex with Ryan. I'd never make it out of the house if I did.

I handed him his glass, and our fingers brushed against each other, sending a shiver running through my body. I could feel the tension pull tight between us, the unspoken desire that hung thick in the air, drawing me to him. Ryan was so close, and I found myself leaning in, needing to feel his lips on mine. But just as I was about to reach out to touch him, he stepped back.

"Let's eat," he said, his voice low and husky.

What the hell just happened? What was I thinking? It must be the wine. I placed the glass on the island. Ryan served up the steaks and potatoes. The meat was cooked to perfection, and the potatoes were creamy and buttery.

I could feel his eyes on me as I ate, and every time I looked up, he was staring at me, his gaze hot and intense. I felt a flush spread across my chest and creep up my neck, and I knew he could see it. I wondered if he could tell how much I wanted him.

"You were right," I said, taking a small sip of wine. "You're not a bad cook."

"I told you," he said, grinning.

We ate in silence for a few more minutes, but the tension was still there, simmering beneath the surface. He was an apex predator in his domain. He was comfortable here and full of confidence that he was in charge.

"I've missed this," Ryan said suddenly, breaking the silence. "Just sitting down and having a meal with someone."

"Really? I would have thought you'd be sick of it, with your brothers and all."

"Nah," he said, shaking his head. "It's not the same. I mean, I love my brothers, but it's not like this. It's loud and busy and often quite messy."

I laughed. I remembered clearing up after the Shaw brothers ate in mine and Jem's apartment.

"This is sitting down with someone you care about and just enjoying each other's company."

"I've missed this too," I said softly. "Just being with you."

Ryan looked at me, his gaze full of an overwhelming predatory intensity focused solely on me.

Uh-oh.

"Mai," he said, his voice deep and rough. "I can't pretend like I don't feel it. You're my mate, my one fated mate."

My heart skipped a beat. Would I ever get used to him saying that?

His presence filled the room, enveloping me, pulling on the invisible thread that bound us together.

"I want to rip your clothes off and claim you on this table. I want to fuck you in every room in this house. I want to feel your wet pussy clench around my cock while I'm fucking you so hard that you're screaming in pleasure. I understand if you don't feel the same way yet, but I needed to tell you."

His words took me by surprise, and for a moment, I wasn't sure if I'd heard right.

"What?" I asked, my voice breathless.

He stood up and stalked toward me, a predator sighting his prey. "I want to lick every inch of you, Mai. I want to know what you smell like when you come. I want to be inside of you, fucking you again and again till you can't walk straight."

"Oh." I looked into his eyes and felt my whole body tremble. Fuck yeah, did I want those things. I'd only been dreaming of them for years. I was wet just at the thought of Ryan fucking me, but adding all of those things? I wasn't sure if I could speak right now. Did I want this? One night of freedom, where it wasn't Mai, Jem's sister, reject of Ryan, and it wasn't Ryan, enforcer, seeker of Mai. No, for one night, it was just us. Following our instincts, no past, no consequences. Just us.

I surged up, closing the distance between us in one step, and kissed him.

Chapter Twenty-Four

Mai

Ryan's lips were hot and firm against mine, and my body responded instantly. His hands found their way to my waist, pulling me closer as his tongue teased mine. I moaned, my hands threading through his hair as he deepened the kiss. It was like we'd been holding back for years, and it was finally time to let go. It was crazy; we were kissing and touching each other like we were running out of time.

He ran his lips down my neck, his hands gliding over my dress, circling my breasts. Suddenly, he lifted me up onto the table and hiked my dress up around my waist. He hooked my underwear with his thumbs and slowly dragged them down, his eyes never leaving mine. I was panting now, desperate to feel him. I yanked him closer, pulled his shirt out of his trousers, and finally got my hands on his bare chest. His fingers went right to my clit and did a delicious swirl. I gasped, and he dipped a finger inside of me.

"Fuck, Mai, you're so wet, you're dripping," he growled as he slid his finger out and then pushed it inside again. His thumb found my clit and stroked it while he finger-fucked me.

"Oh my Goddess, Ryan." My breaths were coming in pants. I put my arms back on the table, giving him more access as he added another finger. I was close. This was Ryan, for fuck's sake, and I was going to come on his kitchen table.

"Ryan," I begged. He added a third finger, and I felt him everywhere inside me. He didn't go faster, though; just kept slowly sliding in and out, setting my nerves on fire.

His thumb did another swirl, and I fell apart on a cloud of stars. The outside world disappeared, and it was just Ryan and me. When I came back to my senses, Ryan slid his fingers out then, never taking his gaze off me, licked each finger. I was going to come again just watching him.

Ryan picked me up and carried me up the stairs. He kicked open a door, and I had the briefest of moments to see his room. It was spacious, with a king-sized bed, a dresser on one side of the room, and a large TV on the other. The walls were painted a soft blue, and there were a few black-and-white photos on the walls. Then Ryan put me down, so I was standing next to the bed.

"Take off your dress," he ordered.

I thought about it for a millisecond, then undid the zip and slid the dress off.

"And your bra."

He was breathing deeply, and I could see his cock straining against his trousers. I took my bra off and threw it on the floor. I was naked, the cool air caressing my skin, and for a moment, I felt vulnerable and stupid, but then I looked at Ryan. His eyes were full of wonder.

"You're so beautiful."

I could feel a blush spreading across my body.

"It starts now, Mai, you and me," he growled.

I nodded, unable to speak. Then he was there, kissing me. His hands tickled my stomach, my ass, then up to my ribs, and finally my breasts. His finger flicked my nipple, and I gasped. He bent down and drew my nipple into his mouth, circling it with his tongue. Then he sucked, and I almost came. My hands grabbed onto his hair, forcing him to stand up and kiss me. He took over, his tongue invading my mouth, demanding and hungry. I ran my hands over his chest, then slid them down, unbuckling his belt. I could feel his cock against my thigh, and my only thoughts were about setting it free. I pushed Ryan back, knelt down, and pulled his clothes down. His cock sprang free of his underwear, and I blinked.

Yikes.

It was huge and beautiful. Pre-cum glistened on the tip, and I leaned forward to lick it. Ryan growled, and it made my insides quiver. I licked it again, tracing the tip with my tongue, then pulled him into my mouth. Ryan rocked back, and I could hear his rapid heart rate.

I sucked, swirling my tongue against him, then used my fingers to stroke his balls. I was loving this, loving making Ryan gasp, when he grabbed me under my arms and yanked me up so I was straddling him, my legs wrapped around his waist. I could feel his cock pressing against my wet opening, and I whimpered.

The tip of his cock pushed inside an inch, then he pulled out again.

"Tell me you want this, Mai. I need to hear you say the words."

I nipped his ear, then whispered, "Of course I want this. I've waited years for this, Ryan. Fuck me. Please."

He did, thrusting up and filling me so completely that I groaned with pleasure. He was so big I could feel every inch of him inside me.

He lifted me up, his cock hitting all my pleasure points as he drew out. Ryan paused, holding me over the top of his cock.

"Look at me, Mai," he ordered.

I lifted my eyes to meet his and was shocked at the intensity in them. His gaze was hot and determined. His eyes never left mine as he lowered me down on his cock. I don't know what he saw, but his expression turned smug.

"You like that, do you?"

"Goddess, yes," I breathed, struggling to think.

He pulled out again, so slowly I thought I was going to die.

"Want more?"

"Yes!"

Then he lost whatever control he had and let loose, slamming into me over and over again. It was delicious and hot. I could feel my orgasm building.

"More," I demanded, and Ryan complied. I don't know how we got there, but suddenly, my back was against the wall. I put my feet against the dressing table, using the leverage so I could drive down even harder onto his cock.

Ryan's pace increased. I met his rhythm, the wet slapping noises of our bodies crashing into each other sending me closer to the edge. I couldn't think. I just knew I needed this.

"Yes!" I threw my head back as Ryan groaned, and our orgasms took over our bodies and souls. The world went black, and I floated in a pool of bliss. It didn't last long, though. My whole body jolted as if I'd been struck by lightning. My Pack bond sprang to life, and the thread that went from Ryan to me shined bright gold, blinding me. It felt so real, so strong, and for a brief moment, I could feel what Ryan was feeling. His joy, his awe of me. Me! His determination that this was the start of us, and nothing could break us apart. I was there with Ryan, and I felt so safe, so loved that I cried out when I was thrown back to my body, and the bond dimmed to a constant thrum inside of me.

Chapter Twenty-Five

Mai

I came to on the floor, Ryan lying next to me. He gently stroked the hair out of my face.

"Mai?"

"What the hell was that?" I asked, struggling to get up. I was covered in sweat and felt weak and empty inside, mourning the loss of Ryan and the loss of feeling the bond, of knowing what Ryan felt.

"Our mate bond. It sealed."

I frowned. "I knew we were mates. I've known that for a long time."

"Yes, but until fated mates have sex, the bond is thin, almost brittle. When we open ourselves up to each other, give a bit of ourselves to the other, then only will it seal."

"Oh," I said, my mind and body reeling from what we just did.

Ryan picked me up and gently placed me on the bed.

"You okay?" he asked.

"Uh-huh." I nodded. Whatever tomorrow might bring, I was going to be dreaming about this night for years to come.

"Good, 'coz I'm not nearly done with you."

Oh, boy.

A sudden sweep of Ryan's arms under my knees and back startled me and made me giggle. He cradled me against his chest. The warmth of his body radiated through my skin, and I couldn't help it when I leaned into him and kissed a trail up his neck.

"Mai," he warned. I ignored him, and my tongue darted out to lick the place where his neck met his jaw.

"Christ" he growled.

Ryan walked into the bathroom and set me down in the shower so I was facing the spray. He reached out and turned on the faucet, steam quickly filling the room.

The sensation of the water streaming over my breasts was intoxicating, each drop awakening a new desire within me.

"Feels good, doesn't it?" Ryan whispered into my ear as he tweaked my nipple with his fingers, the heat of his breath mixing with the steam surrounding us.

"Yes," I breathed, wriggling back into him as he pressed his body against mine. The contrast between the hot water and the solid warmth of Ryan's chest made my senses sing, every inch of my skin alive and begging for more of his touch. I could hardly think straight. Ryan moved my hair to the side and kissed my neck. Then his hand trailed gently down my back, over the curve of my hips, and round to my ass. He caressed my skin, each stroke building the need inside me. But it wasn't enough. I wanted more.

"Ryan," I gasped, feeling his hardness pressed against my ass.

"Open your legs wider for me, Mai," Ryan said, his voice commanding and full of desire.

I complied without hesitation, feeling the anticipation build within me as I spread my legs and tilted my ass up to give him better access.

I could feel every inch of him pressed against me, and it sent a thrill through my entire being.

Ryan positioned himself at my entrance, the tip of his cock teasing me, making me whimper in frustration. He chuckled at my impatience.

"Stop teasing, Ryan... Fuck me," I demanded, desperate for him to fill the void inside me, to claim me once again. I needed him, needed the connection that only he could give me.

With one swift motion, he filled me completely. A gasp escaped my lips as I felt him stretch me, the delicious sensation of fullness making my head spin.

"You feel so amazing," Ryan groaned, his fingers digging into my hips as he began to thrust in and out of me with a slow, measured pace. The water from the shower added a slick warmth to our bodies, making each movement feel like pure ecstasy.

"Ryan..." I moaned, my body writhing in pleasure. The feel of him inside me, the way his body moved in perfect harmony with mine, was almost too much to bear.

"Tell me what you need, baby," he urged, his breath hot on my neck as he continued to drive into me with a growing intensity.

"Harder..." I begged, desperate for more.

His grip on my hips tightened as he began to pound into me with a ferocity that made my knees buckle. I cried out in ecstasy, my voice mixing with the sound of the water as it pelted against my skin.

"Ryan, I'm so close..." I whimpered, feeling the coil of pleasure deep within me beginning to tighten, threatening to snap at any moment.

"Let go, Mai. Give yourself to me," he ordered, his voice thick with need.

And as our bodies moved in perfect synchrony, surrounded by the steam and the heat of the water, I surrendered myself completely to him, knowing that no matter what happened, for this moment, I had Ryan. My Ryan. And there was nowhere I wanted to be more than right here, feeling his fingers grip onto my hips as he slammed into me over and over again.

"Ryan!" I cried out as the world shattered around me, and a feeling of complete bliss, of rightness, swept through me.

"Fuck, Mai," Ryan growled as he came inside of me.

I stayed there, arms against the tiles, panting, as Ryan gently slipped out of me and kissed my neck.

"Are you done with me now?" I whispered.

I felt Ryan grin as he moved his mouth next to my ear.

"Hell, no. Tonight, we're just getting started."

Chapter Twenty-Six

RYAN

Mai didn't stir when the text came in. It made me smile, knowing I had worn her out. If I had my way, we were going to repeat last night many more times.

The smile slipped off my face, though, when I saw what the text said:

He's in the wind, bro. Left three days ago. We're going hunting.

Fuck! All my instincts were screaming at me that Seth was heading here. I wasn't going to let that shithead near Mai. Not again.

"Ryan?" Mai murmured, opening her eyes.

She looked so peaceful, so fucking beautiful. I just wanted to roll her over and plunge my cock into her sweet, tight wetness. Fuck her until she screamed my name again as she came. I was already so hard at the thought that it was painful. But we didn't have time this morning. Tonight, when everything was sorted, I'd suck her clit until she came on my face, then fuck her from behind. She went wild when we tried that position last night.

"Morning, babe." I leaned in and kissed her. It didn't help my hard-on, but no way was I not going to kiss her gorgeous lips in the morning.

I forced myself to pull back as her hand crept down my back, knowing I had to stop this now, or neither of us was getting out of bed today.

"You want breakfast? I can make bacon and waffles."

"That sounds yummy." She smiled at me, and my heart beat faster. Yes, I was going to make sure she had everything she wanted.

I rolled off the bed and pulled on some shorts. "Great, we'll have breakfast together, then I'll help you move your stuff over here."

Mai froze, her eyes going wide. "What do you mean, move my stuff?"

"You've got clothes, don't you? Plus, your work things. I know you don't have much, but I can buy you everything to replace what you left behind."

Mai sat up in bed, her tone serious. "Ryan, what are you talking about? I'm not moving in here. Last night was amazing. Like mind-blowingly awesome amazing, but it doesn't change anything."

I frowned at her. Was she serious?

"Mai, we're fated mates." I held up one finger. "We belong together. I know we have a lot to work out, but we can do that much easier with you living here." I held up a second finger. "Mason and Sam are tracking Seth. He's disappeared, probably heading here to find you. You need to be somewhere safe." I flicked up a third finger. "Jem and Hayley are out of that house more than they're in it. You need to be here. Not only do we have a safe room downstairs, but we can easily arrange it so that one of us is always here with you."

I watched as a mix of emotions crossed her face. A detached part of me was enjoying it, wondering which one she was going to settle on.

"You!" Mai sprung out of bed and started hunting for her clothes. "You absolute prick!"

"Mai—"

"How did you find out about Seth? I sure as hell didn't tell you!"

I decided honesty was the way to go here. "Derek hacked your phone and your laptop."

She paused with only one leg in her panties, her face full of anger. "He... you... he... Oh, my Goddess! I knew coming back was a mistake!"

I felt like she'd slapped me. Her coming back had been the best thing that had happened to me in my entire life.

"Mai—"

"How dare you, Ryan Shaw! These are my private things. You don't get to hack them! If I wanted you to know, I would have told you."

"Yeah? Well, I'm trying to keep you safe. And it would be a hell of a lot easier if you did tell me these things. I need to know everything, Mai, so I can assess the risks and take appropriate measures." I took a step toward her, and she took a step back. The air was full of her scent, both angry and embarrassed.

Why was she embarrassed?

"*I* keep me safe. Not you, Ryan. If I wanted your help, I would have asked for it."

"You don't need to be embarrassed about this, Mai. This is what we do. We protect each other."

"I'm not embarrassed. I'm angry!" she lied, finally pulling her panties on. "You can't just invade my privacy like that!"

"I'm not losing you again, Mai," I insisted, watching her as she stormed around the room, grabbing her things. "I'm not going to take any chances."

"I can take care of myself," she snapped back. "I've been doing it for four years, and I don't need you, or anyone else, to hold my hand."

"I'm not trying to hold your hand," I said, trying to keep my voice level. "I'm trying to keep you alive."

Mai stopped and looked at me, her eyes sparking with anger. "I am not some helpless damsel in distress, Ryan. I'm a werewolf, just like you. And I deserve to be treated like an equal. You can't make these decisions for me."

"I'm trying to keep you safe."

"That's not your job!"

"Mai—"

"No, Ryan. I make my own choices. And right now, I'm choosing to leave."

I watched her storm out of the room, slamming the door behind her.

Okay, that did not go to plan. I sat down on the edge of the bed, rubbing my hands over my face. Seth was still out there. I had to keep her safe, even if it meant she hated me for the rest of my life.

CHAPTER TWENTY-SEVEN

MAI

I darted out of the house and across the street to Jem's place. I needed to get the hell away from here. I couldn't believe Ryan had Derek hack my life. He must know everything about me by now. There were no secrets, no things that I could tell him when I was ready. No, he had to know everything now. How could we start something when the power was so one-sided? He was never going to see me as an equal. I would always be the little girl who needed protecting.

I slipped in the door, ignoring Jem's shout, and went straight to my room. I sat down on the bed as my anger drained away. My face burned, and I cringed, the humiliation of my choices weighing heavily on me. I'd been so stupid to stay with Seth, and now Ryan and his brothers knew it, too. Did they think less of me?

I had thought of coming back here over the years, but I didn't want to come back to the Pack like this. I didn't want them to see me as weak and vulnerable. I'd always thought I'd turn up and show them how strong I was, show them that I had achieved things in my life since I'd left, that I was more than my past mistakes.

"Mai?" Jem's voice called out as he knocked on the door. "Can I come in?"

I took a deep breath and stood up. I didn't want Jem to see me like this, either. If he didn't know already, it was only a matter of time before Ryan told him the truth about Seth. I sighed, knowing I couldn't run from it.

"Sure."

Jem pushed the door open and looked me up and down. "You had quite the night."

It was a statement, not a question, and I knew he could smell Ryan all over me.

I held my chin up higher, daring him to make something out of it.

"I gotta say, Mai, I'm fucking delighted for you and Ryan. As your Alpha, I felt it when your mate bond sealed. You made a good choice. He loves you, Mai. Even more than he loves the Pack."

"He's an arrogant, pig-headed asshole!"

Jem grinned at me. "Yeah, that too."

"How do you put up with him? I want to tear my hair out! Or better yet, claw his eyes out!"

Jem chuckled. "Well, I'm his Alpha, so I can just order him to leave."

"I wish I could order him to leave, or shut up, or even to stop fucking looking at me!"

"You're fated mates, Mai. That's a special bond. You'll work out how to handle him."

I slumped down on the bed. "No, I don't think I will."

I had to leave. It was the only way. Start somewhere new, where I could be myself, where no one knew about the choices I'd made, the rejection, the stupidity. Where no one thought less of me.

"Mai," Jem said, his stern voice bringing me back to reality. "What happened?"

I thought about lying or shrugging it off. But Jem was my brother, and he would know I wasn't telling the truth. "He got Derek to hack into my laptop and phone. He invaded my privacy, Jem. He knows everything about me and didn't respect me enough to let me tell him about my life, in my own way, in my own time."

Jem sat down next to me. "He's scared, Mai. He just found you again. He's desperate to keep you safe. His wolf will be pushing him to keep you near at all times. He's going to be extremely possessive for the next few months. It's normal for a newly mated pair. You know how much he loves his brothers, would do anything for them, yet he's struggling for control whenever they come near you."

"His brothers?" I shook my head. "He knows I'm not interested in them, and they are certainly not interested in me."

"Oh, he knows that. But that's your rational human side talking. To his wolf, it is simple. You are his, and if another male gets near you, he will try to rip their throats out. At least for the next few months. After that, it will settle down. Probably."

Fan-fucking-tastic. This was going to complicate things if I did decide to leave. I would not only have my own wolf demanding I stay, but Ryan would come after me, too.

"You know he raised his brothers. He had to grow up fast, Mai, when their mother died and their dad checked out. Ryan always had a strong protective instinct, but the experience of raising his brothers, of keeping them safe under Oliver, of making sure they had a roof over their heads and food on the table... It honed this instinct into a sharp point. That's what makes him such a good Beta. It's what will make him a brilliant Alpha someday. But right now, it's working against him. He's terrified Seth is going to find and hurt you or that you will run again."

I closed my eyes. Of course, Jem fucking knew about Seth. Did the whole Pack know what an idiot I was?

"There's something important you need to understand about fated mates, about the power that comes with the bond. The Moon Mother puts two werewolves together, but that's it. There is no 'happily ever after' unless we make it so. Fated mates have this potential, but we have to nurture the bond, protect it, and watch it grow." He hesitated, then continued, "Things with me and Hayley are difficult right now."

I nodded. It was hard to miss.

"You know what it was like for her living with her aunt. They treated her like a slave; she was a modern-day Cinderella. I got her out of it as soon as I worked out what was happening, but it shaped her, Mai. It shaped who she would become. Hayley needs constant love, attention, and reassurance. She is only happy if she feels that she is my top priority at all times."

Jem sighed, his expression somber. "After you left, after I was Alpha, I talked with Sofia. I talked to your school. I finally saw what I'd been too busy to see all those years. I realized the mistake I'd made in leaving Hayley to raise you. I confronted her. We fought." Jem paused, his eyes going distant. "We didn't talk for six months. I was busy spending most of my time trying to get the Pack stabilized and organize the search for you. We had to root out the old enforcers, work out who could be trusted. I stayed away because I blamed her for you leaving, even though it was just as much my fault as hers, and it tore our bond. Hayley felt lonely and deserted. For an Alpha pair, it was irresponsible of us. We hid it for a time, but it got harder not to notice the damage we were causing to the whole Pack. Then, a year ago, Hayley cheated."

I sucked in a breath. I couldn't believe Hayley had betrayed Jem in that way.

"It wasn't all her fault, Mai. She found someone who paid her attention and offered her the things she craved. When I found out I... I went crazy. Ryan stopped me from killing him. He knew if I had murdered him, the guilt would have crippled me. Instead, I banished him from the Pack. Since then, I've had to hope that our actions—mine and Hayley's—haven't irreparably damaged our mate bond. That, in time, we'll find a way past this. As the Alpha pair, our weakened bond has affected our entire Pack. It's the little things: fights in the Pack breaking out over spilled drinks, mothers nipping at their kids when they can't keep up, more road rage than normal. The Pack bonds are anxious, on edge, and it's making everyone that little bit more aggressive. It's dangerous for a Pack. They feel this niggle all the time, and instead of feeling safe and happy, everyone is wary of each other. I'm hoping we can fix it, but it's going to take time."

He looked into my eyes, his gaze intense. "I'm telling you this because I don't want you to make the same mistakes I did. If you can trust each other, you and Ryan will become more powerful as a pair than you could individually. But take it from me: if you treat your bond badly, it will weaken you both."

Jem's eyes were haunted. "Talk to Ryan. Work through your issues with him. Don't throw it all away; don't let your bond with your fated mate be damaged over this."

Chapter Twenty-Eight

Mai

M y phone rang. Unknown number. Jem's face had gone hard. He nodded at me. If it was Seth, maybe I could work out where he was or if he knew where I was. I took a deep breath.

"Hello?"

"Mai, girlie!" Wally's voice floated out of the phone.

I watched as Jem smiled at me, then left the room, shutting the door behind him.

"I'm at the bar with Sofia, and we're dying to hear all the gossip about last night! Why don't you make an escape from the tower and come have lunch with us?"

I sighed, thinking. So much had happened since last night; too much to digest right now. I might as well go get something to eat.

"Sure, just let me have a shower first."

I walked into Bottley Bar an hour later. I'd taken time in the shower to think about me and Ryan, and I'd decided I didn't want to think about me and Ryan. I would talk to him, but not anytime soon. Let him stew in his back-stabbing, laptop-hacking office.

Wally and Sofia were sitting in a booth toward the back of the room. It was quiet, only a couple having lunch and a businessman working on his laptop near the window.

"Hey, Mai!" Sofia called, waving at me.

"Well?" Wally demanded as soon as I slid onto the seat next to Sofia. "We want to hear everything. What did you wear, where did you go, what did you eat, what did he say?"

I shrugged, really not keen to talk about last night. "We ate in, actually. Ryan cooked steak at his place."

"You had a date with all the Shaw brothers?" Sofia asked, her eyes bugging out.

"Oo-ee! That would have been one hell of a date!" Wally said, picking up a napkin and fanning himself.

"No! Just Ryan. The others were all out."

"So? How did it go? Did you manage to leave all the history at the door?"

"Mmmm," I muttered. "Maybe too well."

Sofia and Wally stared at me.

"Is she saying what I think she's saying?" Wally asked Sofia. "'Coz if she is, I'm gonna lose it and start squealing!"

"I've got this," she replied to him, then turned to me. "Mai, look at me."

I raised my eyes to meet hers.

"She's definitely looking tired. Tired and worn out. Hell, Mai, we thought you'd have a nice dinner, not fuck his brains out. You did fuck his brains out, right?"

"It's not what you think." Okay, it was exactly what they thought. "We just got a bit carried away with the whole escape-from-who-we-are thing for the night. Trust me, Ryan brought me crashing back to reality this morning."

"That boy," Wally tutted. "He never did know how to keep a good thing."

"I need advice. I don't know what to do. I don't know if I should leave and try to start again someplace new. It all feels too much here."

"You know," Wally replied, a glint in his eyes, "we can only really give advice if we know the whole story. You're gonna have to spill."

I sighed. I knew he was right. "Swear to me on Thomas's doctorate that you'll keep this between us. I don't need the whole Pack knowing about it."

Wally hooked my pinkie with his and made a pinkie swear. Sofia, grinning, did the same.

"Okay, tell us everything!"

So, I did. I filled Sofia in on my life after I left the Pack. I told them about my date with Ryan, the mind-blowing sex, then his demand that I move in with him.

"Wow!" Sofia sat back in her seat. "I knew those Shaw boys had some game, but fuck me!" She had a dreamy look in her eyes.

I clicked my fingers in front of her face. "Hello! Focus! Yes, the sex was awesome, but did you not hear about him hacking into my life?"

Sofia focused her eyes on me. "Sorry, I got a little lost there thinking of the thirty-six orgasms you seemingly had. Okay, so what is it that you're really scared of, Mai? Of being Ryan's mate? I thought that was what you always wanted."

I closed my eyes. "I did. But not like this. I want to be a partner, but he keeps putting me in this bubble-wrapped box that he thinks needs protecting. If I can't show him that I can look after myself, that I won't let Seth hurt me again, how will Ryan ever see me as an equal mate?"

I opened my eyes to see Sofia frowning at me. "You didn't *let* Seth do this, Mai. It wasn't your fault; you have to know that."

Wally put his arms around me. "Mai, someone you loved betrayed your trust. They hurt you. Repeatedly. You are not at fault here. You opened yourself up to another person, and they took advantage of that. You have no control over their behavior, and what they do is not on you."

For some reason, I couldn't stop tears from welling up. I hadn't thought of it that way before.

Sofia put her arms around me, too. "Besides, Ryan doesn't think you're weak. You remember that time when we were fourteen, and I went on a date with Josh Kellen? It was awful, and afterward, he wouldn't leave me alone. Waiting outside my house, calling me all the time. Then he started getting angry that I wouldn't call me back. You remember he cornered me in the park? He had hold of me and was yelling and saying I was a fucking bitch who didn't know a good thing when it was right in front of her, and then you came out of nowhere. You shoved him back, told him if he ever came near me again, you'd break both his legs. He went for you, and you flipped him onto the ground and twisted his arm up his back. I honestly thought you were going to break it. He'd started crying before you let him up. Josh never came near me again, Mai. Because of you. I don't know if you've forgotten, but Ryan was there, too. He didn't jump in; he trusted you to handle it, you remember?"

The memory of that day came flooding back. Sofia was right; Ryan had been there. He'd been on babysitting duty, and instead of getting a pizza delivered, I'd wanted the fresh air, so I convinced him that we'd go and get it. After I'd made sure Sofia was okay and we'd walked her home, the only thing he'd said was that it was a nice flip.

Wally handed me a tissue from his back pocket. "From Ryan's point of view, he screwed up big time. He thought he'd lost you forever four years ago and has been searching for you ever since. Now you're back, obviously hurt, and you won't let him in. You won't tell him what happened. He doesn't know if one person or a whole Pack is chasing you. Are you in danger? Is our Pack in danger? His wolf is probably going nuts, demanding that he lock you in a cage until this is all over. I know you think it is over the top, but if anything like that happened to Thomas, I'd burn the whole country down to find out who hurt him and stop it from happening again."

I looked at Wally, thinking that he was lucky to have found Thomas. Beside me, Sofia stiffened, and her scent turned wary. I followed her gaze to see Brock Madden waltzing in the door. The same sandy hair that had once been kept in a sloppy buzz cut now fell in a tousled wave over his forehead. His frame had filled out considerably, his once lanky body now a firm mass of muscle, an indication that he'd spent the last four years working hard. Despite these changes, he still had a cocky tilt to his chin, a glint of mischief in his eyes, and an air of superiority in the way he carried himself.

An uneasiness gnawed at my stomach as I watched him. Maybe it was seeing him so soon after what had happened with Seth, but just looking at him reminded me loud and clear of a time when I felt small and insignificant. I could feel Wally's eyes on me. Sofia was staring daggers at Brock. I straightened my back. I was no longer that girl he used to bully; I was stronger, tougher, and not about to let the ghost of Brock's past actions haunt me.

Brock paused at the bar, then swirled around on his heel to face our table. "Well, well, well," he said, stalking closer. "I thought I smelled you, Mai. I heard you were back, all broken and pitiful. I honestly didn't think you'd be stupid enough to come back here. I guess I gave you too much credit."

I leaned back in my chair, making myself relax. "Really, Brock? That the best you got?"

Brock's eyes narrowed, and he took another step forward. "What's the matter, Mai? Can't handle the truth?"

"Nothing that comes out of your mouth is the truth, Brock," I replied, meeting his stare head-on. "So why don't you fuck off and let the adults talk?"

Brock's expression turned to fury and then, a split second later, went blank. Interesting. He had better control of his anger now. "Happy homecoming, Mai. I hope you find the place as welcoming as it always was for you."

He gave me a mock salute and strolled out the door.

Chapter Twenty-Nine

MAI

"He's such a prick." Sofia glared at Brock's retreating back as he sauntered out of Bottley's.

"You get many visits from Brock these days?" I asked, wondering if he had changed at all since school or still dropped by to ridicule and belittle Sofia. He always did think he was better than us. That because his dad was close to Oliver, his place in the Pack hierarchy was assured.

Sofia shook her head. "No, thankfully not. He's too busy kissing up to Hayley to bother with me."

I raised an eyebrow. "Really?"

"Yeah, he left just after Jem and Hayley took over. Rumors say he ended up working for the Wolf Council, but I'm pretty sure he was the one who started them," Sofia said, rolling her eyes.

If Brock had somehow managed to work with the Wolf Council, that was big. The Council was our ruling authority. They decided on our laws. They gave Alphas a lot of leeway and trusted surrounding Packs to take care of any who broke the laws, but their priority was to make sure that any problems with werewolves didn't spill over into the human communities. We might be stronger, faster, more efficient killers, but humans outnumbered us significantly, and if they saw us as a real threat to their survival, we'd be fucked.

The Wolf Council was known to be ruthless and protected the peace between the humans and werewolves with vicious efficiency. I'd heard of a Pack out west where the Alphas felt humans were the lesser species. Good for slaves and the occasional meal. The Council got wind of it, and within twenty-four hours, the entire Pack was either dead or had been split up and moved to Packs that had more egalitarian views who would keep an eye on them.

How had Brock managed to end up working for them? Membership of the Council was complicated. There were the core seats, made up of those who shared an ancient lineage of the Bloodrender Pack. They were viewed as a sort of werewolf royalty. They didn't just have the advantages of a normal werewolf. They had some sort of magic that gave them extra strength and other powers—although they had always been highly secretive about these supposed powers—that they believed gave them a right to rule.

Next, ten percent of the seats were reserved for those werewolves selected by the Trial of the Moon competition. Held every ten years, those interested could compete in a test of strength, cunning, leadership, and understanding of Pack laws. Only the best were chosen to serve on the Council. The last competition had been six years ago, so Brock couldn't have got in that way.

Another ten percent of seats were reserved for those whom the Council sought out. These were werewolves who had shown extraordinary service to their Pack or the werewolf community. I knew Brock; there was no way he'd done anything in the service of his Pack or our community.

Finally, once every five years, a selection of Packs could nominate a werewolf to serve on the Council. Come to think of it, I was pretty sure it was the Three Rivers' turn this year to nominate a werewolf for the Council.

"Brock's been back about eighteen months," Sofia continued, breaking me out of my thoughts. "Since then, he's been working his way up the hierarchy. The Shaws don't trust him, I know that. But he works with Hayley's team and stays out of their way."

Wally leaned forward. "Do you think Brock's involved with the Pack's recent troubles?"

Sofia shrugged. "Maybe."

I frowned at Sofia. "What troubles?"

"Jem and Hayley aren't exactly on the same page these days. Everyone feels it. The tension in the Pack bonds keeps on growing. There have been rumors that there are some in the Pack who aren't too happy with the leadership. There's talk that perhaps Jem should take a permanent vacation and let Hayley rule solo."

I felt a chill run down my spine. Hayley couldn't run this Pack by herself for long. There was a reason why the strongest Packs always had an Alpha couple. Packs needed the balance of two werewolves in charge. They kept each other grounded, stopped one from imposing their will over everyone, like Oliver had. Who knew what kind of Pack Hayley would run? What damage she could do?

If there were people in the Pack who were unhappy with Jem's leadership, then that was bad news for all of us. I'd seen first-hand what growing up in an unhappy Pack was like.

I watched as a woman walked in the door. She looked to be in her early thirties, with a mane of lustrous black hair that went down to her waist. She was followed by a small girl, about ten years old, wearing a blue checked skirt and a Minions T-shirt that looked brand new.

"Mom! Can I have a hot chocolate? Please? And a muffin?"

"A small hot chocolate. And a blueberry muffin, Tammy, not the caramel one."

A wide smile spread across Tammy's face as she looked at the different blueberry muffins and pointed at the largest one.

Jem and the Shaw brothers had worked hard to change the Pack, to make it a safe place for kids to grow up. Tammy was here, in this bar, safe and happy because of them. Jem would never voluntarily give up the Pack. His permanent vacation was death. With the Pack feeling like this, though, it would only be a matter of time before someone challenged Jem and Hayley for the top spot. I couldn't leave now. I'd always be on edge, just waiting for the call that told me Jem was dead and that Hayley was undoing all the work that Jem and the Shaws had done. I had to stay and find out what was going on.

"Do you think they will make a move to force Jem out?" I asked, looking at Sofia.

"It's possible," Sofia replied. "More people are talking about it each week. That something isn't right in the Pack bonds, and Jem needs to fix it or leave so someone else can. There isn't another couple who are strong enough to take over, so that doesn't seem to be an option right now. Brock's been busy, saying the weak Pack bonds are all Jem's fault but that Hayley could make it right if Jem was out of the way. So, I don't know whether it would be a direct challenge on Jem or some plan to force him to leave the Pack and let Hayley rule as Alpha alone. Hayley's people have certainly been out and about a lot these last few months, whispering in people's ears."

Wally rubbed his chin thoughtfully. "That's not good. We need to find out what they're planning."

"Surely the Shaws know about this?" I asked, knowing that as enforcers, they were supposed to keep an eye on things like this.

Sofia shook her head. "They're pretty cut off up in the compound. I know there are troubles with the Bridgetown Pack these days. It's kept their focus on that threat, not the one inside. I tried to tell them a couple of months ago, but Derek told me I didn't know what I was talking about and I should stick to making coffee."

My eyebrows shot up. That didn't sound like the Derek I used to know. He always had an eye for Sofia, and even though she claimed she wasn't interested, I'd seen the way she looked at him when she thought no one was looking. I'd always thought they'd end up together. There was definitely more to this that Sofia wasn't telling me. I'd have to corner her later and get her to spill.

"We're going to have to work out what is going on and get proof," I said.

"Oh, detective work! I like it! Do I get to wear a trench coat and smoke cigarettes?" Wally asked, with a glint in his eyes.

"No!" Sofia and I answered at the same time.

I stared out of the door, thinking about where to start. "Brock. He knows what's going on."

Sofia looked at me skeptically. "He's not going to tell us anything."

"No," I agreed. "We'll need to be sneaky."

Chapter Thirty

RYAN

I placed Mai's laptop on the desk, then turned and surveyed the room. Her clothes were either hung up in the chestnut closet or folded into the drawers of the mahogany dresser by the far wall. I'd moved the books that I'd put in her room at Jem's house. She'd liked them when she was younger, and I thought she might find them comforting. I was going to have to find out what books she liked now.

Mai had brought a couple of trinkets, and those I'd placed on the chest next to the bed: a glass paperweight with purple swirls inside, a photo of Mai, Jem, and their parents down at the Westcove beach, and a framed golden eagle feather. I knew what feather it was because I'd given it to her five years ago. I'd gone north for a couple of weeks on a mission for Oliver, meeting the Dresden Pack and trying to get their agreement to buy weapons from us rather than the human gangs.

It had turned messy, and I barely got out of there alive, which I was fairly sure had been Oliver's plan all along. I'd had to hide out in Creek Forest for a couple of days, and for the entire time I was there, I'd been followed by a lone golden eagle. Always high above, swooping on the air currents, but I could feel it tracking me.

On the final day, just before I'd found a road out of there, I'd turned a corner, and the eagle had been sitting on a branch in the tree in front of me. It had stared at me for a long minute, ruffled its wings, then it took off. On the ground, I'd found a feather. As soon as I got home, I'd given it to Mai as a gift. I'd known she was my mate by then, and it just felt right to give it to her. I hadn't thought about that feather in years, but Mai had kept it. Framed it, even.

I'd felt it in our mate bond when she left Jem's house. I'd watched her get into her car and drive off. I'd been scared that she was running again, but she hadn't taken any of her things with her. Tracking her through our bond was easy now that it was sealed. I wondered if she knew I could do that and that she could, too. It would only work on Pack territory, but I felt something ease inside of me, knowing that I could find her now, no matter where she went in the Three Rivers. Maybe it was best if I didn't mention it just yet. No, I had to ease her into this fated mates thing before she got too spooked and took off.

Right now, I knew she was at Bottley's. Probably talking to Sofia and telling her what an asshole I was. She needed a friend to talk to, and I was really glad that Sofia was around and could be there for Mai. She was going to need Sofia when she realized that I'd moved all her stuff into the spare room at our house. I'd thought about putting it all in my room, but I figured that was a step too far right now. My wolf wasn't happy. He wanted her in our bed, wanted her scent on everything we owned. But we needed to take this one step at a time.

My phone buzzed. Mason.

He's heading to you. You need to ask Mai what she told him about the Pack. If we don't catch him, he'll be there tomorrow.

Fuck! Mason was right; I'd needed to talk to Mai. We needed to know what Seth knew. What would he be expecting if he got here before Mason and Sam found him? We had to make sure he was in for a surprise. My phone buzzed again. Jem this time.

You got a minute?

I took one last look around the room, then headed across the street to Jem's house. He was waiting by the door with Derek, both of their expressions grim.

"What happened?" I asked.

"My asset in the Bridgetown Pack came through." Derek drew a hand over his head. "It's bad."

"Come through to the study," Jem ordered, leading the way.

I followed them, and we all sat down around Jem's desk.

"According to my asset in the Pack, they are recruiting for an army. Michael and Camille are going to make a move on us soon. Perhaps even before the end of the year. They claim it's pre-emptive. That we're a danger to their Pack."

"What?" That didn't make any sense.

"I'm trying to get more intel. My asset is in a delicate situation. Something came up before I could get more out of them."

"Push the asset, Derek. We need to know now," Jem ordered.

I leaned back in my chair, thinking. "Even if your asset is right, Michael and Camille would be crazy to come at us. We are well-defended. We might not have the numbers on our side anymore, not since he's been recruiting so heavily, but all our enforcers are highly trained. They'd suffer huge losses. Plus, the humans would get involved. This would be too big of a war for them not to notice. That means the Wolf Council would step in. A war between Packs? When the casualty rates of humans would be high? They won't accept that."

"Not if Bridgetown can prove that they were provoked. Or they can say we are a rogue Pack that can't be controlled, and they had to step in. The Wolf Council would back them." Derek pulled out a file folder, tossing it onto the table in front of us. "Two humans from Bridgetown were found dead this morning," he said, his voice low. "Someone ripped out their throats."

My stomach dropped. Werewolves attacking humans was something we all avoided. We needed the humans on our side, needed them to believe we were tame, harmless. We couldn't afford a war between humans and werewolves. We were stronger, faster, more brutal, but they outnumbered us a hundred times over. "Any idea who did it?" I asked, taking the file and looking over the photos.

Two bodies, both male, lay in their own blood in the middle of a road, their throats exposed to the bone. Muscle and sinew dangled from the massive gashes, wolf teeth marks marring their skin around the bites. The victims were young, barely out of their teens, and their dead, vacant eyes stared out of the photo at me.

Derek shook his head. "A witness identified Carson Hodges running away from the scene."

Carson was one of our enforcers. He was older, probably in his late fifties, and his weathered face bore the marks of time. He was more comfortable on the periphery of the Pack than in the middle of it. He was a good enforcer, observant but didn't crave the spotlight or push himself to the frontlines unless he was needed. His presence was always reliable, and he liked to train the new enforcers. He was the steady heartbeat beneath the often hectic and chaotic lives of the trainees, molding them into a fighting force with his calm manner and strict regimes.

Carson kept his own company, more by choice than circumstance, shunning Pack gatherings unless his role as an enforcer required it. But I had never taken him for a violent man. He was reliable in fights, never letting the adrenaline go to his head, never getting carried away or going too far. He did what needed to be done, not because he enjoyed it but because the Pack demanded it. That's what made him an excellent trainer.

I tapped my finger on the photos. "Where is this?"

"It's at the north end of Dunlavey Road."

"That's what? About a mile from the boundary line between us and the Bridgetown Pack and three miles from Carson's cabin?"

Derek nodded.

"Have you talked to Carson yet?" I asked, my mind whirling with questions and worst-case scenarios.

"I spoke to him before I came over," he said, his voice steady but the worry evident in his eyes. "He swears he didn't commit the murders."

"Does he have an alibi?"

"He claims he was doing some solitary hunting. He says he didn't cross into Bridgetown's land."

"And no one can vouch for him?"

"He was alone the whole time. You know how he likes to go up there to relax. He didn't see or scent anyone else."

An uneasy silence fell over us. Jem turned to me, his gaze probing. "Thoughts, Ryan?"

I ran a hand through my hair. "Either we've badly misjudged Carson, and we've got a murderer among us," I started, "or this is a setup. Michael and Camille might be using Carson as a pawn to stir up trouble and give Bridgetown an excuse to invade."

Neither scenario sat well with me. We were a family, and the thought of Carson doing this stung more than any outside attack. But if it was Michael and Camille, it meant we had a much bigger problem on our hands.

CHAPTER THIRTY-ONE

RYAN

I pushed back the chair, the sound loud in the quiet room. Standing, I moved to the window, staring out at the quiet street that lay bathed in the soft glow of the setting sun. The peaceful sight did nothing to calm the storm brewing within me.

"I don't buy it," I said, turning back to face them. "Carson's not the type. He's reliable. Keeps to himself, yes, but he's never shown any signs of being... unstable." The word left a bitter taste in my mouth.

"And yet here we are," Jem replied, his eyes meeting mine. The weight of his gaze told me he didn't believe it either, but as our Alpha, he had to consider every possibility.

I paced the room, my wolf agitated beneath my skin.

"Has anyone else talked to Carson?" I asked.

Derek shook his head, his face solemn. "I was the only one. He said he's been alone for the last few days."

There was that word again. Alone. It echoed in my head, a stark reminder of the position we found ourselves in. One of our own accused, with no alibi. A setup or a murderer—either way, we were in a precarious situation.

I stared at Derek, my mind churning. "Let's say it's a setup," I began. "If Michael is doing this to provoke a war, then we need to find proof. We can't sit idle and wait for him to make his move."

Derek nodded. "Agreed. But we need to tread carefully. Any wrong move could lead to a confrontation we are not yet ready for."

Jem's gaze was calculating, his Alpha authority permeating the room. "We need to find out more about the humans who were killed. Who they were, if they had any connection to Carson, or if they were random victims."

I picked up the file again, opening it to the pictures. Two young men, full of life, now reduced to gruesome crime scene photos. We owed it to them to find out who had done this. "Derek, I want you to head to Bridgetown tomorrow. Ask around. Check with your asset. See what you can find out about these victims."

Derek nodded, grabbing the file. His gaze was steely, determination etched in every line of his face.

Turning to Jem, I stated the obvious. "We need to prepare for a potential conflict. If Michael is planning to invade, we have to be ready."

Jem was silent for a moment, his gaze lingering on the map of our territory spread across his desk. Then, he nodded. "I'll inform the enforcers and begin training more fighters. We won't be caught off guard."

We all knew what was at stake—our freedom, our territory, our lives.

We nodded our goodbyes, and as I left Jem's house, the weight of it all crashed down on me. There was so much at stake here, and yet I couldn't stop thinking about Mai. She was oblivious to the threats we were facing. She was at Bottley's, likely surrounded by warmth and light, laughing with Sofia, unaware of the dangers lurking at the edge of our Pack.

As I trudged back to my place, my gaze went to the window of the room I'd just set up for her. Seeing the golden eagle feather through the pane of glass, I knew exactly what I was trying to protect. I needed her to be safe, needed her to trust me, to believe in the bond we shared.

I reached for my phone, Mason's text from earlier popping up on the screen. A reminder of the immediate danger from Seth. I needed to speak to Mai, sooner rather than later.

I followed our bond to the Bottley Bar. It was like a cord pulling at me, with my wolf wagging his tail the nearer we got to her. I parked, then paused outside the bar, watching Mai through the window. She was talking to Sofia and Wally, her wavy black hair flung over her shoulder. I remembered how it felt to run my fingers through her hair. How good it felt watching her bounce up and down on my cock, her hair bouncing with her.

I shook my head; I couldn't think of that right now. We had to lock Seth down, make sure the Bridgetown Pack stayed out of our territory, clear Carson's name, find the real man-eater, and find some sort of solution to the Hayley issue. Then I was going to take Mai away for a week and fuck her in every position I could think of, and there was a shitload I'd been dreaming about in the last four years.

I walked in the door and knew the moment she realized I was there. She stiffened, her scent of almonds, honeysuckle, and mint suddenly laced with anger. She didn't turn to look at me, even when I approached the table.

I nodded to Sofia and Wally. They both looked amused to see me.

"Mai."

She shifted her gaze to me when I said her name, and a jolt of passion swept through me.

Focus. I had to focus.

"We need to talk."

"I don't have anything to say to you right now, Ryan," she replied, her voice cold.

"That's okay," I said as I sat down next to her, my body nudging her along the bench seat. "I'll talk, you listen."

I picked up a couple of fries from the plate in front of her and bit into them. Mai looked outraged.

"You know, I need to get back to work," Sofia said, bugging her eyes out at Mai as she stood up.

Wally looked from me to Mai and back again. Then he slid out of his seat. "I'm gonna go, er, over there." He strode over to where Sofia was standing by the bar.

"He really doesn't have the hang of the whole subtle thing, does he?"

Mai ignored my question. "What do you want, Ryan?"

I sighed. This wasn't going to be easy. "I know you're mad at me right now, but I need to ask you some questions about Seth."

She narrowed her eyes. "No. Absolutely not. We are not discussing Seth. We will never discuss Seth. Seth is my business, not yours."

Yup, not fucking easy at all.

Being the Beta of a Pack meant I'd had to sit through countless meetings where Pack members needed a mediator. I knew I couldn't get upset. I kept my tone even, trying to ease into it. "I appreciate how you feel about this. However, the situation that we're in means that Seth is heading this way. Mason and Sam are tracking him, but it's possible Seth is going to get here before they get to him. If that happens, it would be useful for us to know what Seth might be expecting when he arrives. How much does he know about our Pack? About your place in it?"

Mai glanced down at the table. I followed her gaze. Sometime in the last minute, I'd picked up a fork and bent it in two. Huh. I really didn't like saying that asshole's name.

Mai looked up at me and raised her eyebrows. I placed the bent fork back on the table.

"This isn't just about you anymore, Mai. Seth is coming here. He is a threat to the Pack. What if he attacks someone here trying to get information about you? Does he know where you live? Do we need to put extra patrols in that area? Or will he head into town to try to track you down? We need to anticipate his next moves."

Mai stared out of the window as I talked. I knew she was thinking about it, and I could smell how unhappy she was. I hated doing this to her, bringing this up when she obviously wasn't ready. But I had to have the information so I could protect her.

"I understand how difficult this is for you, Mai. I'm not trying to be a dick about this."

"You don't understand anything, Ryan."

My wolf whined inside me. He couldn't understand why she was so reluctant to tell me. In his mind, Seth was a threat to Mai and to the Pack. She should tell us everything so we could hunt him down and kill him. It was simple. I had to contend with my wolf's point of view and balance it with my human side. I knew this made her uncomfortable. I knew she wanted to hide Seth from us, to deal with him herself. But that was not how our Pack operated.

We had worked hard over the last four years making it the sort of Pack where we all had each other's backs. I had to remember that Mai grew up in Oliver's Pack, though. Jem and Hayley were too busy trying to establish themselves as an alternative Alpha couple to pay much attention to Mai. My brothers and I were too busy trying to keep Oliver's enforcers off all our backs and keep them from hurting the weaker Pack members to see what was going on. After Mai left, Sofia told me what life had really been like for Mai at school and with Hayley.

Mai left, and Goddess knew what she had to do to survive before she found a base at Cocrane. She had always had to deal with things herself. Why would she think any different this time? My wolf growled. That was our job. We had to show her that there was a different way. That the Pack protected each other, and we were all stronger for it. So far, I'd done a piss-poor job of it.

Chapter Thirty-Two

Mai

I thought about what Ryan said. He was an arrogant, possessive asshole, but he was right; if Seth was making his way here, he was a threat to the Pack. How did Seth know where I was? I'd never told him about my past. Just said I was from the east, hadn't been close to my family or Pack, and had bounced around the human and Shifter conclave cities for the last few years. He'd never pried too deeply.

Seth didn't like to talk about his history either, so it had been a silent agreement that we left our pasts out of our relationship. Seth was a mid-level enforcer trying to prove himself, with his dad, Korrin, grooming him to take over the Beta spot. Seth had grown up in the shadow of Korrin's legacy, always measured by the towering expectations that came with his father's reputation. But I knew Seth was having trouble living up to it, and it would come out in his increasingly volatile temper.

I had left him. What would my leaving have done to his reputation as he saw it? Did Seth think it showed up a weakness on his part, that he wasn't strong enough to keep a partner? More importantly, was that what Korrin would think? If Seth wanted to prove himself to his dad, to the other enforcers, in his warped mind, would that mean he had to get me back?

I knew I had to share this with Ryan and the Shaw brothers. Seth coming here wasn't just a threat to me; it posed a danger to the entire Pack. I felt a knot in my stomach. How could I willingly expose my underbelly, revealing scars I'd hoped would fade into oblivion?

"He doesn't know much about the Three Rivers Pack," I whispered.

Ryan kept still, perhaps realizing how much this was costing me and not wanting to spook me.

"I never talked about my past."

"Does he know you're Jem's sister?"

I shrugged. "I didn't tell him. But if he knows I'm here, I'm sure he has done some research into the Pack. He has contacts. I don't know what he might have found out by now."

"And the Cocrane Pack?" he asked, curiosity pricking his tone. "How much do you know about them?"

I shook my head, a bitter chuckle escaping my lips. "Not enough, never enough."

The room seemed to grow smaller with the truth I was pouring out, bit by bit. "Seth's father, Korrin…" I began, my voice faltering at the mention of his name, "… he's the Pack Beta. He has always had high expectations for Seth. He's supposed to follow in his dad's footsteps."

The worry in Ryan's eyes deepened. "So, Seth has been groomed for violence since he was a pup?"

His words punctured the silence, hung in the air between us like an omen. I nodded, my eyes downcast, locked onto the patterns of the wooden floor.

"It's not just violence," I murmured. "Seth seeks acceptance and an acknowledgment of his power and dominance."

"I won't let him hurt you, Mai."

I could smell the waves of anger pouring off him.

"No matter what."

I shook my head and forced myself to look Ryan in the eye. "*I* won't let him hurt me, Ryan. And I won't let him hurt this Pack. No matter what."

Of course, that was easier said than done. If Seth was coming, there was nothing I could do to stop him. I would have to deal with him if or when it happened. Until then, I had Brock to contend with.

"Move in with me, Mai."

Not this again.

Ryan held up his hands, gesturing for me to give him a moment to explain.

"Just until the situation with Seth has been resolved. If Seth does make it here, we can draw him there. There are Pack members in and out of Jem and Hayley's every day. Any one of them could get hurt if Seth showed up. At ours, we can contain the fallout. It's just me, you, and my brothers. We know what's coming and can prepare. After that, if you want out, I'll help you move."

I raised one eyebrow. I knew him better than that.

"Okay," he smiled at me. "I'll try my fucking hardest to persuade you to stay, but it's not a prison, Mai. You can leave if you really want to."

Damn it. I hated it when he was right. I couldn't put other Pack members at risk just because I was annoyed at his bossy, arrogant ass.

"Fine. I'll move in. But only until this thing with Seth is resolved."

Ryan's smile turned into a grin. "I'm so glad you said that. I moved your things across this morning."

I glared at Ryan and wondered just how angry I needed to be before my head exploded.

Chapter Thirty-Three

MAI

"Get out of my sight, Ryan," I said through clenched teeth. "Before I do something that you'll regret."

Ryan laughed, then leaned down and kissed my cheek.

"I'll see you at home later, babe. Be safe." Then he stood up, nodded to Sofia and Wally, and walked out the door.

Taking a deep breath, I watched the door swing shut.

"That looked intense," said Sofia as she came and sat next to me.

"I know!" agreed Wally, fanning himself with his hands. "That boy radiates sexual tension! Are you gonna have hot shower sex with him again tonight?"

A thrill jolted through me as the memory of his slick body thrusting into mine popped into my head, and I swear both Sofia and Wally knew it.

Damn it. I had to get this conversation off me and Ryan before my hormones went haywire.

I narrowed my eyes at Wally. "No more talk about Ryan. What I want to know is what's going on between Sofia and Derek."

Sofia shrugged. "There's nothing to tell."

"Bullshit. Derek always had a thing for you. The Derek I knew would never have shut you down if you came to him with information."

"Maybe you don't know Derek anymore," Sofia said softly.

"Again, I call bullshit."

Sofia sighed, looking past me and Wally to the street outside. "You're not going to drop this, are you?"

"Well, if Mai does, I sure as hell will not!" Wally said. "You've been holding out on us."

"I haven't been holding out. There really isn't anything to tell. About a year ago, Derek discharged from the military. He came back here, and we started to get close. We even went on a couple of dates."

"Oh my God, you didn't?" Wally asked.

Sofia frowned. "Didn't what?"

"Do the nasty with Derek Shaw?"

Sofia sat bolt upright. "I did not sleep with Derek! It didn't get that far. It... it was good. Really good. I thought... I thought he was my..." Sofia shook her head. "It doesn't matter now. We had some dates. Then he ghosted me. Wouldn't take my calls, didn't answer my messages. I thought he was hurt or something. I was on my way to see him, to check he was okay, when I saw him walk out of a bookshop with Shya Little."

My brow furrowed. "Who?"

"Shya Little is the Bridgetown Alphas' daughter," Wally explained. "That doesn't mean anything, Sofia."

"He hugged her. Like really hugged her. Then kissed her forehead. My wolf went nuts. It was all I could do to stay on the road and not jump out of the car and rip his balls off."

"Maybe—"

"Maybe nothing. Derek barely says hello to me anymore, and that's just the way I like it."

"I'm so sorry, Sofia." I reached over and pulled her into a hug.

"Don't worry about me, I'm over it," she lied. "Anyway, enough about me. We have to work out what we're going to do about Brock."

"Brock's not going to willingly spill his guts," Wally said.

"We'll need to follow him," I agreed.

Wally rubbed his hands together. "I can tail him without being noticed."

"And I know some of the Pack members who work with Brock. They might be able to give us some information," Sofia added.

"Good. Let's do that," I said. "But we need to be careful not to get caught. Brock won't be happy if he finds out we're snooping around."

Wally smirked. "Don't worry, Mai. I'm the master of disguise. No one will recognize me."

Sofia rolled her eyes. "Just make sure you're not too obvious. And no trench coats!"

We spent the next hour ironing out the details of our plan. Wally and I were going to follow Brock. Sofia listed the people she thought might have noticed something and those who would be willing to talk to her.

As we left the bar, I couldn't shake off the feeling of unease that settled in my stomach. We needed to find out what Brock was up to, but I hated the thought of putting Sofia and Wally in danger. The stakes were high. A misstep, a moment of bad luck, and we could land in a heap of trouble. My heart twined around the fear of what could go wrong, tugging at the edges of my determination.

"Stay safe," I implored, my gaze locked onto Sofia. "If something feels off, leave it. This is about finding out what is going on, not playing heroes."

With a nod, Sofia pulled me into a hug. "We'll be fine, Mai. You worry too much. Just take care of yourself, okay?"

Sofia slipped into the afternoon shadows as Wally touched my shoulder. "She'll be okay. She's good at talking to people."

I nodded, my gaze lingering on the street Sofia had taken.

"Come on, Mai. My car's over here."

I followed Wally to a dark blue Mercedes and got in the passenger side. As he started the engine, I leaned back in my seat and took a deep breath.

Our plan hinged on Brock being where we thought he was. At this time of day, Sofia had figured our best bet was to wait outside the betting shop on Broadway.

Wally's car was a sanctuary, a bubble of warmth against the afternoon chill. I twisted a frayed thread on the cuff of my jacket. Wally drummed his fingers on the steering wheel in tune to some silent beat only he could hear.

He glanced sideways at me. "So, what's it really like? Being back in the Pack?" He spoke softly, the kind of soft you use when you don't want to startle a fawn.

"I never thought I'd come back here. But now that I am, I'm glad I did," I admitted, eyes flickering back to the betting shop. "I didn't realize how much I'd missed everyone, you know? Jem. Sofia..." The words stalled on my tongue, an unspoken name caught in my throat.

"Ryan?" Wally's smirk was more knowing than teasing. I sighed, the sound escaping me like the echo of a forgotten dream.

"Yeah... Ryan. It's just so complicated now."

Before Wally could respond, the betting shop door creaked open. Brock walked out and slid into his car, a shiny, ostentatious black thing that screamed of overcompensation.

"Okay, Wally, stay cool. We don't want to tailgate him, all right?" I cautioned, my heart sounding a drumroll in my ears as Brock pulled out into traffic, and we followed him.

Wally shot me an incredulous look. "Do you think I learned to drive yesterday?"

"Um—"

"I watch all the police shows, Mai. I know how to tail someone without getting caught."

"Really? 'Coz he just turned right, Wally."

"Fuck!" Wally slid the car round the corner at the last second, only swerving a little into the oncoming lane.

We were both silent as he picked up Brock's car ahead.

"Do you want me to drive?"

He shot me a look that made his answer plain.

I decided to shut up and let him drive. But after a few minutes, I couldn't help myself. "So, in your head, if there was a 'Fast and Furious: Werewolf Drift,' you'd be Vin Diesel?"

He laughed. "Damn fucking right, I'd be Vin Diesel. I suppose that makes you Michelle Rodriguez?"

"Well, I do have the attitude," I shot back.

Brock settled into a predictable rhythm, pulling over every few blocks to chat with a passer-by when he saw someone in particular. The conversation was always brief, like fleeting whispers in the wind. I recognized a couple of people but Wally, his senses attuned more to the subtle nuances, confirmed my suspicions.

"They're all wolves, Mai. That one is Harper Creek, the one before that was Dixon Main, and the first person was Elliot Muyat."

My mental notebook filled with faces and names. These were people Sofia and I would seek out later, hoping to unravel Brock's web of secrets.

Brock seemed in no hurry and didn't appear to have a destination in mind. He weaved through the town in a random pattern, heading south down one street, then turning at a junction and going north along the next street. He did this for an hour, slowly crisscrossing the Three Rivers, before stopping outside The Nouveau Table, a restaurant right on the edge of town.

"Looks like he's going in," Wally said, leaning forward so he could get a better view. "You been here before?"

I shook my head. "I didn't even know it existed." My life before I left didn't really involve many eateries.

"It's an upmarket restaurant, this. It's the place to take your date if you want to impress them. Thomas took me once. They make their money with the evening trade. It's a little early for that, though."

Even so, they were definitely not closed. Brock walked up to the door, and it whooshed open for him. I shrugged and settled back to wait.

It was two hours later, and Brock still hadn't come out. Wally and I perched in the front seats of his car, parked outside the restaurant. People had started to trickle in there in the last couple of hours, but not many. Despite Wally's assurances that this was one of the places to be seen in the evenings, so far a buzzing restaurant, it was not.

"Do you think he saw us? Slipped out the back, maybe?" Wally fretted, a furrow deepening between his brows.

"Well, with your Formula 1 aspirations back there, we might as well have had flashing lights and sirens."

Wally groaned. "I should go in and check."

"No." I shook my head. I couldn't let him put himself in danger. This was all my idea. If anyone was going in, it had to be me. "I'll go. I need you here in case we need a quick getaway—you can Vin Diesel us to safety."

It took me another five minutes to persuade Wally to stay in the car. I didn't want Brock to see us together. It might be useful for our surveillance if Brock didn't realize Wally and I knew each other.

I got out of the car and walked quickly to the door. I wanted it to seem like I knew where I was going and had a reason to be there.

Inside, the restaurant was a mélange of mouth-watering aromas and soft music. The walls were all light mint and pastel blues. Structural posts, large plants, and decorative slat dividers were strategically placed so that each table had a measure of privacy.

I glanced around the mostly empty tables. I couldn't see Brock until I stepped behind a dracaena plant. He was sitting at a table in the back, talking with three unfamiliar werewolves.

The first, a man in his late thirties with a shaved head and trimmed goatee, was glaring at Brock and radiating waves of being severely pissed off. The woman next to him, with her auburn hair cascading around a delicate face, was smiling, yet her cool gray eyes suggested an undercurrent of steel. The third, another man, was dressed as the epitome of a businessman in an expensive suit and striped tie.

"Good afternoon, do you have a reservation?" a waitress queried, snapping me out of my reverie.

"No. I would like to look at the menu. I have a date next week, and I'm trying to work out where to take him," I replied. Out of the corner of my eye, I saw Brock's face snap up at the sound of my voice. I kept looking directly at the waitress. I didn't want him to know that I'd seen him. Brock stood up, excused himself from the table, and made a quick beeline for the back exit.

I had a choice now. Brock had pretty much run out when he saw I was here. Why? Because he suspected I was following him? Or because he didn't want me to see him with those other werewolves? I could go back to Wally, see if we could pick Brock up when he went back to his car. Or I could try to find out what was so special about the group here. I said my thanks to the waitress when she handed me a menu, then settled into an empty booth next to the werewolves, pretending to study the menu.

"Why the fuck did Brock just up and leave like that?" the goateed man grumbled, his voice low but carrying a current of unease.

The businessman replied, "Fuck Brock! We came all this way to broker the alliance. I thought Brock had more respect. Or at least that he needed this. I still don't understand what Bridgetown is doing getting involved in this."

If they were from the Bridgetown Pack, they should have been talking to Jem or Hayley, not Brock.

The woman sighed audibly. "It doesn't matter what you think. Our job was to take the meeting and report back to Tristan."

A chill swept over me. This wasn't a casual meeting. If the

Bridgetown Alphas were getting involved and taking sides against Jem, then this was more serious than I thought.

Chapter Thirty-Four

RYAN

The sharp ping of a text message from my brother Derek reverberated in my pocket, piercing the stillness in my car. I couldn't listen to my usual music; it drowned out my thoughts, and right now, I needed to hear myself think. I fished out my phone. Carson was at Jem's place. It was time to turn over some stones.

I drove quickly, parking at my place and jogging over to Jem's. I found Derek and Carson at the dining room table.

"We alone?" I asked my brother as I walked in.

"Yes, everyone's out. I made sure before I brought him here."

I nodded, then took a good look at Carson. His face was pale and drawn. He was clutching his hands together and staring at the table, but otherwise, he looked like the calm figure I'd always known him to be.

"Carson," I began, "thank you for coming. You know why you're here?"

He gave a quick nod of his head.

"Okay. I need to ask you some questions. I know you've gone over this with Derek already, but I need to hear it from you."

Carson stared at my nose, not meeting my eyes and not saying anything.

"You know where the bodies were found?"

He nodded this time.

"Were you there anytime in the last week?"

His answer came back like a recoiling spring, swift and tense. "No. I've been at my cabin. Since last Wednesday."

I studied him, trying to navigate the uncertain waters between truth and deception. "Why would anyone claim they saw you fleeing the scene, then?"

His eyes sparked with anger. "I've no idea, Ryan. I don't know why someone would want to pin this on me."

No, I didn't, either. I had to work out if he was being framed or if he really was our killer. "What do you do up at that cabin of yours, Carson?"

The hint of a weary smile shadowed his face. "I enjoy the quiet, Ryan. Being away from humans, not needing to pretend all the time. I can be myself up there. Shift to a wolf, hunt when I want…"

"Hunt?" I asked, keeping my voice even.

He shot me a look that said he knew what I was really asking.

"Squirrels, rabbit, sometimes deer. Never humans. You know me, Ryan. You know that's not who I am."

The trouble was, I did know. Whoever killed those boys, it wasn't Carson. But we had no proof.

"Who knew you were up at your cabin this week?"

Carson took a moment to answer. "Everyone knows I go there, but I guess only Jem and Mattie knew I was there this week."

"Mattie Bowster? She owns the convenience store on Russell?"

Carson nodded. "I always stop at her shop for supplies before I head up."

I sighed. "I gotta say, Carson, you don't have a lot of information for me to go on."

His smile was bitter. "Don't I know it. What happens now?"

I looked up at Derek, sitting across from me, close enough to Carson, in case he made a run for it or tried to attack me. "Keep Carson here, under lock and key, until we find out more. I don't like this. I think it's best if we keep an eye on Carson for his safety."

Carson watched me, a quiet resignation etched on his face. His gaze held an understanding of the gravity of the situation, the wolf in him recognizing the Pack's need for the truth.

"You have my word, Carson. We won't stop digging. We'll find the truth. This isn't over."

The Alpha's house always had a cage room. No matter what the issue—a rogue werewolf, a man-eater, a grieving werewolf, a teen who didn't know how to control themselves, or an older wolf letting off steam that got out of hand—the Alpha was the best person to contain them. Ours had been updated since Oliver's time and now housed an impressive array of steel cages, padded walls and floors. Everything was built to withstand the strength and power of the most stubborn werewolves while also being comfortable and calming for the confused and distressed.

I waited while Derek locked Carson inside.

Derek looked grim as he came back into the dining room, and we headed outside. My boots crunched the gravel underfoot as we left Jem's house.

Derek broke the silence first, his voice a low rumble. "So?"

"Did you check with Mattie?"

Derek nodded. "No one else was in her store when Carson was there and she didn't mention it to anyone."

I shot him a sidelong glance. "You think he did it?"

"Carson's been with us for years. We've seen what he is and isn't capable of. I've worked next to him for the last year. He's not our guy."

"Agreed."

"So, what now?"

"Any news on the victims?"

"Paul Abbotsford and Kaz Wheston. Both nineteen. Graduated together from the human-Shifter high school in Bridgetown. Known to run dodgy deals with both humans and Shifters. Drugs mostly."

"They could have pissed off one of their suppliers. Had an argument with a client. Lots of motives. Any connection to Carson?"

"None that I've found."

"Keep digging. In the meantime, we need to talk to the witness."

He quirked a brow at me. "We might be able to get in and talk to people in Bridgetown, but there is no way Michael's going to let us talk to the witness. Especially not if this whole thing is a setup."

I shrugged. "We'll need to go around him."

Derek stared at me, not saying a word.

"It'll mean war if Michael finds out," he eventually said.

"The other option is to hand over Carson. It'd be a death sentence. What do you want to do?"

He was silent for a while, staring at the Alpha house with a thoughtful expression. Then, without turning his gaze, he said, "He's Pack. We protect our own. If there's a chance to clear Carson's name, we have to take it. And if it means marching into that prick's den, then so be it."

The conviction in his voice made me smile, but even more than that, it was the undercurrent of compassion for Carson that struck me. Derek, for all his military hardness, carried a deep empathy for his Packmates.

"I knew there was a reason I kept you around," I teased as we got in my car and I pulled out into the street. His lips twitched upwards in a grin.

"And here I was thinking it was my cooking," Derek shot back.

"You can't cook for shit, man."

"Yeah? You still eat it."

I did. I'd eat anything my brothers made.

"Talking of cooking, did your cooking skills work their magic on Mai?"

I paused, wondering how much I wanted to tell him.

Before I could answer, Derek continued, "Bear in mind, I have been home today. The whole place reeks of you two, so I know they worked something. Of course, it was laced with Mai's distinct scent of anger, so I know you also fucked it up somehow."

"Your confidence in me is heart-warming, you know that?"

He gave me a sideways glance. "Bro, I know you. I know how much Mai means to you. I also know you haven't been in a relationship in

203

years, and you are stubborn as fuck, so I don't have any doubts that you messed it up in some way. Tell me, Ryan. Maybe I can help get your head out of your ass long enough that you can fix this."

I hated that he was right. I hated that he knew me so well. And I really fucking hated that he could predict I would mess things up. I sighed and told him about this morning.

He laughed for a full five minutes. I timed the fucking bastard.

"You done?" I finally asked.

"I can't believe you told her that I hacked her phone! What did you expect would happen? You thought she was going to thank you and demurely move all her stuff into our house?"

I kept my face blank.

"Oh fuck, you really did, didn't you?" He laughed again.

"No, but I didn't think she'd storm out. It's not an issue now, anyway. She's agreed to move into the spare room, at least until this thing with Seth is settled."

He turned and looked at me. I could feel his eyes studying my face. "I want you to be happy, Ryan," he said, his tone serious. "You deserve to be happy. But you have a lot to learn about women. A lot to learn about Mai. You need to respect her boundaries. You need to talk to her about shit like this before asking me to wade through her entire life. Don't fuck this up, okay? We're all counting on you."

Counting on me? "What does that mean?"

He hesitated, and I could sense he was debating something with himself. Finally, he turned away as he said, "Nothing. Just that we all want you and Mai to be together. You guys have waited a long time for this."

CHAPTER THIRTY-FIVE

RYAN

O ur car sliced through the night, the buildings of Bridgetown growing denser as we drew closer to its heart. Derek's eyes had remained glued to his phone screen for the last ten minutes, his fingers a flurry of movement. The silence hung heavy, punctuated only by the quiet hum of the engine and Derek's intermittent murmurs as he dug deeper.

Finally, his phone beeped, and Derek exhaled, glancing at me with a spark of triumph in his eyes. "Found him," he declared. "Name's Eddie Keller. Works at the local sawmill. Apparently, he's also a regular at a dive bar called 'The Black Hound.'"

"Guess we're going for a drink, then," I said, steering the car toward our new destination.

Nestled in the outskirts of Bridgetown Pack territory, The Black Hound was a gritty bar with grimy windows. This was not one of the approved places in town that tourists were encouraged to visit. This was a place for those werewolves too real for the tourists to see. The outside of the bar was dimly lit by a neon sign of a huge black dog. I could see silhouettes of men and women through the glass. The place was busy tonight.

As I parked the car, the raw scent of a rival Pack filled my nostrils. No way we could go in there and talk to Keller without word getting back to Michael.

"We wait. He has to leave at some point. We'll follow him home and talk there."

Three hours later, under the dim, scattered lights of the parking lot, the bar's door swung open. A man of wiry build with closely cropped sandy hair stumbled out into the night. He was wearing worn jeans that had seen better days and an old T-shirt that read, "Hell yeah!"

Derek's eyes narrowed in on him. "That's him," he affirmed in a low voice, his gaze trailing Eddie as he stumbled toward a beat-up Chevrolet.

We shadowed Eddie through the streets of Bridgetown. The human tourists were still out and about, sampling the Shifter nightlife, at least the one that Michael and Camille wanted them to see. We headed into the suburbs, and then the houses gradually thinned out, replaced by an array of trailers. Eddie stopped in front of a small trailer with a metal exterior, rust creeping up along its edges. It had a small yard out front, unkempt and dotted with assorted debris. A single wooden chair sat on a makeshift porch alongside a battered cooler. No lights were on inside.

"According to my research, this is his home," Derek whispered.

"Anyone live here with him?"

Derek shook his head. "His records have him living alone."

As Keller stumbled inside his trailer, I nodded to Derek. This was it. We slipped out of the car and circled the trailer. There were no exits around the back, and the windows looked too narrow for even someone with Eddie's frame to fit out of. The place smelled of werewolf, old, rusted metal, and greasy food.

Derek knocked at the door.

"Who's there?" Eddie's voice was gruff and defensive.

"We just want to talk, Eddie," Derek responded, his tone carefully neutral.

Silence. The door creaked open a fraction, a suspicious gaze peering at us through the gap. "Don't know you. Fuck off."

"We believe you have information that we'd be keen to hear," I interjected, holding up a wad of cash. Eddie's eyes flickered between us and the cash before they narrowed.

"Nah, ain't interested."

Before he could close the door, I moved. I was inside his trailer before he had time to think. I grabbed his arm and twisted. His yelp of pain echoed through the trailer, and I could see fear creep into his eyes.

"Alright! Alright! I'll talk," Eddie wheezed, looking at the ground and trying to make himself appear smaller.

I let go of him. Eddie, wincing from the pain, held his arm awkwardly.

"We want to know about the murders. What exactly did you see?"

"Alright," he repeated, his breath reeking of alcohol. "I... I don't remember much about that night. I was drunk. Can't even remember how I got back home."

Derek glanced at me. I shook my head. I was going to let Eddie talk;

we needed him to tell us everything.

"I... I was up there 'coz..." Eddie trailed off, grimacing. "I was meeting someone. A guy who sells me... stuff. You know, out of town, where no one looks."

There were all kinds of transactions happening where the road led into the forest marking the boundary between our territories. Transactions best kept away from prying eyes. That explained why Paul and Kaz were there, though.

"Did you know the victims?" I pressed, my voice steady.

"Kaz and Paul? Sure, I knew them. They were into some heavy stuff, man. Selling drugs and shit. They said they had the good stuff, you know, the stuff that works on Shifters."

I frowned. Alcohol worked on Shifters just fine. Drugs were more hit-and-miss. Painkillers took the edge off. Antibiotics were rarely needed, given our healing capabilities. Recreational drugs, though, could either make us feel like we were flying or slide right off us with no effect. Often, the reaction you had was individual—a drug that worked for your sister might do nothing for you. There had been rumors lately, though, of a new drug on the scene, one that guaranteed a reaction from every Shifter. Theriothiamine, or "ripple," as it was known on the streets, was supposed to be highly addictive for Shifters. The southern conclave cities were reporting dangerous side effects and some deaths associated with it. I hadn't thought that ripple had reached the Three Rivers yet, but if what Keller was saying was true, then it was already here.

"Did you see the murders, Eddie?"

He shook his head. "No. I heard some noises, though. Struggles, you know. Screams. Then someone running away. Fast."

His eyes look haunted for a moment.

"So, you didn't actually see Carson Hodges at the scene?" I nudged.

Eddie shrugged. "Told you, man, I was drunk. All I remember is some figure bolting away. I reported it like I'm supposed to. Called it in to the voicemail."

I looked at Derek.

"They have a hotline here for Bridgetown members to report anything that might cast an unfavorable light on the Shifter community. It means they can keep that stuff away from the human tourists with their pockets full of money."

Unfavorable light? Yeah, I guess two men getting their throats torn out would cover that.

"Enforcers came round after," Eddie continued. "They showed me a picture of this Carson guy later, told me it was him."

"But you can't be sure it was him?" Derek questioned, his gaze fixed on Eddie.

Eddie swallowed hard, a bead of sweat trickling down his forehead. "No, I... I can't. I just... I just said what they told me to say."

"Why?" I asked.

"I don't know, do I? They... they offered me money to say it was Carson. A lot of it."

"Money?" My voice turned dangerous. Keller had set up Carson to be killed for fucking money.

Eddie dropped his eyes and nodded.

"Who did you really see?"

"I don't know, I told you that. But here, look, whoever was there, they dropped this." Eddie shuffled over to his wallet and pulled out a twenty-dollar note. "It must have slipped outta his pocket when he...

you know."

When he killed the men. I took the note from Eddie and sniffed it. There was a blend of scents on there, Eddie's scent being the strongest. But scents on bank notes tended to stay for a long time. People touched the notes with their fingertips, transferring their pheromones onto the paper. They soaked in, layer after layer of everyday emotions, of fears, joys, hunger, excitement, and even desire. I took a moment to sort through the smells.

"Brock Madden."

"Brock?" Derek turned to me. "You sure?"

I nodded. We were werewolves; we could remember the scents of over a thousand different people.

"There are other scents there as well. No one else I recognize."

"It could be that Brock handled this note in the last few days. It doesn't confirm it was him at the murder scene."

"Yeah, but we need to talk to him."

This time, Derek nodded.

Eddie reached out to take the note back.

"You took this from the scene?" I asked.

"Yeah, man. No one else there needed it."

I looked around at the inside of the trailer. It was the size of a small bedroom, with both living room and kitchen shoved into a single space. Christmas lights from years past hung from the ceiling, their cords exposed and frayed. The furnishings were old, of the kind found in thrift stores. A television set with a black-and-white screen and a single wooden stool in front of it, a few mismatched chairs, and an old, worn couch were all the furniture I could see.

"What did you do with the money the enforcers offered you?" I asked.

"I don't have it yet, man. I gotta wait until the whole thing dies down, don't I? That's just common sense, man," Eddie said, still clutching his arm.

I doubted they were ever going to pay Eddie. He'd probably find himself face-down in the river sometime in the next couple of days. Something like this, they'd tie up all loose ends. My guess? They didn't think we'd make a move so soon and thought they had time to dispose of Eddie.

"The situation dies down, or Carson dies?" Derek asked. His face was blank, but I knew my brother and the hard line of his jaw and the way he held himself told me he wanted to finish the job for the enforcers himself. That Eddie would betray one of his own kind for cash, knowing it was a death sentence, went against everything Derek stood for.

"I don't know, do I? They just told me I had to wait." He stood up and took a step toward Derek. "I need the money, man. You see me living the high life? I gotta start somewhere, man. I gotta start somewhere."

Derek looked at me, and I nodded. We weren't going to get anything else out of Eddie.

"Leave him some cash."

Derek raised his eyebrows at me. I knew he didn't approve. I didn't respond to his look, and Derek pulled out his wallet, throwing a few bills on the floor next to Eddie.

"Thank you," he mumbled as he scrambled to pick up the notes. "I won't tell them that you were here. I promise I won't."

"Use the money to get out of here for a while, Eddie. Those

enforcers, they'll be back to make sure you don't ever talk."

I walked out of the trailer. Outside, the trailer park was eerily quiet, the hush of the night broken only by the distant hum of a lone car engine. My wolf's hackles raised in alert. Derek's body stiffened. I scanned the trailer park, my instincts screaming that we weren't alone. I took a step forward and stopped dead. The scent hit me then, strong and familiar.

There, casually leaning against my car as if he had all the time in the world, was Michael, Alpha of the Bridgetown Pack. His broad figure was outlined in the soft moonlight, and his eyes glinted with a predatory gleam.

Chapter Thirty-Six

RYAN

"Ryan. Derek." Michael's voice held a tone of cool amusement, an incongruous smile shadowing his face. He had First Nation heritage in his lineage, and it showed in his tall, lean frame, strong muscles, and sharp features.

"You boys are a long way from home."

I sighed, letting my body relax, showing Michael that I didn't think he was a threat. I knew Derek would be looking for other wolves sneaking up on us, so I could keep my focus on Michael.

"We're thinking of buying a trailer, aren't we, Derek? Thought we'd stop by here and see what they're really like."

Michael scoffed, then his eyes went hard. "Did you leave my boy in there in one piece?"

Okay, he was done messing around. That was good because I was, too.

"In one piece, yeah. Of course, I don't suppose that matters, given that Eddie isn't long for this world, is he?"

Michael's body went still. "Is that a threat? Against one of my own?"

"From us? We got what we needed. But I'm sure your enforcers are going to take real good care of him, aren't they?"

Something flickered in Michael's eyes as he glanced toward Eddie's trailer, gone too fast for me to work out what it was.

"You got what you needed, huh? Look, I'm sorry about Carson, but he murdered two of my men. They were human, but they were under my protection. Your Pack is out of control, and it's leaking into my Pack now. I can't let this stand."

I laughed. "Fuck, Michael, you sound as if you really believe your own horseshit. You and I both know Carson didn't do this. We both know you're using this as a cover so you can launch a war, but we ain't gonna make it easy for you. You attack us, we'll be ready."

Michael shook his head. "Surely, you can see the damage Jem and Hayley are causing your Pack? They aren't strong enough to hold it. You want it to turn out like it did under Oliver? Those were some tough fucking years you guys had, but Oliver held his shit in his lands. Jem can't even do that. Now, me and Camille have to clear it up. You might not see it right now, but we're doing you a favor."

"We don't need any favors, Michael. And you're mistaken if you think we'll let you undermine Jem's leadership with concocted murder charges."

Michael's expression hardened further; a flicker of surprise and then something close to anger shadowed his features. "You really are sticking with them, aren't you?" he asked, disbelief tinting his voice.

"Yes, we are. Just like you would stand by Camille," I shot back, refusing to give ground, to show any weakness. There was a tense silence, the air charged with unspoken words and brewing conflict.

Finally, Michael pushed off from my car, running a hand through his hair as he glanced toward the night sky. "I didn't want it to come to this, Ryan," he said, his voice almost regretful. "I don't want to go to war with you, but I will if it means protecting my Pack."

"No one wants a war," I said, standing my ground. "If you have a problem with Jem and Hayley, you bring it to the Pack leaders, you don't blame Carson for something he didn't do."

Michael's eyes flickered to Eddie's trailer again. Something wasn't right about this, but I couldn't work out what.

"Get out of my territory, both of you. You don't step a toe over the line without my permission. I see you here again, I'll kill you and your brothers."

With that, he turned and began to stride toward Eddie's trailer. I had the feeling it wasn't going to go well for Eddie. I shook my head, motioned for Derek, and we headed to my car.

We kept silent as we pulled out of the trailer park, both of us alert and ready for any attack. This whole thing with Michael was too easy, and neither of us trusted that he had just let us go.

We had crossed over to our territory before Derek broke the silence.

"Michael shouldn't have been there alone." His voice was steady, eyes set on the dark expanse of road ahead. "An Alpha, in that area of town, at this time of night. He shouldn't have been alone," he repeated.

"You sure he was?" I questioned, my gaze flickering to Derek.

"I didn't see or scent anyone else. You?"

I shook my head. A sense of unease grew within me. Michael was many things, but reckless was not one of them. Something was definitely off about this whole situation.

I steered the car onto the main road, the shadows of the night swallowing us. The streetlights flickered by intermittently, their glow washing over us in a spectral dance.

"We'll update Jem, see if he has any insights," I said finally, my focus still on the road.

Derek's confirmation was a simple nod, a line of tension etching his features in the dim light.

Chapter Thirty-Seven

Mai

I stepped out of The Nouveau Table, my eyes going immediately to Wally's car. Darkness cloaked the interior, making it impossible to see inside. Good, I didn't want Brock to have noticed Wally when he left.

"Mai, fancy seeing you here."

I turned to see Brock leaning against the restaurant wall.

"This place is a bit upmarket for you, no?" he said as he straightened himself and walked toward me.

"Brock," I returned evenly. "I see you've crawled out from under your rock to bless us with your presence tonight."

"Ah, the little bitch still has some claws." His gaze was unsettling, but I refused to look away. "Seen anyone interesting tonight?"

I frowned. Was he fishing to see if I'd seen him with the Bridgetown wolves?

"I'm not really interested in who's who these days, Brock. I've got better things to do than check out what people are wearing and what skank is dating which dickhead."

He shrugged. "Just making conversation. You know how it is."

"Do I?" I raised an eyebrow. "Well, don't let me keep you from your nocturnal activities."

A flash of irritation crossed his face, but he masked it quickly. "Give my regards to your brother."

I stared at him with a bored expression on my face, then flicked my fingers in a "you're dismissed" gesture.

He clenched his jaw but managed to keep his cool. "See you around, Mai."

"Count on it," I murmured, watching as he walked away, his figure retreating into the darkness.

Once he was out of sight, I made my way to Wally's car and slipped inside, tension still vibrating through my veins.

"Are you sure about this?" Wally asked. He had turned off the engine and the headlights, and we were bathed in a quiet sort of gloom. After my little chat with Brock, Wally and I had texted Sofia to see how she was getting on. She'd sent one reply:

I'm busy. Will be in touch when I have something.

She'd then turned her phone to "do not disturb"—I knew this because not only did my new super-duper phone tell me, but she ignored all my texts and calls. We'd spent the next couple of hours driving around all the places where we thought she might have gone. Finally, I'd called time and said we needed to go back to Jem's.

"He needs to know, Wally," I replied, unfastening my seatbelt and turning to face him.

"We don't have any proof. You said yourself, you didn't hear Brock even talking to them. Only saw he sat with them, and then what they said after he left. And we haven't heard back from Sofia yet and what she might have found." His voice was laced with concern.

"I know, but this is bigger than we thought. If Brock is trying to form an alliance with Michael and Camille to push Jem out, or worse, kill him so Hayley can take over, then we need to prepare. Now."

Wally nodded, but his face was unhappy. "Okay, just be careful. Sofia said she was shot down when she tried to bring this up. You don't know how he's going to react to the news that members of his own Pack are plotting to oust him."

I put my hand on his and squeezed. "It'll be okay. Just find Sofia and see what she knows. We need to work out how big this is and who else is involved."

I got out of the car and walked toward the Alpha house. After a moment, I heard Wally start the engine and drive off.

As I opened the door, I noticed Hayley's scent was conspicuously absent, but Jem's lingered in the air, a marker of his presence. That scent guided me, and I followed it, letting my instincts lead the way through the quiet house.

The muffled echo of my footsteps was the only sound as I padded down the corridor, heading toward Jem's study.

I found him at his desk, bathed in the warm glow of a desk lamp. He was leaning back in his leather chair, lost in a sea of paperwork, his brow creased in thought.

"Jem," I began, hesitating at the doorframe.

He glanced up from his papers, eyebrows furrowed, but his gaze softened when he saw me.

"Mai! Sorry, I was lost in these papers. I didn't even realize you were home."

I frowned, stepping into the study. Jem was a werewolf; he should have heard the door, heard my footsteps, smelled me long before I came into the room. He was a Pack Alpha. I shouldn't have been able to surprise him.

"We need to talk."

Jem nodded, putting the papers down. "Of course. Is this about you moving in with Ryan? I noticed all your stuff is gone. I've got to say, Mai, I'm glad you decided to stay a while and over the moon that you're giving Ryan a chance."

My foot faltered from one step to the next, but Jem didn't seem to notice.

"No, this isn't about that. I need to talk to you about some things I've heard. About a plot against the Pack." I looked at Jem, my gaze steady, even as my heart pounded.

He paused, pen held in mid-air, and locked eyes with me. "Mai," he began, his voice almost a sigh, "you know better than to pay attention to Pack gossip."

"This isn't gossip, Jem. This is about you." I swallowed hard, gathering my courage. "There are members of the Pack who are trying to oust you."

His brow furrowed, eyes narrowing. "You've got your wires crossed, Mai. You must have heard wrong," he said, his voice firm yet controlled.

Jem's dismissal didn't surprise me. But the blatant denial, the refusal to even consider the possibility, stung.

I took a deep breath, determined to make him listen to me. "Jem," I began again, "I'm not wrong. I followed Brock tonight. He met with three werewolves from the Bridgetown Pack at a restaurant downtown. They were talking about brokering an alliance."

Jem looked at me, taken aback. "Are you sure?"

"Of course I'm sure. I wouldn't have come to you with this if I wasn't sure, Jem," I stated.

Jem stood up and came to sit on the front of the desk. "Okay, I'm listening. Tell me what you know."

I told him about Sofia's rumors, about us deciding to follow Brock, about the two-hour meeting with the Bridgetown Pack members, and what they said afterward.

"So, you never heard Brock mention an alliance?" he asked.

I shook my head. "No. I know what you're thinking—this could be a ruse by the Bridgetown Pack to make you think that Brock is betraying you. Hoping to sow doubt in your mind, make the Alpha bond even weaker. But how did they know I would be there? That I would overhear what they said?"

Jem shrugged. "I'm sure news of your return has reached the Bridgetown Pack by now. I'm also sure they would recognize you—we've had your photo on flyers and websites all over the state for the last four years. Maybe they weren't even there with Brock, but he stopped to see what they were doing in our territory. Then they saw you in the booth next to them and decided to take advantage of that."

"You know that's unlikely," I replied.

"Unlikely, maybe, but possible. You don't know anything, Mai. You have no evidence, no hard facts, just speculation and guesses. I can't accuse Brock of trying to get rid of me with this. Besides, Brock isn't a threat. He doesn't have a mate, and only an Alpha pair can challenge for the Alpha spots of a Pack."

I started pacing across the study floor. "Okay, so we get evidence. We talk to Brock. Find out why he was there. There is something going on, Jem. Brock doesn't need to challenge you; he only has to oust you so Hayley can rule alone. The Pack is not healthy, it's not happy. People are talking, whether you like it or not, and you need to get your head out of your ass and see what is happening right in front of you."

Before he could respond, the front door opened and shut quietly, and familiar voices echoed down the hall. Ryan and Derek were here.

The comforting scents of Ryan and Derek washed over me as I watched Jem's gaze shift toward the study door.

Ryan appeared first, his tall frame outlined by the low light. His ice-blue eyes swept the room, landing on me. His gaze softened for a moment, a silent question if I was okay. I gave a slight nod, assuring him I was. His relief was clear, even as he moved to stand protectively near me. Derek followed, his expression grave.

"We tracked down the witness," Ryan began without preamble, his gaze never straying far from me. "He didn't see Carson leave the scene."

What witness? What scene? Who the hell was Carson?

I opened my mouth to ask, when Ryan continued, "There's more. The witness picked up a banknote dropped by the murderer. It had Brock Madden's scent all over it."

"Ah-ha!" I said, pointing to Jem.

"Ah-ha, nothing," Jem replied gruffly. "You don't even know what we're talking about."

Okay, he had a point.

"Did the witness actually see Brock there?" Jem asked.

Ryan shook his head.

"It's circumstantial at best, then."

"We also ran into Michael on the way out."

"Michael?" Jem echoed, his surprise evident. "You okay?"

Ryan nodded, his gaze flicking from mine to Jem's. "Yeah, but something was off about it. He was alone, and he really seemed convinced that Carson did it. He thinks you've lost control of this Pack, and it's leaking into his territory."

A tense silence filled the room. I could almost see the gears turning in Jem's mind.

"Someone's been feeding him bad intel on us," Jem said, his voice speculative.

Ryan nodded. "I think so. It would explain why he's been recruiting—if we had an unstable Pack on our borders, we'd do something about it."

"Someone's trying to start a war between our Packs," said Derek.

A chill ran down my spine at Derek's words. Jem stared at them. "But why? To what end?"

"And is Brock in on it?" I added.

All eyes in the room turned to me.

"What do you know?" asked Derek.

I repeated my evening for Derek and Ryan.

Ryan walked over to the table. "Two groups: one in the Bridgetown Pack—it might be Michael and Camille, or it might be some of their enforcers—looking to take over the Three Rivers Pack. The other group is in our Pack."

"We need more information," Jem stated.

"Sofia is talking to some people, those she thinks might tell her what's going on. Maybe we'll know more when she reports in."

Derek's head whipped around at the mention of Sofia's name. "You have Sofia involved in this? Where is she?" he demanded.

"I don't know. Wally's tracking her down."

"Fuck!" Derek dragged a hand through his hair, then looked at Jem. Jem nodded, and Derek strode out of the room.

"You two should head home," Jem said, going back around the desk and sitting in his chair. It wasn't a question.

"But—"

"No, Mai, there is nothing more to say tonight. We'll know more in the morning when Sofia and Derek have checked in. Be here at eight. We can meet over breakfast." He looked at Ryan, who nodded.

Ryan walked toward me, and I sighed, knowing Jem was dismissing us. He needed to think about what we'd all said. I got that. I just wish we could brainstorm it together. But maybe he was right. We needed more information before we could decide what to do.

As Ryan got closer to me, his eyes changed from serious to warm and full of intent. My wolf went on alert.

"Come home with me?" he asked. I felt a quiver in my vagina, and heat flushed up my body.

I ignored the sensations my traitor body was having. "We might be staying in the same building, but it's not my home."

I spun around, walked out of the house and across to the Shaws' home. Ryan got to the door before me and held it open for me.

"You sure you don't want to forget our past for the night?" he asked, his tone dark and seductive.

I glared at him. "Where's my stuff?"

"In the spare room. Mai—"

"I can find it. Goodnight, Ryan," I said firmly and stormed up the stairs. I could feel Ryan's heated gaze follow me, and I could have sworn I heard him chuckle.

CHAPTER THIRTY-EIGHT

MAI

T he first rays of the morning sun washed over the living room as Ryan paced the floor. He was close enough that I could smell his earthy, pine scent—a tantalizing aroma that sent an unwanted shiver down my spine.

Last night, I'd checked my mail, making sure none of my clients had emailed with an emergency. None had, but there had been a message from Seth. I wrapped my arms around myself as I remembered the words:

I miss you. But soon we'll be together again. Count on it, Mai.

I hadn't told Ryan. Hadn't needed to. I'd come down this morning, and Ryan had told me that Derek had forwarded the message to him. Apparently, Derek would be monitoring my phone and email until the situation with Seth was resolved. If Seth was coming here, then I understood the need for Derek and Ryan to invade my privacy like this. The Pack had to come first; I knew that. But it riled me. This was exactly what I'd been afraid of, of having others go out of their way to protect me because I couldn't protect myself. And Ryan seemed completely oblivious to my feelings.

Ryan stopped pacing and instead stood dangerously close to me, his scent pervading my senses, sending a pulse along our bond that shouted, "Fuck me, fuck me," in time with my heartbeat.

There would be no fucking. Not now. Not ever.

Ryan was in full protector mode. There was a raw power in his presence, an aura of authority that drew me seductively to him. I folded my arms across my chest and glared at him.

"Mason and Sam are closing in on Seth. But if Seth makes it onto Pack lands, we have to keep him away from Jem's house. I've let it be known in town that you're staying with me, so he'll probably head here. I don't want you here alone. Anytime you enter this house, you need to always have either me or one of my brothers with you, okay?"

I nodded, wondering how long I was going to have to put up with this.

"If you are at the house, and you get any sense, any sense at all, that Seth is around or something isn't right, you come here."

Ryan led me to an inconspicuous-looking panel on the wall. He pressed a switch hidden in the wall, and a door slid open, revealing a fortified room. "This," he said, motioning to the room, "is the safe room."

It was spacious, going back the length of the living room, and was well-equipped. Shelves lined the walls, stocked with food and medical supplies, and a couple of thick blankets. A computer, TV monitors, and a satellite phone were on a desk by the wall. "You get here, lock the door with this button, and alert us using this," he said, pointing to the phone.

"Okay," I murmured, letting his instructions sink in.

Satisfied that I understood, he led me back out to the living room. I could feel the heat of him next to me, his presence both comforting and infuriating. The tension between us crackled in the air, a live wire of emotion. I was angry at him, still stinging from his invasion of my privacy, but as I looked up at him, the memory of our bond sealing zinged through me.

Before I knew what I'd done, I took a step toward Ryan, the invisible pull between us dragging me forward.

Ryan's eyes bore into mine, the desire in them unmistakable. I licked my lips, wanting to taste him, and reached out—just as an alarm on his phone went off.

"Fuck!" Ryan said, his voice rough. "It's eight o'clock."

I took a step back and swallowed hard. I couldn't let my hormones rule my head on this. I stomped toward the door and glanced back at Ryan. His face was closed, angry, but his eyes followed me with a hungry longing that made a rush of heat go straight to my core.

We stepped inside the Alpha house, welcomed by the mouth-watering aroma of fresh coffee and bacon. Ryan and I strolled into the dining room just as Sylvie was setting down the last of the dishes. Steam wafted up from fluffy scrambled eggs, the edges just slightly crisped, while a plate of bacon and a stack of buttermilk pancakes drizzled with maple syrup stood beside it. In the center of the table was a fresh fruit platter, the vibrant colors of sliced melons, berries, and citrus fruits making a beautiful display.

Sofia and Derek were already seated at the long wooden table. They sat across from each other, not talking and not looking at each other. Derek looked unhappy, and Sofia avoided my eyes when I walked in.

"Morning," I said, aiming for nonchalant and cheery. I needed them to focus on something other than whatever was going on between them. "Everything smells delicious, Sylvie."

Sylvie beamed at the compliment. "Oh, you flatterer. You're just like your brother. Sit down and enjoy your breakfast."

Ryan pulled out a chair for me. I took one glance at it, walked past him, and sat down in a chair next to Sofia. Out of the corner of my eye, I saw Ryan shake his head and sit down in the chair he'd pulled out, just as Hayley and Jem walked in. There was no hiding the tense silence between them. Hayley's face was stony, her lips a thin line. Jem's jaw was tight, and his eyes burned with barely concealed anger.

I frowned, not liking that Hayley was here.

When Jem didn't say anything, Ryan broke the silence. "How is everyone this morning?"

"Fine," Jem grunted.

Hayley scoffed at his response, her hands clenched into fists.

My eyes darted round the room, looking at each of them. This wasn't going to work. We had to be able to work as a team. Jem angry and distracted, Hayley winding everyone up, Sofia and Derek barely able to be in the same room together, me annoyed with Ryan while also trying to rein in my stupid hormones that just wanted to jump him—none of it would help us work out what was going on and be able to save the Pack. Maybe if I made nice with Hayley, made sure she was the center of attention for the meal, she'd leave as soon as she'd finished eating.

"Hayley," I said, bringing my gaze to her. "It's lovely to see you this morning."

"Don't start with me, Mai. I know what you're up to."

I raised my eyebrows at her.

"You think I'm involved in this. That I'd take on Jem and push him out."

I shot a glare at Jem. I hadn't thought that. Hayley had many faults, but she loved Jem. All she ever wanted was to have Jem's full attention. What would she have to gain from pushing Jem out and ruling alone? But I guess Jem had thought of it. If she cheated on him, any trust between them must be fragile. It would take a lot to regain that. But Jem was the Alpha; he was supposed to put the Pack first, and that meant not confronting Hayley and telling her what he suspected until we had the evidence. But he'd put his mating bond first; he'd acted as a husband wanting the truth from his partner. If he was right, and Hayley was involved, he'd tipped our hand. She would warn Brock that we were onto them. They would delay or change their plans. We no longer had the element of surprise.

"I don't know what to think, Hayley," I replied, keeping my voice calm.

"Well, I do. You're back and causing trouble again. Trying to jam a wedge between me and Jem. Trying to make Jem think less of me. Well, it won't work, Mai. Jem is mine, and I'm never letting go, no matter what bullshit you come up with to drive him away from me."

"Hayley—"

"Save it," Hayley snapped, pushing back her chair and standing up. "I can't stand being in the same room as any of you right now."

She shot Jem one last icy look before she turned on her heel and marched out of the room. We were all silent as we listened to her close the front door, then Jem picked up his fork and started poking at his food.

"Well, that was one way of getting rid of her."

"You shouldn't have told her," Ryan growled.

"I'm Alpha. She's the Alpha, too, or did you forget that? I did what I thought best." Jem stared directly at Ryan, and there was a warning in his voice, telling Ryan to back off. Ryan was right, though. Jem shouldn't have told her. I put my hand on Ryan's thigh and squeezed. We couldn't afford to be at each other's throats right now. We needed to sort this mess out, and then afterward, we could discuss what we should and shouldn't have done. It took Ryan longer than it should have to look away from his Alpha.

"Michael called this morning," Jem continued when Ryan had backed off. "He wants to meet. Said he wants to discuss the murders and Carson."

Ryan had filled me in on the murders this morning, so I knew who Jem was talking about this time.

"It could be a trap," Derek said.

Jem nodded. "Yes, but I have to take that risk. Carson didn't do this. If Michael and I can clear this up, then we can neutralize one plot against us."

"When?" Ryan asked.

"Today at noon. On neutral ground, in the human town of Maxly."

"I don't like this," Ryan and Derek said at the same time. I had to agree with them.

"You don't have to like it. I'm going."

Derek leaned forward. "My source in the Bridgetown Pack says

Michael is honorable and can be trusted when hosting meetings, but we don't know what is going on with their Pack right now. He's—."

"Of course she would say he's honorable and trustworthy!" Sofia chimed in.

Derek swung his head around to look at Sofia. "She? I never said my source was a woman."

Sofia scoffed. "I know who your source is, and if you think she wasn't sent here to seduce you and feed you false information, then you are a lot more stupid than I thought you were."

"Seduce me?"

I swear, if Derek had been a wolf, all his hair would be standing on end.

Sofia folded her arms across her chest and leaned back in her chair, looking away. "Don't play dumb, Derek. It's not a good look on you."

"Sofia, you and I need to have a conversation—"

"I agree," interrupted Jem, "but now is not the time. No matter what Michael's intentions are, if there is any chance of him giving us information to clear Carson and shut this down, we need to take it. I'll bring Derek and Ryan as backup. Who else can we trust?"

Derek kept staring at Sofia for a moment before he shook his head and looked at Jem. "At this point, no one. We don't know who is involved or how big this thing is. If Brock is involved, he had to have help. We can't trust our enforcers."

Jem switched his gaze to Sofia. "What did you find out?"

Sofia cleared her throat, glanced quickly at Derek, then said, "I spoke to a few people who I've seen or heard were close to Brock. I figured these were the people Brock would recruit for any plot against the Pack. None of them are fans of Jem's, and all have been

getting more vocal about their dislike of how the Pack is being run."
She shot an apologetic glance at Jem. He waved his hand for her to
continue. "There are definitely others involved in this, but most of
them clammed up."

"You were too soft on them," Derek interjected, earning him a
sharp look from Sofia.

"I was getting there, Derek. It's called subtlety. You might want
to look it up. I didn't want them to alert Brock that I was asking
questions. You turned up like the big bad wolf and scared them off."

"Sofia, I was in military intelligence. I'm the epitome of subtle."

Sofia scoffed, but Derek ignored it and continued. "You have to
read people and know when subtle isn't gonna work."

"I got Maria-Anne talking, didn't I?"

Ryan leaned forward. "Maria-Anne Dubliss? Brock's on-again,
off-again girlfriend?"

Derek nodded. "Definitely off-again."

"They had a fight two nights ago about Brock seeing her sister, of all
people. But," Sofia said, smiling, "it meant Maria-Anne was suspicious
enough to listen in on his conversations, and she overheard that Brock
has a meeting today with Tristan Heller."

Ryan raised his eyebrows. I got the feeling the name meant
something to everyone here.

"The same Tristan who the three werewolves I saw yesterday were
reporting back to? Who is he?"

Jem put his fork down. "He's Michael and Camille's Beta."

Okay. That was big.

"Did she say where and when the meeting will be?"

Sofia nodded. "Reynold's Sushi and Meat Bar. Two o'clock."

"We have to be there," I said.

Jem nodded. "We have to be there."

CHAPTER THIRTY-NINE

RYAN

J em and I sat in a corner booth of a nondescript highway diner. The droning of a worn-out jukebox in the background, along with the occasional clatter of diner staff and the distant symphony of crickets outside, were the only sounds right now. The sunlight cast long shadows that mirrored the growing unease in my gut. Derek was hidden outside, guarding us against the possibility that this was a set-up. He'd warn us if Michael arrived with an army. Though, at this rate, I was betting Michael was a no-show; he was twenty-five minutes late.

With Sam and Mason still tracking Seth, and not knowing who in the enforcers we could trust, we'd left Mai at the house with Sofia, Jase, and Wally. They had strict instructions to lock the doors, not go out, and not answer anyone who came by. Jem, Derek and me were going to check out Brock's meeting after seeing Michael. Though, if we wanted to make it to Brock's meeting, we had to leave in the next fifteen minutes.

"Jem, he's not coming."

As if in answer, the door swung open, and in walked Michael.

His dark eyes were sharp, scanning the room, locking onto us. Right behind him was Tristan Heller. Tristan was a towering figure, broad-shouldered and muscular, his shoulder-length brown hair pulled back in a tight plait. His hazel eyes flicked around the room before settling on me.

Interesting. We would need to wrap this up quickly if Tristan was going to make his meeting with Brock.

"Jem. Ryan." Michael nodded to each of us as he sat down. "Do you know Tristan?"

Tristan held out his hand, and we both shook it.

"Please to meet you both," he drawled, though he looked anything but pleased.

"My apologies for our lateness. We got held up on another matter. Thank you for waiting."

Jem didn't say anything; just continued to look at Michael, waiting to hear what he had to say.

"I asked for this meet firstly to discuss your wolf Carson."

"Michael," I began, "these allegations... Even you must see that they don't seem right."

His response was immediate and gruff. "Easy for you to say, Ryan. You're not dealing with the fallout or telling those men's families how they died. They want justice. I want justice."

I took a sip of my coffee, the bitter taste grounding me, focusing my thoughts.

Jem interjected, his normally light tone replaced with an uncharacteristic edge. "I know that you have always relied on evidence, on facts. Not hearsay, emotions, or assumptions. Carson deserves the same."

Michael's mouth twisted into a grimace, seemingly mulling over Jem's words. "I talked to Eddie. He told me about my enforcers. Unfortunately, they've gone AWOL, and I haven't been able to track them down yet to get answers."

He sounded angry. Furious, even. It couldn't be easy for him to admit he'd lost some of his enforcers.

Tristan leaned forward. "That doesn't mean we believe you. You're right. We do rely on evidence, but we haven't seen any that Carson is innocent. Besides, Eddie told Michael you scented another one of your wolves on the note he found. So, even if it wasn't Carson, it was someone else from your Pack. You've got a man-eater who is using our territory as an all-you-can-eat buffet.

"Everyone knows how weak you are. You can't keep your Pack in line. Hell, you can't even keep your own mate from cheating. You're letting down your Pack, and now your fuck-ups are bleeding into our territory."

Jem went still. It was not a good sign. I'd seen it before, right before Jem had ripped the person's throat out. What the fuck was going on? Was Tristan trying to start a fight right here between our two Packs?

I tensed, ready to launch myself in front of Jem if Tristan or Michael made a move, but Michael placed his hand on Tristan's forearm.

"I apologize for the words of my Beta. He is keen to find the murderer of our men. But I called you here not just to talk about Carson. I suspect there is a plot against both of our Packs."

A jingle sounded at the diner's entrance. I turned to see who the newcomer was. Surprise ran through me when I recognized the person stepping through the door—it was Shya, Michael's daughter.

She was a striking figure, with an aura of strength of someone much older than her twenty years. The light streaming in from behind her cast her curly auburn hair in a fiery halo, and her large, almond-shaped emerald eyes, identical to her father's, sparkled with determination.

Tristan looked and smelled furious, but a strange mixture of emotions flickered across Michael's face—surprise, concern, anger. "Shya? What the hell are you doing here?"

Ignoring her father, she leveled a serious look at Jem. "We need to talk."

Derek stalked in the door and headed for us. "Our phones have been jammed. No communications in or out. I can't tell where it's coming from. We need to leave, but you have to listen to Shya, Jem, to what she has to say."

I looked sharply at Michael. Was this all a set-up?

Michael pulled out his phone and pushed some buttons. "It isn't us. My phone's jammed, too."

He stood up and grabbed Shya's arm. "We need to go."

"No!" Shya yanked her arm free and slid into the booth. "Dad, you need to hear this, too. It's Tristan—he's the one behind all this."

All of us went silent, then Tristan growled, "Shya, I don't know what game you're playing, but you need to leave."

"Don't even, Tristan!" she spat back at him.

"Tristan is right, Shya, you have no business being here," Michael said, his words full of anger.

"You always do that, Dad. Just dismiss what I have to say. I tried to tell you that things were not right in our Pack. That Tristan was working against you. But you wouldn't listen to me. Too hell-bent on getting me to accept Tristan as my mate because you decided he was the best choice for me. But you have blinkers on, Dad. Every time you decide something, you ignore what anyone tells you that contradicts that decision. This is why I went to Derek six months ago. It's why I've been his informant since then."

Oh, boy.

"You've been what?" Michael spat out, his voice rising in a mixture of disbelief and fury. He turned to Derek, betrayal etching lines into his forehead. "And you—"

"Hear her out, Michael," Derek interrupted calmly, though I could see his jaw clenching. The revelation that Derek's informant was Shya was a shocker, not just for Michael but for all of us.

"You involved my daughter in your games of subterfuge, Derek?" His voice was low, but the tension in his muscles pointed to a wolf about to break free.

Shya met her father's gaze without flinching. "This isn't about games, Dad. This is about our Pack. Tristan has been playing you. You know something isn't right in the Pack. You know, that's why you're here. But Tristan's been feeding you lies. He's the one behind the unrest in our Pack. He's the one who's been stirring things up between the Packs, pitting us against each other. Telling you crap about the state of the Three Rivers. It's not true, Dad. None of it is. But he's fed you that crap, and you believed it. He wants you to attack the Three Rivers Pack. To start a war."

"What the hell are you talking about?" Michael demanded.

"Tristan's been conspiring with Brock Madden from the Three Rivers." Her eyes flickered over to Jem before going back to her father. "They've been working together. They were the ones who framed Carson." The words hung in the air, heavy and irrefutable, and I felt the tension in the room spike.

241

Michael scowled, disbelief etched into his every feature. "Tristan?"

"Yes, your precious Tristan, Dad," Shya affirmed, her voice unwavering. "They've been orchestrating all of this for months."

Michael swung his gaze to his Beta. Tristan was leaning back in his seat, watching the show. He didn't look or smell worried. If anything, he smelled excited.

"You know, Shya," Tristan smirked at her, "you really shouldn't get yourself involved in these things. When we're mated, I'll make sure you're not allowed to run around sniffing into other people's business."

"What the fuck, Tristan?" Michael demanded.

"What the fuck, indeed," he replied. "I got tired of waiting, Michael. Shya's my mate. I told you that for two years. She should have been wrapped up in a bow and delivered to my bed. Instead, you told me to wait. That she would come around. Well, she didn't come around, Michael, and I've been left holding my dick for two years when I could be an Alpha."

"You want to be the Alpha? Challenge me like a proper wolf!"

"Oh, I intended to, once I got the power boost coming my way from having Shya in my bed twenty-four-seven. But that didn't happen. Not yet, anyway. Now, I'll just have to take what I'm owed. And then I'm going to show the world that we're not some prissy little Pack that caters to every human who strolls in here wanting a good time. We're werewolves, not a Disney show. I'm going to make sure every human knows that."

Michael's face snapped into a calm mask. "You're out of your mind if you think you're getting out of here alive."

"Sure, I will." Tristan smiled, then flicked his fingers.

It was a sign. As soon as he made that gesture, the front and back doors banged open, and ten, no fifteen, werewolves flooded in.

Chapter Forty

Mai

Anxiety gnawed at me as I sat in my car, parked inconspicuously a little down the street from Reynold's. I could feel the pulse of my heartbeat in my fingertips, the tension of the situation looming over me like a tangible thing. Jem had taken Ryan and Derek to meet with Michael. Jem would need both Shaw brothers if things went south. They were supposed to be back in time to check out the meeting between Brock and Tristan.

Jem's meeting with Michael was at noon. It was one-fifty now. Ryan promised he'd call as soon as the meet was over, and they were on their way back. I'd waited until one-fifteen, then persuaded the others that someone had to be here to check out Brock. Despite Ryan's instructions not to leave the house, Sofia, Jase, and Wally hadn't taken much persuading, to be honest. They all loved Jem and knew how important this was.

Unease snaked its way around my stomach. My eyes kept straying to my phone, set on the dashboard. Each time, the screen remained blank; a fresh wave of worry washed over me. I pushed the unease away for the umpteenth time. I had to focus. I was here to do a job, and I had to make sure things didn't go wrong at this end. Our plan was simple: listen in to the meeting between Brock and Tristan and report back. I wasn't going to be seen, and I wasn't going to engage, not unless it was absolutely necessary.

Brock had booked a table on the rooftop terrace. My car was angled so I had a clear view of the glass elevator that led up there, its ascent and descent marked by a soft, golden glow. You could only access the elevator from the inside of the building, so we kept an eye on the front entrance opening and closing as people ventured in for an early meal or a few drinks. Sofia and Jase, their car parked around the back, were the fail-safe. They could see the rear door into the restaurant and could tag Brock if he slipped out the back again. If he did, they were going to follow him, nothing more. We needed to know where he went after this meeting.

Sofia and Jase knew the manageress of Reynold's. She'd dated a guy on Jase's football team. They'd been able to persuade her to part with the table number that Brock and Tristan would be sitting at. Apparently, whoever made the booking had specially requested that table. Sofia checked it out—it was in the back of the terrace and out of sight of the road. Someone had been here before and knew which table to ask for.

Jase had gone inside armed with a tiny listening device I'd found inside the safe room. Given that Derek and Ryan had hacked my entire life, I figured it was only fair if I helped myself to their tech. We couldn't hack into the diner's security feed, as cool as that might be, as none of us had a clue how to do that. The bug would have to do.

Jase had returned from his mission and slipped into the backseat of my car with Wally. Sofia had seated herself with me in the front.

"Fucking hell, you should have seen me!" Jase beamed. "I was soooo smooth. I picked a spot close to their table, pretended to tie my shoelace, and bam, baby! Dropped the bug on the underside of the table. It was a work of art, really, how easily it went."

I'd glanced at Sofia, and she'd grimaced. "He wants to be here. He's trustworthy, and it's not like we had any other options."

That was all true. Still.

"Aw, come on, Sof! Admit it. I did a fuck of a good job."

"Stop saying fuck!" Sofia and I had said at the same time.

Sofia had turned to face him. "You did do a good job, Jase. Now, tone down the jabbering five-year-old."

I hadn't gone into the restaurant, conscious of the fact that if Brock were to catch my scent in there, it could compromise our whole plan. As much as I wanted to ensure the bug was placed perfectly, the risk of being discovered was too high. So, I'd stayed put, occupying my anxious mind with what I could do on my end—keep watch and listen.

After that, Sofia and Jase had gone back to Sofia's car to wait for Brock's arrival.

"You don't need to be here, you know."

Wally looked sideways at me. "Why? Because I'm relatively new to the Pack?"

I shrugged.

"Do you know how many Packs I've belonged to over the years?"

I shook my head.

"Six. And not one of them made me feel safe. Not one. I'm a gay werewolf, Mai. And I somehow managed to find some of the most homophobic, asshole Alphas this country had to offer. I've always had to hide the real me. What Jem has built here, in the Three Rivers, is special. For the first time in my life, I feel safe to be who I am. To follow my heart. There is nothing that would stop me from being in this car with you right now. I will protect this Pack. I will protect your brother with my life. And if that means I get to wear a trench coat, then I'm all in!"

After Ryan had called him this morning, told Wally what was going on, and asked if he could come round to help babysit me, Wally had turned up at the Shaws' place wearing a full-length black leather trench coat. With his dark skin and piercing eyes, he looked bad-ass in it. Not that I was going to tell him that; it would only encourage him.

A flash of movement in my rear-view mirror caught my attention. It was Brock, pulling into the parking lot in his black SUV. He stepped out, a picture of casual confidence in jeans and a white and blue striped shirt, and started toward the restaurant. I ducked, bending under the wheel to make myself as small as possible. After a moment, I sneaked a peak. Brock sauntered in the front door without a glance in my direction, and I breathed out in relief.

I picked up the walkie-talkie I'd also swiped from the safe room. "Guys, do you copy?"

"Team Trench Coat, we copy loud and clear, over."

Team Trench Coat? I guess I wasn't the only one to notice.

"The target is in the building, over."

"Copy that, out."

⚜

Forty minutes later, there was still no Tristan. No news from Ryan or

Jem, either. I had a really bad feeling about this.

"I don't like this," Wally whispered next to me.

"Me, either. If Tristan was coming, he'd be here by now."

I held up the walk-talkie. "You guys still there?"

After a moment, the walkie-talkie hissed. "Still here, though I think we're on the verge of going to sleep."

"Any movement back there? Could Brock have slipped out the back?"

"Nope. Nothing apart from a waitress having a smoke."

Shit.

"You want me to go in there, suss it out?" Wally asked.

I looked at the restaurant door. The sign above it announcing that it was Reynold's Sushi and Meat Bar was slick and understated. It was crafted in matte black lettering against a brushed steel backdrop. Its modern, clean lines seemed to promise an experience as refined as the font itself.

"No, it's too dangerous. We regroup back at the house and come up with a new plan."

Just then, the walkie-talkie crackled. "Hey, are you listening in to Brock? His phone's ringing."

I picked up the earpiece that would let me listen in on what Brock was saying and popped it in my ear just as Brock answered.

"Yeah?"

There was a muffled voice on the other end. I couldn't make out what they were saying.

"Sure thing. She's here."

Who was there? I hadn't seen any women on their own enter the diner since we'd arrived. Did he mean a waitress?

"Of course, man. She's all yours. Just like we agreed."

Maybe he was talking about a car?

"You've got five minutes. Then I'm leaving."

I got on the radio. "Sof, how trustworthy is Maria-Anne? Is there a chance we've been set up?"

Silence. I frowned, radioing Sofia again, but she didn't respond.

Chills shot down my spine.

"Come in, Sofia! Jase? Do you copy?"

Nothing.

Fuck!

I threw the door open and jumped out. I had to get to Sofia and Jase.

"Mai!" Wally yelled at me. "Get back in the car."

I had taken two steps away from the car when another voice stopped me.

"Ah, there you are."

I spun around, my legs suddenly shaking.

Behind me, Seth stood next to my car. He looked the same as I remembered, his wavy blond hair falling around his face, and his familiar grin sent fear coursing through my body.

Before I could say anything, he opened the driver's door, punched Wally in the head, and dragged him out of the car.

I leaped, aiming straight for Seth. He lunged under me, a glint of something black and metal in his hand. Pain buzzed through my arm, and my vision swam. I hit the ground hard as the world around me blurred, and then everything went dark.

Chapter Forty-One

RYAN

I didn't recognize any of the new werewolves, but from the growl that escaped from Michael's throat, I was guessing some of these were his missing enforcers.

The scent of sweat, adrenaline, and anticipation from the werewolves surrounded us, tinged with the sharp scent of fear from Shya. My wolf snarled beneath my skin, desperate to break free and tear into the threat. We couldn't Shift. Not now. There wasn't time, and we'd be vulnerable until the Shift was over.

Tristan had jumped up when the others came in, and he was now outside the ring, arms crossed over his broad chest as he glanced at the scene. His gaze landed on Shya, a smile twisting his lips. "Kill the rest, but bring Shya to me."

Shya lunged at Tristan with a snarl. Michael picked her up effortlessly with one arm.

"Not yet," he whispered. "They'll take you if you cross the line of fighters."

Tristan smirked. "No worries, Michael. I'll get her soon. I'd love to stay, but I have places to be." Then he turned to his fighters. "The Beta spot for whoever brings me Michael's head."

Tristan strolled out of the diner as a howl went up from the werewolves surrounding us.

Jem moved first, launching himself into the werewolf closest to us, claws ripping through flesh as he tore the bastard's throat out. Jem had partially Shifted. Only Alphas could do that, Shift only one part of their body, and Jem was using it to his full advantage. Blood sprayed, the coppery scent intensifying the frenzy thrumming through my veins.

Two males in wolf form leaped at Jem while another in human form charged straight for me. He was big, had at least a couple of inches on me, and had a ragged red beard that covered most of his face. I jabbed my fist into his face, feeling the satisfying crunch of bone as it connected with his jaw. He stumbled back but came again, his hands doing a one-two punch. I leaned back, feeling the air swoosh across my face as his fists went past.

I ducked beneath another blow and kicked out, sweeping his legs out from under him. As he fell, I grabbed him by the neck and slammed his head into the linoleum floor, once, twice, until he went still.

There was no time to think before the next one was on me. A woman with blond, braided hair and a fuck-off solid steel bat swung at me. I ducked, drove my shoulder into her stomach, then kicked her in the head as she fell to the ground.

The scent of blood was overwhelming now. I scanned the chaos for the others. Jem was in the center of the fight, face hard as he launched a brutal front kick at the wolf attacking him. It caught the wolf in the chest as he jumped at Jem, and the wolf went flying back, knocking into two other attackers. Michael and Shya were fighting together, their movements in sync as they rounded on two fighters who looked to be identical twin sisters. Derek staggered back, clutching his arm, blood streaming down it.

A battle cry echoed through the diner as Jem threw himself forward, slicing through two of his opponents with his partially Shifted claws. Michael, who was following Jem's example and using his claws as well, with Shya at his back moved in Jem's direction, sending werewolves scattering ahead of them. I hauled Derek up and shoved him after them, then turned, picked up a chair, and brought it down on the head of a man charging toward us.

We were holding our own for now, but we were tiring. If we didn't end this soon, we'd be dead.

A werewolf rammed into me from behind, sending us tumbling to the floor. The scent of him was a mix of stale coffee and fresh sweat. I twisted as we fell, but I felt a blade slice along my ribs. I kicked out. My boot connected solidly with a knee with a loud crack. And I jabbed my hand into his windpipe to make sure he would stay put.

As I got up, I saw all the attackers were down, either dead, unconscious, or moaning on the floor. Michael walked over to a man slumped against the wall, clutching his stomach, trying to stem the blood that was leaking out.

Michael didn't say anything, just drove his fist into the side of the man's head. He went limp and slid to the floor.

Okay, then.

"We need to move," Jem said quietly. "Before reinforcements arrive."

Michael stood up, glanced at his daughter, then back at Jem. "I have a request. Take Shya back to the Three Rivers with you. Protect her."

Shya stepped toward her dad. "What are you talking about?"

"I need to go hunting, Shya. Deal with Tristan. Root out all the traitors. I need you safe." He gestured around the room. "You won't be safe in Bridgetown until I can work out what the fuck is going on and how many of our people are involved in it."

"I'll protect her with my life," Jem replied.

The piercing ring of my phone cut through Shya's colorful reply.

"The jammer must have been shut off," Derek said.

No shit.

I snatched my phone up, answering without glancing at the caller ID.

"Ryan," came the voice of Jase. His voice was ragged, thick with fear, and my heart froze. I knew before he said anything that it was Mai.

"Mai... She's gone."

The words hit me like a physical blow, and I felt my grip on the phone tighten until my knuckles turned white.

"Kidnapped," he clarified, his voice a choked whisper. "She's—"

I didn't hear any more. There was just white rage in my head as I ran for my car.

Chapter Forty-Two

Mai

I blinked my eyes open and found myself staring at the back of a seat. My head felt fuzzy, my limbs weren't working, and I couldn't remember where I was or how I had gotten here.

"Wharrrrttt," I gurgled.

I guess my tongue wasn't working either.

Seth looked over his shoulder at me and smiled. My gaze caught on the steering wheel that he was gripping. My thoughts came slowly but I realized that we were in a car.

"Hiya, sleepyhead."

"Fuuucccck yuuu," I slurred, my tongue only just coming back online.

Seth laughed. "I always did love that mouth of yours."

It took about ten minutes before I could feel all my limbs again. My hands were tied in front of me by an old rope that smelled of fish, but I managed to pull myself up so I was sitting.

"Feeling better, are we?" Seth mocked from the driver's seat.

I was about to swear at him again when I saw a passing sign.

"Sampton?" I whispered, not believing it. That was over two

hundred miles from the Three Rivers.

"You've been out, Mai. I gave you a little something to make you sleep. Just enough to give me time to put some distance between us and your old Pack."

I dropped my head against the backrest. Two hundred miles. There was no way Ryan, Jem, or Sofia would be able to find me. I was on my own. My stomach cramped as I remembered Ryan not calling after his meeting, and the silence on the end of Sofia's radio.

My hands were still tied to each other, but I leaned forward and grabbed Seth's hair, yanking his head back. "What did you do?"

He slapped my hands away. "Sit your ass back, Mai."

"Tell me what you did to them!" I growled.

"Me?" He laughed again, and I wondered how I ever liked that sound. "I didn't need to do shit. I got contacted by someone in your Pack. Told me you were in the Three Rivers. Said your brother wouldn't be Alpha for long, and they would clean house afterward. So, no need to worry about anyone coming after us."

My heart tried to burst out of my chest. He couldn't be right, could he? My wolf howled inside of me, wanting me to Shift, wanting to be in control. I took deep breaths and forced her back down.

"I... I'm going to throw up," I gagged, fighting to keep the bile down.

Seth whipped his head around to look at me. Whatever he saw, he didn't like as he hissed, "Fuck!" and swerved the car over to the side. He grabbed the keys, jumped out, opened my door, and pulled me out by my hair, dumping me on the ground. I threw up, barely missing his boots, and sending him scurrying back a few paces.

"Fuck!" he repeated.

I had to get away from Seth. I had to get back to my Pack and see if Ryan, Sofia, and Jase were okay. I had to stop whoever was planning to take out my brother. My wolf squirmed, and I felt her pushing against my skin. No! I'd be too vulnerable Shifting now. As soon as Seth saw it, he'd stun me again. I had to stay human, at least for now.

"You done?" Seth growled at me, his disgust obvious.

I wiped my mouth and nodded, waiting on all fours until Seth came closer. The tips of his black motorbike boots came into view, and as soon as they did, I drove up, smashing my fists, still bound together, into his face. He reared back, and I followed, kicking him in the gut. Seth doubled over, and I sent my knee into his face, feeling the satisfying crunch of bone under my kneecap. He hit the ground, clutching his nose and writhing in pain.

With shaking hands, I patted my pockets, but my phone was gone. I sprinted to the car, quickly searching it. My phone wasn't here, but Seth's was. I punched in his code, but it didn't work.

Shit! He must have changed it.

I eyed Seth, still on the ground. "What's the new code?"

"You're not very good at this, Mai," Seth said, slowly getting to his feet, his hand clutching his bloody nose. I charged him. He sidestepped at the last second, grabbing my arm and flipping me onto the ground.

I looked up at him standing over me as he said, "I'm going to enjoy showing you how it's done. Then I'm going to enjoy teaching you your place, Mai."

Seth was bigger and stronger than me. In a fight, with Isaac's training, my odds of winning against Seth were maybe forty-sixty. But I'd been stun-gunned, given sleeping pills, and my hands were still tied together with rope. There was no time to try to get the ropes off me. I looked at Seth and saw the determination in his eyes. Out of choices, I launched myself at him, kicking and hitting.

Seth blocked my punches and slammed his fist into my solar plexus. I stumbled back, gasping for air, but he gave me no time to rest. He kicked my knee, and I yelled in pain as it collapsed, and I stumbled to the ground. Seth didn't stop there. Pain jolted in my ribs and made me gasp for air as starbursts of agony blossomed behind my eyelids every time Seth struck.

"You gotta learn, Mai," he said, panting heavily as he stood and stalked back to the car.

I lay on the ground, trying to take shallow breaths—anything deeper sent spikes of agony into my chest. Seth fumbled around in the car, then came back toward me, holding something that glinted black and metal. Not again.

I tried to push myself up, but my left arm collapsed under me, and my face smacked into the ground. I felt Seth's boot kick me in the shoulder so that I rolled over onto my back. I watched, helpless, as Seth brought the barrel of his stun gun toward my chest until it touched against my skin, and with blood dripping down his face, he smiled. A bolt of electricity jolted through every inch of my body like white-hot lightning. The world dimmed around me as pain overwhelmed all my senses; then, I felt nothing at all.

When I came to this time, everything hurt. I managed to turn my head slowly. It was dark, with just a sliver of light peeking through from an opening in the wall. The floor was concrete and cold. The air smelled musty. A basement, perhaps? There were no other sounds or smells that gave any clues as to my whereabouts. I was alone. I had no help and knew none would be coming. Wherever I was, I was going to have to get myself out of here.

With slow movements, I brought my hands to my face, wincing as I touched the bruises and cuts that littered my skin. My left eye was swollen, and I couldn't see properly out of it. Blood was caked on my shirt and pants, and I could feel the stickiness of it on my skin. At least a couple of my ribs were broken, and it hurt to breathe. Taking small, shallow breaths, I felt inside for my bond to Ryan. Nothing. My heart squeezed tightly, and it felt like a bowling ball had landed in my stomach. No. It didn't mean anything. The bond was new. I don't know why I thought I'd be able to feel him. I just wanted to feel his comforting presence. To know that he was okay, but I had to get myself back to my Pack to do that.

My wolf pushed against my skin, urging me to let her out. She was right. I should Shift; it would heal a lot of my injuries, and I would rather face Seth again in my wolf form. I felt too vulnerable as a human right now. But I knew I stood a better chance of finding a way out if I stayed in human form. I reluctantly shook my head at my wolf.

Not yet.

I don't know how long it took, but I finally managed to sit myself up. The room spun in a dizzying whirlwind. My mind felt foggy, my right knee wasn't working correctly, and my vision swam. I closed my eyes and tried to take a deep breath, but it sent sharp, shooting pains along my ribs.

Fuck!

I sat there, my body shaking with pain and exertion. My wolf was howling inside of me, furious that I was still in human form. She wanted out; she wanted to hunt and hurt Seth, to take revenge for what he had done to us, for taking us away from our mate.

I made my way to my feet, swaying as pain shot through my knee. It took my weight though. The room shifted and swam again, and I almost fell back down. I gritted my teeth and held myself steady. I wouldn't give up. Not now. I took a few faltering steps forward, my hand outstretched to feel my way around.

The room was small, with no windows and only a single door that was solid and heavy-looking. There was no furniture or furnishing, just six concrete posts that held up the house above us. Nothing that I could make a weapon from. I stumbled, and I let out a cry of pain as my injured knee hit the ground. Tears pricked at the corners of my eyes, and I hung my head.

I couldn't give up, not now, not ever. I struggled to my feet again, holding onto the wall for support. I needed to find a way out, and fast. I couldn't afford to stay here any longer.

I reached the door and pressed my ear to it, listening for any sounds outside. It was silent, except for the sound of my own rapid breathing. I tried the handle. Locked. Of course, it was locked. Why wouldn't it be locked? I didn't have any tools or anything to pick the lock with, and even if I did, my hands were still bound together. I was trapped. That was when I heard movement outside. My heart pounding, I leaned against the door. I could hear footsteps coming closer. Panic squeezed at my chest, but I pushed it down. I had to be ready for whatever was on the other side of that door.

CHAPTER FORTY-THREE

RYAN

The engine's rhythmic beat synced with the frantic pulse throbbing in my veins. My wolf was going crazy. To think that someone could have taken Mai from us... It drove him to the brink of madness. I could feel his emotions coursing through my veins, intertwined with mine. Rage surged, and the urge to shift was strong, so strong that the hair on my arms began to stand up as I fought the compulsion.

It felt like a wild beast inside me clawing to escape, ready to blow the city apart in search of Mai. Every muscle in my body was primed for action, and I could feel its power surging through me, yelling at me for release.

My wolf was capable of so much destruction that if I let him take over completely, our mission would be doomed before it even started.

Soon, I promised him. *It will be your turn soon.*

A glance at the dashboard confirmed what I already knew—I was pushing two hundred. Still, not fast enough. I had to get back to the Three Rivers Pack, had to find Mai. My foot bore down harder on the gas pedal, nudging the speedometer needle a notch higher.

My phone jittered on the seat next to me, Mason's name flashing across the screen. I grabbed it, keeping my gaze locked on the road ahead.

"Talk to me, Mason."

Mason's voice crackled through the speaker, strained with tension. "We're at Reynold's. Her scent ends here, but Seth's scent is everywhere. He had to have known exactly where Mai would be."

"Why was she even there? I told her to stay at the house."

"They hadn't heard from you or Jem. They were worried. Wanted to help."

"Fuck!"

"I can tell you this, bro," Mason cut in, "Seth was confident. He didn't bother to cover his tracks."

I was going to kill that motherfucker.

"What about Sofia, Jase, and Wally? They were supposed to be with Mai."

"They're all pretty banged up."

A curse slipped past my lips.

"Where are they now?" I asked, a spike of fear for Mai's friends slicing through the icy rage building within me.

"Thomas has them," Mason reassured me. "They're hurt, but they'll live."

Before I could respond, a beep indicated another incoming call. "Hold on," I said as I switched the line.

"We're five minutes behind you," Jem announced, his voice laden with an urgency that matched my own. "We've got Shya."

"I don't need looking after!" a voice in the background shouted.

"News from the Pack isn't good, Ryan," Jem continued.

The knot in my stomach grew tighter.

"Brock has taken advantage of us being out of the territory. He and his supporters are moving against us. I've managed to get in touch with some of our enforcers. They're under attack, and I can't get hold of Hayley," Jem said. I could hear the worry in his voice.

A growl ripped from my throat, the fury within me rising with each piece of bad news. Brock, Seth... they were all going to pay.

"Tell Mason and Sam to meet me at the northern gate," Jem said suddenly, an unmistakable command in his voice. "I need them. Your only job right now is to find Mai and bring her back safely."

"The trail ends at Reynold's," I told him. "Seth must've taken her in his own car. She could be anywhere by now."

There was a beat of silence on the other end of the line. "Find her, Ryan," Jem said, the line going dead immediately after.

I stared at the phone for a moment before tossing it onto the passenger seat. Swallowing hard, I tried to reach out through the bond I shared with Mai. A weak pulse told me that she was still alive, but nothing else. No tug of a direction, no access to her feelings.

Damn it. If only Mai had embraced our bond, I could have felt more.

I turned the car around and pointed it at Cocrane. It was the most likely place that Seth had taken her. I would tear apart every Pack, every town, every street if that's what it took to find her. Mai was mine, and I was going to bring her back.

Chapter Forty-Four

MAI

S eth stood in the doorway, between me and freedom. His hand drifted to the stun gun at his side. I braced myself for him to lunge at me, but instead, he just smiled.

"I'm glad you're awake. I was worried there for a while," Seth said softly as he stepped into the room.

My breathing came in shallow pants as Seth's footsteps came closer; my eyes darted around for a way out, even though I knew there wasn't one. I hated being this scared.

"Don't worry, I'm not going to use this on you again. Not unless you make me," Seth said, stepping closer. "I'm sorry for earlier, but you forced my hand. All I've ever wanted is for us to get along. You know that, right?"

This was how he'd behaved in the past. We'd argue, he'd go somewhere to cool off, then come back all gentle and apologetic while explaining how it was my fault and I needed to be more careful. But he'd broken my arm, then turned up at Three Rivers, stun-gunned me, and beat the shit out of Wally. This wasn't something he could just turn on the charm with, and I'd take him back. He had to know that, right? He couldn't be that stupid.

I kept my face emotionless and didn't reply.

His eyes narrowed at my lack of response. "You pushed me, Mai. You ran away. You never gave me the chance to explain or to say sorry. I know things got out of hand, and I need to make that right. But you didn't need to run. And to the fucking Three Rivers, of all places."

I took a small step to the right, eyeing the open doorway. Could I reach it and get it locked before Seth was on me?

"I did some research on you, you know. I should have done it at the start, but I liked the mystery of Mai. Now I know all about your brother and that dickhead who rejected you. Why did you go to them, Mai? After all they've done to you?"

"They're my Pack, Seth. My family. It's where I feel safe," I whispered, edging closer to the door. I wasn't just saying that, either. The Three Rivers was where I belonged. It was just my shitty luck that I finally worked that out in a basement with my scummy ex-boyfriend.

"Bullshit." Seth's face twisted in anger. "You're not thinking straight. It's your Pack bonds. It draws you back there, clouds your mind. But we'll take care of that."

"It's not the Pack bonds, Seth." I kept my voice gentle, hoping to get through to him. "It's us. We were never right for each other."

He shook his head. "You'll see the truth as soon as we break the bonds."

"Seth, that's not going to happen. I'll never sever my bond with the Three Rivers."

"You don't need to, Mai. I'm going to take care of that for you."

I'd never heard of anyone being able to forcibly sever the bonds of someone else. That was an Alpha's power, and Seth was no Alpha. He had to be just saying that to frighten me.

"Then we can put all of this behind us," he continued. "You and me again, Mai. It was good, wasn't it? Between us. We can have that again."

I stared at him, wondering what I ever saw in him.

"I get you're angry with me. But you'll see, Mai. It'll all be good again, I promise. Come on," he gestured to the open door, "I'll take you to get cleaned up."

I weighed up my options. Refuse and stay in the dark, cold basement, or play along and get as much information as I could about where I was and how to get the fuck away from Seth.

I shuffled forward, half expecting an attack, but as I got nearer, he just rested his hand on my lower back. The heat from his touch seeped through my shirt, and my stomach turned upside down. I pushed down the bile rising in the back of my throat and arched forward, not wanting any contact between us as I climbed up the stairs and arrived in a kitchen. It was an old set-up. The countertops were a dark brown, the cabinets a shade lighter, and the floor was gray and black tile. A small table, big enough for four people if they squeezed together, sat in the middle of the room. A cream-colored fridge stood alone near the back wall.

Where the hell were we? I didn't recognize this at all.

A window with a large wooden frame that was peeling white paint was open to let in the air. I caught the scent of rain and dirt, maple, green ash, and pine trees through the window, but the house itself smelled of Seth and Isaac. I'd always liked Isaac, had enjoyed our training sessions when he'd push me hard and then grin manically when I took him down. He'd always been the voice of reason when

Seth's temper flared. Why was he here? I didn't think he would go along with Seth hitting me or kidnapping me.

Seth steered me toward the hall and then stopped in front of the bathroom. He gave a small smile before stepping aside and ushering me inside. The room was small and coldly sterile, the chillingly bright overhead light reflecting off the white tiles. A mirror hung above a simple porcelain sink, and an enclosed shower stood in the corner. No windows.

Seth had laid out fresh towels and even placed some travel-sized toiletries on the shelf above the sink.

"Get cleaned up." Seth leaned forward and untied the rope still binding my hands. I watched the rope fall to the ground and fought the urge to claw his fucking eyes out. I needed to be smart about this. Seth would be expecting an attempt to escape.

I could feel Seth studying me, waiting to see what I would do.

After a moment, he said, "I'll make us some food." Then he turned and shut the door.

I hesitated before locking it. The door wouldn't keep a werewolf out, but by locking it, at least I'd get a warning.

My eyes darted around the room, scanning for anything I could use as a weapon. The pickings were slim—the room was practically bare except for the essentials.

I ran the hot water in the sink and cleaned my face and arms. I felt too vulnerable to take a shower with Seth just outside. Instead, I cleaned up the best I could while keeping an ear out for any sounds of Seth returning.

I dried my face on a scratchy blue towel that Seth had left out, then stared at my reflection. It wasn't pretty. My left eye was swollen, my lip was cut, and I had a hell of a bruise on my cheekbone.

"You can do this. You'll survive. You'll escape. You'll get back to them," I murmured to myself, trying to see past the fear and uncertainty mirrored in my eyes.

My fingers dug into the towel as tears formed in my eyes. Nope, I wouldn't cry. Not here. Not like this. I lowered my head, unable to look at myself anymore, and focused on the towel. Could I wet it, twist it tightly, and use it against Seth? Until I knew where Isaac was and if he was here to help me or Seth, I couldn't take the chance.

Drawing in a deep breath, I schooled my face into a calm, compliant expression and opened the bathroom door. Seth was there, leaning against the opposite wall. I walked past him, my head held high and my posture suggesting a false sense of calmness.

"You look better," Seth said, his eyes glinting with satisfaction.

Uh-huh. I gritted my teeth and kept walking.

"You'll feel better, too, after you've eaten."

I limped with my injured knee back to the kitchen, where the aroma of chicken and rice wafted toward me. My wolf growled in response, reminding me that I hadn't eaten in hours. I kept my distance from Seth as he dished out two plates of food, then placed them on the table. I picked up my plate and moved to the seat furthest away from him.

We ate in silence. I didn't know what his plan was. How long did he think he could keep me here? Did he seriously think he could break my bond with the Three Rivers? The breaking of a bond was irreversible. I would do everything possible to stop him from severing it.

There were so many questions I wanted to ask, but I didn't know what might set him off. I needed to heal and get fighting fit if I had any chance of getting out of here. I couldn't afford to get another beating, not until I knew I had a chance of winning.

As I scraped the last of the rice off my plate, Seth glanced at his watch and then up at me.

"Time for bed, Mai. I'll show you to your room."

He stood up and gestured for me to follow him. I left my plate on the counter and trailed behind him.

He led me back to the corridor and up some stairs. A dark, patterned, threadbare carpet covered the steps, making me think that this was the house of someone elderly. I remembered my grandparents' house before they died; it had carpet on the stairs to help their grip when they went up and down them.

"Where are we, Seth?"

He glanced back at me over his shoulder. "An old hunting lodge. It used to belong to Isaacs's uncle. It's not exactly a penthouse, but it'll do for now."

I searched my memory, trying to remember Isaac ever talking about his uncle. Was he in the Cocrane Pack? If so, we were probably on Pack lands. That was good. If I could escape, I could probably find my way to the town and find help from there. I couldn't recall Isaac ever mentioning an uncle. Hell, this lodge could be in Alaska.

At the top of the stairs, Seth turned right, down a narrow corridor, and stopped in front of a thick wooden door. He opened it, revealing a small but airy bedroom. A double bed sat in the center of the room, covered in clean, white sheets. A window, barred from the outside, overlooked the forest. The room stank of Seth, and I knew he'd been sleeping here.

I whirled around. "I'm not staying in the same bedroom as you!"

Seth grabbed my arm, and I flinched. I hated myself for it. Hated the fear that scurried through my veins every time he came close.

"It's here or the basement floor."

I stared at him for a moment, then put some steel into my voice as I said, "The floor was comfy. I'd like to go back there."

The scent of his anger spiked in the air, and I braced for the hit I was sure was coming. Instead, his face went blank before he said, "As you want, Mai." Then he turned and dragged me back to the basement.

CHAPTER FORTY-FIVE

MAI

T he bitter chill of the basement seeped into my bones. The hard concrete bit into my skin, completely indifferent to my discomfort. My whole body ached from Seth's assault, and I had the headache to end all headaches.

Was Ryan okay? Was Jem? Were they searching for me? What about Sofia and Jase? Had Seth killed them before he'd snatched me? Grief flooded my senses. Goddess, I'd been so stupid. So stupid to leave my Pack four years ago, to keep running, to get involved with Seth, and to stay for as long as I did.

Stupid for not realizing Brock was plotting something. Stupid for letting my guard down. I could feel the tears streaming down my face and tried desperately not to sob. I let it all wash over me and sank into my despair. I don't know how long I lay there for before I fell asleep, but exhaustion and the call of the sweet release of sleep finally got to me.

I opened my eyes to find myself in Ryan's arms. He felt so real, his scent overwhelming, his strong arms enclosing me, and I knew, I knew I was safe.

"Shhh," he whispered, stroking my hair.

It was a dream, but I didn't care. I didn't want to wake up. I wanted to stay here forever.

"It's all going to be okay," he promised.

I nodded, agreeing with him. It would be okay, just as long as I didn't ever wake up.

The feel of his body against mine sent need ripping through me as I yearned for him. He bent down until our lips were a whisper apart, and I basked in the warmth radiating from his body. His fingers teased the buttons on my shirt apart. As soon as he touched my skin, that was it. All I could think of was him, his body, the need for his hard cock to be moving inside of me. I ripped at his clothes just as he tore mine from my body. We both paused, me in awe of his beautiful cock, his hard muscles, and strong thighs. Then he rolled on top of me and slid inside. It was so sudden and so delicious that I gasped in shock as waves of pleasure shot through me. His eyes bore into mine, seeing me, the whole of me, right into the depths of my soul.

"Goddess, Mai, you're so beautiful," he murmured, his voice husky.

I writhed under him, needing more. More contact, more friction. He responded immediately, moving against me, pulling out until just the tip of him rested inside, then bucking his hips, pushing deep inside of me.

"Yes," I purred, urging him on.

I wrapped my legs around his waist, tipping my hips and giving him deeper access. He didn't hesitate. Drawing out and thrusting back in, coaxing my pleasure higher and higher.

"You're going to come for me," he whispered, clutching my head between his hands, never once breaking his gaze on me.

"Yes," I agreed, unable to say more than one word at a time. I was having trouble thinking, all thoughts having fled in the face of the unrelenting feeling of him filling me up, touching parts of my inside that had never been touched before.

"Yes," I repeated, and his shit-eating grin covered his face. He was so fucking pleased with himself. I didn't care, just trailed my nails down his back and across his bottom. I squeezed his cheeks, urging him on.

Then it hit me: powerful spasms racked my entire body, sending wave after wave of orgasmic joy coursing through me. Ryan came a moment later, spilling himself inside of me, and the feel of it pumping into me sent another orgasm flooding through me. It felt so right, a moment so perfect that I never wanted it to end.

Suddenly, Ryan froze. He looked at me, panic etched across his face. "I'll find you." His voice was full of urgency and need.

My eyes snapped open at the sound of hushed murmurs drifting down from the top of the stairs, pulling me away from sleep.

No!

I shut my eyes again, willing myself to go back there. To be back, safe in Ryan's arms. The voices got louder, and I stifled a sob. I had to get up. I had to do everything I could to get back to the real Ryan. I strained to listen; the low rumble of Seth's voice unmistakable. There was another voice, one I couldn't immediately recognize. They were talking, their conversation just a touch too quiet for me to grasp the words. Was it Isaac? And if it was him, what did that mean for me?

I rolled to my feet. Sleep could wait. My injuries could wait. My priority was to survive, to escape and find my Pack.

CHAPTER FORTY-SIX

RYAN

Cocrane was a town with modern architecture, high-rises, and a complex network of asphalted streets. The heart of the city pulsed with life, resonating with the murmurs of traffic and sounds of a busy and thriving town. The smell of food wafted from a string of restaurants, blending with the slightly tangy odor of city air.

On the outskirts of this urban milieu stood a stark aberration—the Alpha's house. Unlike the steel and glass structures dominating the cityscape, the house was more like a fort, nestled amid a lush expanse of woods. Its towering stone walls gave off an ancient aura, a throwback to times when power was displayed through fortifications and territorial markers. They were making a statement—to other Packs? Or to the humans here?

I steered my truck into the driveway. Two guards stood at the entrance, a solid steel door with no obvious handle on this side. I stepped out of my car and stopped when I was two feet from them. Their gaze on me was unflinching.

"I need to see the Alpha."

One guard, the older one of the two with a closely shaven face and calculating eyes, stepped away and spoke into his radio. After a moment, a muffled reply came. The guard turned to face me and nodded as the door swung open. I strode past them into a wide reception area decorated with fresh flowers and a six-meter fish tank. The tank was empty, but I caught a whiff of fish and coral coming from it. A woman with white hair pulled back into a bun and a gray business suit was waiting for me.

"Your name?" she asked.

"Ryan Shaw, Beta of the Three Rivers Pack. I'm here to see the Alphas about Seth Morin. He's kidnapped my mate, Mai Parker."

The woman jerked her head, shock crossing her features before she schooled her face.

"Wait here, please," she ordered, then turned and walked quickly to an inner door, her heels tap-tapping loudly.

I clenched my fists, urging myself and my wolf to remain calm. My best bet was to get the Alphas on my side.

A moment later, the woman returned.

"Follow me."

I trailed behind her through the inner doorway, down a hallway, and into a conference room. A thick carpet muffled my footsteps as I stepped inside, its deep red hue complemented by gold trim throughout the room. Gleaming mahogany furniture formed a semi-circle at one end, while onyx chairs lined the other side. At the head of the table sat a female werewolf. She was tall, with sculpted features, emerald eyes that stared coldly at me, and tresses of deep black hair that fell down past her shoulders. Next to her had to be Ajak. Steel-gray hair was combed back from his high forehead. He had a wide nose, prominent cheekbones, and a small scar under his left eye.

Whereas the woman's power felt cold and contained, Ajak's presence filled the room. He was an imposing figure, and I suspected he used that to impose his will on others. To his left sat an older werewolf. Strong, powerfully built, with a hard face that suggested he would not suffer any excuses, his resemblance to the photos of Seth that Derek had sent me was undeniable.

"Ryan Shaw," the woman at the head of the table said, her silky voice filling the room. "I'm Kara and this is Ajak." She indicated the werewolf sat next to her. "We are the Alphas of the Cocrane Pack. This is Korrin, Seth's father."

I nodded to them all.

"My mate, Mai Parker," I began, cutting straight to the chase, "was assaulted by Seth a week ago. She fled home to the Three Rivers Pack. She and I sealed our mate bond. Yesterday, Seth attacked three of my Pack and kidnapped her."

Heavy silence filled the room. Kara, Ajak, and Korrin were too experienced to show whether my news shocked them.

"You have proof of this?" Korrin's voice was hard.

"Why don't you help me find Mai, and you can ask her yourself?"

Korrin waved his hand. "So, you have nothing. Your word against my son's. We don't know you. Go back home, Ryan Shaw, and mourn the loss of the female you rejected."

I didn't show my fury, but Korrin must have sensed it.

"Yes, we've done our homework on you and your Three Rivers. You should go home before you don't have a home to go to anymore."

"I'm not leaving without Mai. You're right. I might not have a home anymore. I have nothing to lose. I'll go through your entire Pack until I find her. In fact, tell me to go home one more time. I've got a lot of anger to work off."

Korrin slammed his hand onto the table in front of him. I tensed, ready for him to come at me, but Kara shook her head.

"Seth has been troubled for a while now," Kara's voice was measured and calm, "and we do not condone his violence toward Mai. She is a valued member of this Pack—"

"Was," I interrupted. "She is a member of the Three Rivers Pack and my mate."

"Lies. She's been with my son for months."

"Her scent is all over me. I know you can smell it."

I felt Ajak studying me and shifted slightly to face him.

"What do you want from us?" Ajak finally asked.

"I want your help," I replied. "I need to know where Seth is."

Korrin scoffed, "Even if I knew this information, I would not help you kill my son."

Ajak held up a hand, silencing Korrin. "We do not know Seth's whereabouts—he left Pack lands a week ago, and we have no knowledge of where he might be heading," Ajak said firmly and evenly. "I'm sorry we could not be of more help." His tone made it clear he was dismissing me.

My wolf growled. Something told us that Ajak spoke the truth.

Fuck. They didn't know any more than I did.

I stared at them, storing their faces and scents in my brain. If anything happened to Mai, I was coming back here and would exact my revenge. Then I turned and walked out.

A hushed whisper reached my ears as I left the house, a soft, tentative voice calling my name. "Mr. Shaw?"

I turned to see a young girl, barely fourteen, with curly red hair tied back in a messy ponytail and a smidgen of freckles across her pale face. Her wide eyes flitted nervously around, as if she was worried someone would see us together.

"Can I speak with you? Kara said it was okay." Her voice was barely above a murmur.

"Of course," I said, softening my tone. "What's your name?"

"I'm Anna," she said, drawing in a deep breath. "Isaac is my brother."

Isaac. I searched through my memory of the file Derek had sent me when we'd first learned Seth was the one who had beaten up Mai.

"Isaac is Seth's friend?" I asked.

"He's Seth's best friend." She glanced around again, tucking a stray strand of hair behind her ear. "They've always been inseparable. If Seth is involved in something... Isaac would be right there with him."

"Anna," I leaned in closer, "do you know where they might be?"

She hesitated for a moment, looking torn. Finally, she nodded, a determined glint in her eye.

"We have an old hunting lodge. It used to be my uncle's. It's deep in the forest, west of the Pack lands. If they're hiding... that's probably where Isaac would go."

A surge of hope ignited within me. It was a lead, as slim as it may be, but it was better than nothing.

She handed me a note with a handwritten address on it.

"Thank you, Anna," I said, my voice sincere. "This could be really helpful."

She gave a small nod, biting her lower lip. "I just... I just want Isaac to be safe. And... Mai. She was nice to me. She doesn't deserve... whatever Seth is doing."

"Thank you, Anna," I said again. "I'm going to do everything in my power to bring Mai back."

She gave me a small, uncertain smile, then turned and disappeared into the shadows. So, Kara wanted me to know where Isaac and Seth might be, and she didn't want to tell me in front of Ajak and Korrin. Was it a trap? It didn't matter. I'd go through every last one of them if it was.

Chapter Forty-Seven

MAI

The door banged open, and a person I didn't recognize strode through it. I thought it was a man because of his size, but I couldn't be sure as he had a dark hood pulled over his face. He smelled of herbs, old paper, and something spicy that made me want to sneeze.

Friend or foe?

Seth appeared in the doorway behind the man. He seemed relaxed, glancing from the man to me and then back again.

Foe, then.

I darted to the left as the man paced toward me. He started chanting in a foreign language, then threw something that looked like old leaves that had been chopped into tiny pieces into the air.

What the hell?

I sneezed, and then everything went black.

My wrists were bound tightly to one of the support posts by coarse ropes that dug into my skin. Blood trickled down my arms, leaving a trail of pain. My feet were bare, and my ankles were tied, too, the cord biting into my flesh. Every movement felt like needles stabbing me.

I figured I'd been out about half an hour. When I'd come to, the hooded man had disappeared, and I'd been tied to the support post. Since then, I'd been trying to work my way loose, but these ropes were tied tight. Seth had been busy, too. He'd taken a piece of chalk from his pocket and drawn a circle around me, then another around himself. He connected the two circles with a bridge-like line. My breathing became shallow and erratic as I watched him, unable to tear my eyes away.

"Whatever this is, you don't have to do it, Seth."

Seth kept working, making little lines spiral out from the bigger of the two circles. "You know, I thought it was me. That I wasn't good enough. That was why you never gave yourself fully to me, to us. That this relationship was another thing in my life that I couldn't get right. But it's not me, Mai. It never was. It's your bond to the Three Rivers," he spat the words of my Pack. "It tied you in knots, so you couldn't be you. Not really. With it gone, you'll be able to take the Cocrane bond. It's pure, Mai. Not corrupted. Not twisted. Everything will become clear once it's gone, I promise. Then we can go back to how we used to be."

He was delusional. That had to be it.

"The bond isn't the issue, Seth," I said, trying to stay patient.

"Ah, but we won't know for sure until it is broken, will we?"

I watched him add more lines to the chalk circles and tried to make sense of them. "How long have you been working with the witches?"

Seth's hand hesitated. Werewolves were not supposed to work with the witches. Not since Simon Webster had tried to create the spell to put all werewolves under his control.

"Long enough to see the truth about our bonds. There are only some left that are pure. We have to destroy the others."

I blinked. Where was this coming from? He'd been keen for me to sever the bond to the Three Rivers when we were together, but he'd never said anything about bonds being impure.

"It's time, Mai. Are you ready?"

"Seth, this isn't going to work." I pulled against the rope.

"I have to try. I have to save us. I have to prove it's not me."

Seth began to chant, the sound echoing in the room. The air around us seemed to hum with energy, the hairs on my arms standing on end. An odd tingling sensation started in my chest and spread out through my body. The tingling ramped up until it was like thousands of tiny needles pricking at my skin, making me want to scream and claw at my own flesh. My wolf started howling; she didn't like what Seth was doing or how it was making her feel.

The chanting got louder, and the shadows seemed to dance along the walls, twisting and contorting into grotesque shapes. My stomach churned, bile rising in my throat as the thought that Seth might actually be able to snap my bonds hit me full force.

"Stop!" I yelled. "Seth, don't do this!"

He ignored me, chanting faster now. My vision blurred, the world around me shifting and swaying as if I were caught in the eye of a storm. The pain in my body was everywhere, from the tips of my fingers to the soles of my feet. It felt like I was being torn apart from the inside out, and I couldn't help but let out a raw, guttural scream.

It didn't matter that I'd spent so much time away from the Three Rivers Pack or that I'd once wanted nothing to do with them. All I

285

knew was that I loved them—Ryan, my Pack, the land I'd grown up on, everything. And I couldn't bear the thought of losing any of it.

The air crackled with energy as the bond between me and the Three Rivers Pack began to manifest before my eyes. It was a web of shimmering silver threads, each one connecting me to the land I'd grown up on and the wolves I'd known all my life. I focused on it, on the little details—on the light seeming to come from inside each individual thread, on the patterns that each thread made, almost tribal in detail, and on the perfect way they weaved amongst each other to make up my bond—and as soon as I did, a feeling of warmth and security washed over me. It was there, not broken, not severed.

Then I watched, horrified, as a single thread frayed and began to unravel, slowly and deliberately, as if they were being pulled apart by an unseen force.

No! This could not be happening.

Another thread unraveled. Then another. Panic surged through me, and I cried out, desperate to stop Seth's ritual from destroying everything. I couldn't let this happen.

"Seth, stop!" I begged, my voice barely audible above the sound of Seth's chanting.

More threads frayed and came loose. Seth was going to do this. He was really going to break my bond with the Three Rivers.

I looked away. I couldn't watch. But then my eye caught on another bond—the mate bond between Ryan and me. It was a vibrant, pulsating golden strand, full of love and promise. Could Seth see it, too? He was concentrating on my Pack bonds, intent on his task. I mentally willed it to hide, curling it into a small ball deep within my psyche. Safe, for now.

"Damn it, Seth!" I yelled.

There had to be something I could do. A loose thread fluttered on the air currents, spiraling in front of me. It was mine. It was part of me. I reached out with my mind and gathered it to me. I had to keep it safe. Maybe if I collected all the threads, I could rebuild the bond. I moved the thread back to the bond, trying to weave it back into the main current. A tiny spark of light flashed at the spot where the thread was absorbed. This wasn't supposed to be how bonds were formed, but it was working.

The threads started to weave themselves back together, faster than before, as if they were responding to my determination.

"Is this really what you want, Mai?" Seth said through gritted teeth. Sweat was trickling down his face. "To cling to your old life? To remain shackled to a Pack that will never truly accept you? They rejected you, for fuck's sake!"

"Fuck you, Seth," I spat, channeling all my anger and fear into repairing the damaged bond. "You'll never break it."

The front door above us creaked open, and both Seth and I froze. Footsteps echoed through the house above us. My gaze went to the ceiling as if I could see through the boards to whoever was up there. Was the witch back to help Seth finish the job?

"Seth?" a voice called. "You here?"

Not the witch. Isaac. Was he here to help me or Seth?

"Damn it," Seth muttered, his eyes narrowed as he glanced toward the ceiling. Then he stood up, and the pressure on my bond collapsed. "Don't think this is over, Mai. I'll be back to finish what I started."

CHAPTER FORTY-EIGHT

MAI

S eth was gone a long time. Enough that I dozed off. After Seth went upstairs, I heard him and Isaac walk outside. I'm guessing it was so I wouldn't be able to overhear their conversation. Someone had come back about ten minutes ago. I could hear their footsteps moving around upstairs. The footsteps drew nearer to the basement door. I swallowed down my panic. I had no idea how I was going to stop Seth from breaking my bond. If he tried again, it would be a contest of stamina. Who tired first, Seth pulling them apart or me mending them. I was sure I could keep at it for a few hours, but after that, it was only a matter of time.

The door opened, letting a yellow glow in from the stairway. I squinted, adjusting to the sudden influx of light, as a figure began to descend. Isaac. A knot formed in my stomach, anger rising in me at the sight of him. I thought we were friends.

He wore his usual fitted black crew-neck T-shirt that clung to his torso just enough to hint at the strength beneath. A pair of rugged, dark jeans hung low on his hips, broken in from years of use. Around his wrists, he had on a couple of brown leather bands, worn and weathered. They were important to him, and he never took them off. His boots were military-grade, scuffed at the toes. His hair was cropped short, a no-nonsense cut that required minimal upkeep. But what always stood out and made the girls take a second glance at him was the dark stubble framing his jaw.

Isaac's face was weary, his movements were hesitant, and his gaze avoided mine as he walked down the steps.

He carried a tray with a sandwich, a water bottle, and a first-aid kit. Placing it on the floor, he straightened up, his gaze still not meeting mine.

"Thought you might be hungry," he mumbled.

My stomach churned with hunger at the sight of food. I pulled my hands against the rope and glared at him.

"Oh, right. Here let me." Isaac pulled a Swiss army knife from his back pocket and set about slicing through the rope.

The ropes snapped apart, and the rush of blood into my hands hurt like fuck.

"Ow!"

I rubbed my hands against my thighs, trying to get the circulation going.

"Sorry," Isaac said, and he set to work on my feet. "Seth should have released you earlier."

I glared up at him. "Seth should never have tied me up in the first place."

Isaac held my gaze for a moment, then nodded. The ropes came apart in his hands, and he gestured to the tray of food.

I crawled over to it; the feeling in my legs hadn't returned yet, and I didn't trust them to support me if I stood up. Falling on my ass like a newborn fawn was not a good look. Picking up the water bottle first, I unscrewed the cap and took a tentative sniff.

"It's clean."

"Like I can trust anything right now," I replied, then took a sip, my eyes never leaving Isaac.

"The food, it's ham and tomato. I remember you liked eating that after our sessions."

I would be so hungry after I trained with Isaac. He pushed me hard, and afterward, I could never make it all the way home before my stomach started growling at me. So I got into the habit of making a sandwich at home, taking it with me, and eating it on the bench outside the club while Isaac, my ride home, was writing out my training program for our next session. He liked to keep everything written down to see how much and how fast I was progressing.

"Why are you here, Isaac?" I asked as I took a big bite. The food tasted dry in my mouth, but I knew I had to eat. Had to build my strength up.

"I was looking for Seth. I didn't know, Mai, what he was planning. You gotta believe me. I never would have gone along with this." He waved his arm around the basement.

"Well, now you know."

The implication was clear: now that he knew what fucked up shit Seth was doing, what the hell was he going to do about it?

Isaac rubbed a hand against his shaved head. "It's not that easy."

"Of course it is. This is wrong. You know it, Isaac. Are you really going to let him do this?"

Isaac blinked, considering. "I... I'm sorry, Mai," he said finally and turned to go.

Damn it.

It was now or never. As he moved toward the door, I stumbled forward, launching myself at him from behind. He grunted in surprise as we tumbled to the ground, knocking the tray scattering in one direction, its contents skittering across the floor in another. Adrenaline surged through me, drowning out the pain of my injuries. I grappled with Isaac, a desperate kind of fury fueling my every move. He was caught off guard, flailing beneath me, his breaths ragged with shock.

My hands found their way to his throat, squeezing with as much force as I could muster. He choked, hands clawing at mine, but I held on, my vision blurring with the effort.

"Mai," he gasped, his voice barely a whisper. I could see the surprise in his eyes, the panic. But there was something else, too. Regret? It didn't matter. I tightened my grip, his pulse fluttering beneath my hands. He should have thrown me off by now, but he didn't. Just gripped tightly onto my wrists.

I hated this. Hated choking my friend, but I needed to get free. I slammed my knee into his stomach, aiming for his solar plexus. The air whooshed out of him, and his eyes bulged. I yanked my hands away from his throat and slammed the side of his head against the concrete floor.

Isaac's eyes rolled back, his body going limp underneath me. I slumped next to him. He could have stopped me at any time. We'd practiced this exact situation in training, though it was usually me being choked and throwing Isaac off. He let me choke him. He wanted me to escape.

Damn it. Why didn't he just let me go? Did his loyalty to Seth mean this was the only way he could square it with himself?

I didn't have time to work it out now. I jolted into action, rummaging through his pockets. No keys. No phone. Just a wallet and a few crumpled notes. I grunted in frustration, casting a glance at the open door and the steps leading up to the next floor. My only way out was up there, where Seth was, but it was a chance I had to take.

Muffling my footfalls, I tiptoed up the stairs, each thud echoing the words, "escape, escape, escape." I peered into the hallway, empty for now. The wooden floor felt cold beneath my bare feet as I padded down the corridor, my breaths shallow and quiet. When I reached the main door, I pressed my ear against it. Hearing nothing, I twisted the handle, the cool metal a stark contrast to my sweaty palm.

The door swung open, and, with one last glance at the house, I bolted into the dark night, my only thought to put as much distance between me and Seth as possible.

CHAPTER FORTY-NINE

RYAN

T he lodge was silhouetted against the moonlit backdrop, its old timbers worn and weather-beaten. Two cars were parked to one side, and I wanted to roar my challenge to any who might be inside. I could smell Mai, and it was driving my wolf crazy. No one seemed to be around. The only sounds came from the forest and a lonely ring of a phone from somewhere in the lodge. It stopped mid-ring. Then started again. Someone was keen to get in touch.

I forced myself to move cautiously, even though every muscle in my body was coiled tight. I'd already done a circle of the lodge, making sure there weren't any unpleasant surprises waiting for me. Both the hoods of the cars felt cold, so whoever was in there had been there for a while.

I came at it from the east, sliding along the veranda, and tried a side door. Unlocked. This felt too easy. I stepped inside and followed the persistent ring of the phone. I found it on a kitchen table, Korrin's name flashing on the screen. Ignoring it, I moved deeper into the house. My wolf was still, his rage tightly coiled and primed for what we might find here. The scent of Mai was stronger now. I followed my nose and circled back to the kitchen and an open doorway with steps leading down to the basement.

The soft, regular sound of someone breathing drifted up. I knew it wasn't Mai; my wolf would have told me if it was.

I slipped silently down the narrow staircase, feeling the air change as I descended. It turned colder, and the scent of damp concrete and fresh chalk mingled with the stronger, distinct smell of Mai. It was full of pain and panic. She's been hurt here. My wolf snapped at me.

Soon, I promised him.

A werewolf in human form lay unconscious on the concrete floor. Tall and muscular. Seth? I kicked him over.

Not Seth. Isaac, then.

I slowly spun around, taking in every detail of the room, trying to piece together what had happened here. A tray lay in the corner, food and drink splattered across the room. So, Isaac brought Mai food. They fought. And Mai, my fucking courageous little wolf, won. I looked up the stairs. There was no sign of Mai or Seth up there. The house upstairs was empty. A shiver of anxiety snaked down my spine, and my wolf nudged me on. He'd already put it together. Mai was on the run, and I was wasting precious time.

I sprinted upstairs and out of the lodge. The two cars were still there. My eyes narrowed on the forest. She'd run. And Seth was chasing her.

I ripped off my clothes and let my wolf take over. I felt my bones crack and realign, my senses sharpen to a razor's edge. We raised our nose, and as soon as her scent hit our lungs, the bond flared to life. We could feel her fear, her desperation, coursing through our veins, setting every nerve alight. She was on the run, and the bond was tugging us westward. We didn't hesitate. Our paws hit the damp earth, and we raced off into the darkness.

CHAPTER FIFTY

MAI

The cold night air whipped against my skin as I sprinted into the forest, the rough terrain a blur beneath my feet. My wolf was scratching at my insides, demanding to be let out, to take control. I held her back. Not yet. I had to stay human for a bit longer, had to get more distance between me and the house.

I had made it about a mile when a howl shattered the night. Seth. He knew I was gone. Panic clawed at my insides. I had to Shift. Now. Stripping off my clothes, I let my wolf out. The Shift was quick, my body twisting and reforming in less than a minute. It hurt, fuck did it hurt. But I welcomed the pain, welcomed the adrenaline that surged through me, urging it to make my Shift quicker.

I stood as a wolf and howled my defiance into the wind. Rage filled me, anger at the audacity of Seth to think he could take me.

I mentally slapped my wolf.

Enough. Not now.

Now I had to run. She shook her head, her rage subsiding. As a wolf, the forest became a spectrum of smells and sounds, each one telling a different story. I sensed water ahead and sprinted through the undergrowth, my powerful limbs carrying me with ease. If I followed the water, eventually, I'd come to a settlement.

Another howl pierced the night air. Seth, coming in fast from the east. He was stronger, faster. Even as a human, he could outrun me. As a wolf, I had little chance of beating him. My wolf growled, disagreeing.

I zigzagged through the forest, using the undergrowth and trees to my advantage. If I could lose him or even just slow him down, I might have a chance to reach help.

I could sense Seth behind us, pounding ever closer. I used the fear to spur my legs faster. Branches whipped against my fur, and leaves crumpled underfoot as I ran. I could feel every twig snap beneath my feet, every thorn that grazed me. I changed direction, running to the left before doubling back. As I ran, I brushed against trees and bushes, leaving traces of my scent in the hopes of misleading him. I doubted it would work, but it might slow him down. Then I turned right, toward the water. The river came into view, its dark waters churning and frothing. Dead leaves and twigs swirled around in circles, forming ungainly eddies in the movement.

I didn't hesitate, leaping straight into the freezing current. The cold shocked my system, knocking the air from my lungs. My muscles seized up, and I struggled to keep my head above the surface as the river pulled me along.

I kicked furiously, fighting against the current that wanted to drag me under. My sodden fur weighed me down, but I pushed on, swimming diagonally toward the far bank, each stroke making my limbs grow heavier, the chill of the water sapping my strength. I had to get out of this water.

I saw our chance a moment later. A thick branch on the side, partly fallen into the river. I headed for it and swung a paw over the end. I kicked and heaved, dragged myself along the branch before collapsing on the muddy bank in a heap. My breaths came in ragged gasps, the cold air burning my lungs. I was utterly spent, my chest heaving as I gulped down air. A howl sounded from the other bank, piercing the night air.

Fuck!

Why couldn't he just leave me alone? Scrambling to my feet, I shook the water from my fur and glanced back across the river. My heart froze at the sight. Seth was there in his wolf form. Even from this distance, his silhouette was imposing. His body, wrapped in charcoal-black fur, bristled with raw power and intimidating muscle. His massive paws scratched the ground, the tension rippling through his muscular frame as his eyes narrowed on mine. He'd found me, and I knew I couldn't outrun him. I was exhausted, cold, and wet. I was out of options. If this was my fate, then so be it. I would face Seth head-on and teach him there were consequences to messing with Mai Parker of the Three Rivers Pack.

I snarled, the sound reverberating through the forest. It was a declaration. A challenge. I wouldn't be a victim any longer. Seth's eyes hardened, and his lips curled. With a muscular flex, he leaped into the river, his powerful strokes cutting through the water. I steeled myself, my legs tensing, as I gathered every scrap of strength left within me. As soon as he scrambled up the bank, I lunged, my teeth aiming for his throat. He ducked, spinning around to snap at my exposed flank. I yelped as pain blossomed, but managed to rake my claws across his face.

He charged. I braced myself, digging my claws into the earthy forest floor. He came at me like a living missile, an intimidating mass of fur and fangs. I stood my ground, my focus never leaving him. I dodged at the last moment, his momentum causing him to overshoot and giving me a brief opening. I took my chance, snapping at his exposed side, my teeth finding his flesh. His surprised yelp echoed in the forest and gave me a glimmer of hope. Seth came at me again. My mind became a blur of pain and determination, my body reacting purely on instinct. I could taste his blood in my mouth and knew he was injured. I could feel my strength ebbing, though. The initial adrenaline was wearing off, and the effects of the last few days were making themselves known as my limbs grew slower.

Seth, his fangs exposed in a sneer, seemed to sense my waning strength. In his eyes, I saw only his will to dominate. He crouched, ready to spring, his body tensed, just as a new howl pierced through the air. It was an anguished cry filled with rage and desperation. Its raw power froze both of us in place. It was a voice that was both strange and familiar, one that filled my heart with dread and hope.

Ryan.

I sought out the bond that connected Ryan and me. I howled, calling to him.

It was now a race against time. I saw the moment Seth realized he would soon have two werewolves to fight against. His eyes focused on me, and he let out a savage growl.

Chapter Fifty-One

Mai

S eth lunged at me with newfound ferocity, his teeth aiming for my throat. I danced away, making him overshoot. He swung around, barreling toward me again. I kept moving, evading, and herding him in the direction Ryan would come from. My legs trembled beneath me.

I realized I'd been here before, Seth attacking me. Me, weak and helpless.

Not this time.

My bond flared to life, and a warm rush of energy flooded me, washing over me like a calming wave. It was the essence of Ryan—his courage, his resolve, his love. The connection pulsed in rhythm with my heart, its strength surprising me. I'd been resisting this bond for so long, afraid of what it might mean, afraid of what I might lose. But now, I realized its true potential. This bond didn't bind me; it empowered me. It wasn't a chain; it was a lifeline.

I felt rather than saw Seth tower above me. Then Ryan, my Ryan, his massive wolf form, larger and more imposing than any of us, barreled into Seth, sending them both snarling and snapping across the forest floor. I yipped in alarm for Ryan, then raced after them. I was no longer just Mai Parker of the Three Rivers Pack; I was a part of something much more significant. I was part of a mated pair, a force to be reckoned with, and Seth had no idea what was coming his way.

We attacked Seth from both sides, our movements perfectly in sync through our bond. Seth fought with a desperate ferocity, but he was tiring. Ryan moved with a lethal grace full of his power and fury. I felt a tug in our bond, a silent signal, and I moved, darting in from one side as Ryan leaped, his body a blur of motion, and in a fraction of a second, he was on Seth.

Ryan's jaws snapped shut on Seth's throat. There was a sickening crunch, followed by a choked-off yelp. I watched as Seth's eyes widened in shock, his body spasming under the force of Ryan's deadly grip. He struggled for a moment, his body writhing in an effort to free himself. Ryan's jaws tightened. Seth's movements slowed, his eyes starting to glaze. His body twitched one last time before finally going still.

CHAPTER FIFTY-TWO

MAI

Before I could go to Ryan, my legs collapsed under me. Each breath was a struggle. I was a mess of cuts and bruises, my pelt matted with dirt and blood.

Immediately, Ryan was there, nuzzling my face. I could feel his relief surge through the bond. He started licking my wounds and whining. He nudged me, urging me to get up, but I just needed a moment to rest.

A twig snapped to our left. My body tensed, my eyes scanning for the source of the noise. Isaac stepped out from the undergrowth.

I saw him take in the scene and the moment when his eyes landed on Seth's body. He took a step toward it, but stopped when Ryan growled a warning.

Isaac backed up, hands raised. "I don't mean you harm. I'm sorry, Mai," Isaac said, his gaze moving from me to Ryan and back again. His voice held a note of regret, of sadness. "Seth loved you. But what he did was wrong. I knew it then, and I know it now. I thought he'd come to his senses. See what he was doing to you and realize his mistakes. But I'm done covering for him. I wish you hadn't killed him," his eyes flicked over my injuries before continuing, "but I understand why."

I got a warning before it happened, a slight pull on our bond, then Ryan Shifted. Bones crunched and realigned, limbs stretched and lengthened. Then he stood as a man, a beautiful, completely naked man.

"You couldn't have had this epiphany when Seth was beating the living shit out of her?" Ryan growled.

Isaac hung his head. "I—"

I whined, telling Ryan to let it go. We had no time for this.

"I'll take care of Seth," Isaac said, his voice barely above a whisper. "You both need to leave. Korrin will want revenge for this."

His words stirred a fresh wave of fear within me. We weren't safe yet. Exhaustion pulled at me, and I knew I wouldn't be able to shift into my human form, not now. My body was at its limit.

Without another word, Ryan walked over and gently picked me up, cradling me in his arms. The last thing I remember was seeing Isaac weeping beside Seth's body. Then I closed my eyes, and everything went black.

My eyelids felt heavy, exhaustion coursing through my veins. Everything was sore, even the soles of my feet. I was back in human form. The familiar scent of Ryan surrounded me, as soothing as a lullaby. My eyes fluttered open. I was in Ryan's car. Leather seats, Ryan's mix of cologne and wolf. I was safe.

"You're awake," Ryan said. It wasn't a question. He glanced my way, his gaze sweeping over me in a quick but thorough examination.

His eyes were tired. I didn't need our bond to tell me he was just as worn out as I was.

"Yeah. How are you doing?" I managed to ask, my voice hoarse. Ryan squeezed my hand lightly.

"I'm alright. We're on our way back to the Pack," he said softly, his voice almost drowned out by the hum of the car.

"Sofia and Jase? Wally?" I asked, suddenly filled with the need to know they were safe, too.

"They're okay. Hurt but okay."

I slumped back against the seat. "Good."

"The news is not all good."

He looked at me, and I got the impression he was giving me a moment to steel myself. I nodded, wanting him to continue.

"You were right. Brock's aiming to take over the Pack. He's launched an attack from within. He was working with Tristan the whole time to destabilize both Packs."

His words felt like a punch to the gut.

"We have to get back there," I said.

Before he could respond, Ryan's phone buzzed from the console. Derek's name flashed on the screen. Ryan put him on speaker.

"Ryan," Derek's voice was strained with grief and anger. Something was seriously wrong. "Do you have her?"

"I do. She's been badly beaten, but she's alive. We're heading back now. What's the situation there?"

"I... I can't, Ryan. It's just so fucking awful."

"Derek, what happened?" Ryan demanded.

"Jem's dead. Hayley killed him. She and Brock, they've taken over the Three Rivers Pack."

Find out if Jem is really dead and what's next for Mai and Ryan in Book 2, The Renegade Mate.

Want to know what happened on Derek and Sofia's hot and dangerous first date? Sign up to my newsletter at www.kiranightingale.com for a *free* prequel novella!

COME JOIN US IN THE SHIFTER REALM!

Kira Nightingale

Mystically Dark, Wildly Romantic...

Sign up to my newsletter and get Fairground Fling, a free prequel short story about Derek and Sofia's first date!

As an author, I write paranormal romance books that are mystically dark and wildly romantic. I send out my newsletter every week, and in it you can get exclusive content and snippets from my current work-in-progress, news about what I'm up to, and sometimes even photos of my clumsy cat, Scout. You can sign up to my newsletter at www.kiranightingale.com

Fairground Fling, Shifters of the Three Rivers 0.5

No way will I let fate decide my destiny, but Derek Shaw is back and proving impossible to resist

Sofia

All I wanted was to run my coffee shop in peace, avoid my fated mate, and forget about our Shifter bond. Is that too much to ask for?

Apparently it is, because Derek Shaw just walked back into my life, all rippling muscles and piercing eyes. The man sets my blood on fire, but there's no way I'm giving in. I've seen what happens when "fated mates" are torn apart, and I won't let that happen to me.

Derek left to join the military, turning his back on our bond. Now he's back in the Three Rivers Pack, determined to win me over. But I've built walls around my heart that even an Alpha wolf can't break through. At least, that's what I keep telling myself...

Derek

I left Three Rivers to serve my country, but I never forgot Sofia. Every day, her fiery hair and captivating scent haunted my thoughts.

Now I'm back, and the pull towards Sofia is stronger than ever. My wolf won't rest until I claim what's mine. But Sofia's determined to keep her distance. That's okay, though. I'm a Shaw, and we never back down from a challenge.

Also by Kira Nightingale

Shifters of the Three Rivers series

The Runaway Mate

The Renegade Mate

The Resolute Mate

The Rescued Mate

The Reluctant Mate(coming 2025)

The Relentless Mate (coming 2025)

A Three Rivers Holiday Tale: A Shifters of the Three Rivers Novella

Boxsets

Shifters of the Three Rivers, Omnibus of Books 1-3 (ebook only)

Mai and Ryan's story with *an exclusive epilogue!*

Audiobooks

The Runaway Mate (available on Audible and Amazon)

Coming in 2025

The Renegade Mate
The Resolute Mate

THE RENEGADE MATE

Want to find out what happens next for Mai and Ryan?

❧───···❀···───❧

The Renegade Mate, Book 2 in the Shifters of the Three Rivers series

Mai and Ryan's fated mate bond may be sealed, but their troubles are just beginning...

Mai

I'm on the run. Again. Only this time Ryan and his brothers are with me, and we're being hunted by members of our old Pack. Betrayed and consumed with grief, all I can think about is getting vengeance. But we're struggling to regroup and strike back. Then a bombshell drops - Jem wanted Ryan and me to succeed him as the Alpha pair.

I'm overwhelmed and don't know if I'm ready to lead, but with danger closing in and the Pack in turmoil, I may have no choice but to embrace my destiny to protect the ones I love.

Ryan

My wolf just wants to protect Mai and keep her safe. But she doesn't make it easy. She's always had a fierce independent streak and now my protective instincts are in overdrive as we navigate our changing relationship and the threats coming at us. I'd do anything to protect Mai, but can our bond withstand the impossible choices we face?

Time is running out for our wounded Pack as a battle for control of the Three Rivers looms. Mai and I must unlock the power of our fated mate bond and rally our allies before others destroy everything we hold dear.

THE RESOLUTE MATE

The Resolute Mate – Book 3 in the Shifters of the Three Rivers series, and the finale of Mai and Ryan's story.

The Resolute Mate

Their bond is undeniable, but the challenges they face could tear them apart forever...

Mai

Just whenI thought Ryan and I had finally got our revenge, our world is thrown into chaos once more. A deadly drug is wreaking havoc among the Packs, and to make matters worse, someone I thought was dead is being held hostage by Brock. He wants us to nominate him for a seat on the Wolf Council, but if Brock wins, it's not just us that he'll be coming after—he wants every Shifter community under his control. This Alpha gig is not proving easy, and if Ryan and I can't work out how to rule together, we could lose everything.

Ryan

Protecting Mai is a constant battle; my mate has made some dangerous enemies. With my wolf demanding I stop at nothing, and Mai fighting my every move, I have to navigate our new situation with care—something I'm not exactly good at. Only now we're in a race against time, and if I don't get this right, it could destroy all Shifters. But I'll do anything to protect my mate, my pack, my family.

Filled with heart-pounding action, sizzling romance, and unexpected twists, The Resolute Mate is a breathtaking conclusion to Mai and Ryan's epic journey in the Shifters of the Three Rivers series. Will their love withstand the ultimate test, or will the shadows of their past destroy everything they hold dear?

About Kira Nightingale

K ira Nightingale is a Scot living in Canada. She has always wanted to be a writer, and can't believe how lucky she is to finally be able to write romance stories all day long. She lives with her husband, her two children and a massive cat called Scout. Kira loves to drink tea (her favorite is Long Island Iced Tea, but unfortunately she only gets to drink this occasionally) and likes to dunk cookies in it (yes, even the Long Island kind.)

ACKNOWLEDGEMENTS

Putting together a book for publication is no small project and involves many steps after the author has written 'The End.' A huge thank you to my wonderful editor, Brigitte Billings. Any mistakes are mine. The cover was created by 100 Covers, and I would like to express my heartfelt thanks to Jamie Ty for his unwavering support and help to get such an awesome cover.

Printed in Great Britain
by Amazon

56692850R00189